Also by Melody Carlson

As Young As We Feel (Cook)

Limelight (Multnomah)

Love Finds You in Pendleton, Oregon (Summerside)

A Mile in My Flip-Flops (WaterBrook)

The Christmas Dog (Revell)

HOMETOWN TIES

HOMETOWN TIES

=== *BOOK TWO* ===

MELODY CARLSON

transforming lives together

HOMETOWN TIES
Published by David C. Cook
4050 Lee Vance View
Colorado Springs, CO 80918 U.S.A.

David C. Cook Distribution Canada
55 Woodslee Avenue, Paris, Ontario, Canada N3L 3E5

David C. Cook U.K., Kingsway Communications
Eastbourne, East Sussex BN23 6NT, England

David C. Cook and the graphic circle C logo
are registered trademarks of Cook Communications Ministries.

This story is a work of fiction. All characters and events are the product of the author's
imagination. Any resemblance to any person, living or dead, is coincidental.

LCCN 2010930102
ISBN 978-1-4347-6495-9
eISBN 978-0-7814-0554-6

© 2010 Melody Carlson
Published in association with the literary agency of Sara A. Fortenberry.

The Team: Don Pape, Erin Healy, Amy Kiechlin, Caitlyn York, Karen Athen
Cover Design: FaceOut Studios, Tim Green
Cover Images: iStockphoto, royalty-free

Printed in the United States of America
First Edition 2010

1 2 3 4 5 6 7 8 9 10

062910

Chapter 1

CAROLINE

Caroline knew better than to trust her mother. Even before Alzheimer's, Ruby McCann was undependable at best. Now she was unpredictable, unreliable, and sometimes downright sneaky. Today she was just plain missing. Caroline had been less than an hour at the grocery store, getting some milk, eggs, bread, and fresh produce in the hopes she could entice her mother to eat something. She'd left her mother contentedly watching a dog show on Animal Planet. And now she was gone.

But Caroline wasn't that surprised. Her mother had wandered off twice last week, and both times Caroline found her on the front porch of what used to be the Wilson house. Marge Wilson had been her mom's best friend, and Caroline supposed that some old wrinkle in her mom's brain sent her there for coffee or a cup of sugar or something. Each time, the current homeowners had appeared to be at work and, despite her mom's incessant ringing of the doorbell, no one responded. However, Caroline's mother was not on that porch this morning.

"Don't come undone," Caroline told herself as she continued through her mom's neighborhood—the same neighborhood Caroline had walked through hundreds, maybe thousands of times in the sixties while growing up. It should have been as familiar as the back of her hand, and yet it was different … changed by time. She looked at the back of her hand. Well, it had changed some too. And what appeared to be the beginning of a liver spot had her seriously concerned. Hopefully her hands weren't going to go all blotchy and speckled like her poor old mother's. Good grief, Caroline was only fifty-three. That was ten years younger than Goldie Hawn, and Goldie still looked fantastic. Of course, Goldie had lots of money to keep her good looks looking good. But what Caroline lacked in finances, she hoped she could make up in savvy. Which reminded her: Wasn't lemon juice supposed to bleach age spots?

"Caroline!"

She turned to see a figure on a bike zipping toward her, waving frantically. Jacob, her mother's neighbor, the preteen boy who'd rolled up his sleeves and assisted her with clandestinely emptying her pack-rat mother's stuffed spare room, was quickly coming her way.

"Hey, Jacob," she called out. "What's up?"

"I think I just saw your mom," he said, slightly breathless.

"Oh, good. Where is she?"

"Down by the docks in Old Towne."

She frowned. "Really, that far? Wow, she was feeling energetic. Thanks for tipping me off."

"Yeah … but … I … uh …" Now Jacob appeared to be at a loss for words, and his cheeks were blotched with red, which might've been from a hard bike ride … or was it something else?

"What's going on?" Caroline studied him. "Did my mom do something weird?"

He nodded with wide eyes.

She braced herself, hoping that her mom hadn't gotten into some kind of verbal dispute with a hapless bystander. Her mother, who'd always been a reserved and somewhat prudish sort of woman, was now capable of swearing like a sailor. Just one more unexpected Alzheimer's perk. "Okay, tell me, Jacob, what's she done this time?"

"She, uh, she doesn't have her clothes on." His eyebrows arched, and he made an uneasy smile.

"Oh." Caroline felt like the sidewalk was tipping just slightly now, like she needed to grab on to something to keep her balance. "You mean she doesn't have *any* clothes on?"

He shook his head. "Nope."

"Nothing?" Caroline tried to imagine this, then shook her head to dispel the image. "Not a stitch?"

"Nothing. Not even shoes."

"Oh." She turned around and started walking back toward her mom's house, still trying to grasp this. "Well, now that's a new one."

Jacob nodded as he slowly half walked, half pedaled his bike by the curb alongside her. "People are trying to help her," he explained, "but she keeps yelling at them to stay away or she's gonna jump."

"Jump?"

"Yeah, into the bay."

She started jogging now. "I better hurry."

"She was heading out on the dock, the one by the big tuna boat, when I last saw her."

Caroline ran faster now, glad that she was still in relatively good shape despite missing her yoga classes down in LA for the past few weeks. "Thanks for letting me know."

He smiled apologetically. "Yeah. Sorry that it was kinda bad news."

"Hey, don't ever be sorry to bring me news about my mom, Jacob. Believe me, I don't usually expect it to be good." And she broke out into a full run.

She ran into the house, which she'd left unlocked just in case her mom wandered back while Caroline was gone. She hurried down the dim hallway, quickly unlocked the deadbolt she'd installed in her bedroom (to keep her mother from going through her things), grabbed up her purse, and, remembering her mother was naked, pulled the yellow and white bedspread from her bed. On her way to the front door, she noticed her mom's favorite purple paisley shirt neatly folded on top of a pile of old magazines and books cluttering the worn coffee table. That should've been Caroline's first clue. Where her mom's other clothes had disappeared to was still a mystery. But Caroline's plan was to wrap her mother in the comforter, escort her to the car, and quickly get her home.

It only took a couple of minutes for Caroline to drive her SUV down to the docks, where she parked in a no-parking zone near a patrol car, then jumped out and, with purse in hand and the bedspread flapping behind her, ran down the boardwalk toward the tuna boat. A small crowd of spectators had already gathered on the wharf to witness this interesting event, and a couple of uniformed police officers with perplexed expressions stood at the edge of the dock.

"Hello!" Caroline called breathlessly as she hurried toward them, peering past them to see if she could spot her mother. She cringed at the idea of spotting a naked old woman wandering around with that bewildered expression in her faded blue eyes.

"Stay back!" the female officer yelled at Caroline, as if she were about to perpetrate a crime.

"I'm here for my mom," she told them, pointing down the dock. "I heard she's down there."

"That's *your* mom?" The woman looked at Caroline suspiciously, like Caroline was somehow responsible for the bizarre behavior of her senile parent.

"Yes. She has Alzheimer's and—"

"Hey, are you Caroline McCann?" the other cop asked.

She nodded, glancing curiously at him. He appeared to be about her age, although he wasn't familiar. "Do I know you?"

He grinned. "Probably not. Steve Pratt. I was a couple years behind you in school. But I remember you, all right. Coolest senior cheerleader at CHS and—"

"And don't forget we're on duty here," his partner reminded him.

"So"—Caroline squinted to see down the dock, which was looking alarmingly deserted—"about my mom? Where is she?"

"She's holed up in a fishing boat down on the end," Steve told her.

"Said she was going to jump if we didn't back off," the woman filled in.

"So we left"—Steve glanced over to the parking lot—"and called for backup."

"Backup?" Caroline grimaced. Did they plan to take her mother by force?

"A professional," he said quietly. "Someone from the hospital is bringing ... uh ... a counselor-type person to talk her into coming peacefully."

"Well, that won't be necessary," Caroline said as she folded the bedspread over her arm and moved past them. "I'm sure I can entice her to come with me." Okay, she wasn't as sure as she sounded, but she would at least try. Sometimes her mother knew and responded to her. Most times she didn't.

"We'll still need to file a report," the female cop called out as Caroline pushed past them and onto the dock. "We need your information."

A report? Caroline tried to imagine filling out their forms with her frightened, naked mother in tow. Didn't they realize this would be tricky at best?

"All I ask is that you try to stay out of the way." Caroline directed this at Steve, since he actually seemed a bit infatuated with her, which might've been flattering under different circumstances. "Police uniforms frighten her," she explained. "And if she sees you two again, she might really jump, and I'm sure it wouldn't take long for someone her age to get hypothermia. You wouldn't want to be responsible for that, would you?"

"We'll keep a low profile," he told her. "You just take your time and see if you can calm her down and get her safely out of there. Just yell if you need help."

Of course she needed help, she thought as she walked down the dock. As calm as she had tried to appear for the sake of the police, she knew her rescue attempt could go a number of directions. And so she whispered a desperate plea for real help. "Please, God, let my mother come peacefully." She was near the end of the dock now. "Peacefully and painlessly. Please!"

"Mom?" she sang out in a sweet voice. Not that her mother normally responded to either *Mom* or a sweet voice, but it couldn't hurt to try. "It's Caroline," she called again. Still no answer. At least she wouldn't be catching the poor woman unawares. Her mother hated to be surprised.

Fortunately, there was only one boat on the end of the dock, and since it was tied off close, it was easy to climb aboard. Caroline hopped onto the deck and called in a pleasant tone, "Ahoy, Mom, are you aboard?" She heard a shuffling sound on the other side of the cabin area and suspected her mom had heard her calling, was fully aware that Caroline was there, and yet didn't want to reveal her whereabouts, which meant this was going to be a game of hide-and-seek. It had been one of Caroline's favorite games as a child. Not that her mother ever had time for such games back then—back when Caroline could've appreciated it. Now her mother liked to play it a lot. Unfortunately, it was never much fun now.

"It's okay, Mom. It's just me—your daughter—*Caroline.*" She noticed a dirty bait bucket and wished she had something to tempt her mother with, something to entice her out of hiding. If only she'd had the foresight to bring a Milky Way candy bar, which she tried to use only on the rare occasion when her mom was being completely unreasonable. The best way to her mom's heart was via a McDonald's cheeseburger and fries and, in really desperate situations, a milkshake. A vanilla shake would come in quite handy right now.

"Are you hungry, Mom?" she called out, hoping it wouldn't backfire on her when her mom discovered that Caroline had come empty-handed. "How about a cheeseburger and fries, Mom? And a vanilla shake, too?"

No answer. Just the sound of a westerly breeze snapping the pirate flag on one of the masts. "Are you cold, Mom? I brought something for you to wrap up in." Now Caroline opened the bedspread as if it were a net, deciding to go ahead and make her approach. Worst-case scenario, she could wrap up her mom, forcibly remove her from the boat, and herd her back down the dock, calling out for reinforcement from the police. Surely the three of them could wrangle her into the back of the SUV. Caroline tiptoed around the side of the cabin, careful not to startle her mother by stumbling over the heavy ropes loosely coiled at her feet.

As she quietly rounded the corner and spotted the hunched figure of her mother, Caroline felt a shockwave of recognition run through her. Turned away from Caroline, the old woman was crouched in a fetal-like position with her arms pulled tightly together in front of her, fists clenched in a protective and defensive way. But her parchment skin was so pale and her body so skinny, with shocks of white fuzzy hair sticking off the top of her head, she almost didn't seem human. From a distance, and in a lesser light, she might've been mistaken for an alien.

Caroline felt a lump in her throat and a sickening in the pit of her stomach. Was this what it finally came down to? Was this how Caroline would end up one day? Naked, frightened, alone, and confused? Where was the purpose, the meaning in this? Why did some old people have to suffer so?

"Oh, Mom." The words came out in a quiet sob as she wrapped the bedspread around her mother's scrawny frame and held her tight. At first her mother struggled against her, but with little strength, and she eventually gave in. She was obviously spent—too tired, too cold to resist. Caroline continued to hold her mother in her arms, pulling her close, hoping some of her own body warmth would soak through the bedspread and into her mother. Caroline rocked her gently as if soothing a frightened child. She gently crooned to the tune of an old seventies song: "It'll be all right, it'll be all right." Slowly, her mother relaxed.

The question now was how to get her mom off the boat, down the dock, past the police and curious crowd, and into her SUV. It seemed impossible. And her mother seemed very weak. How far could she realistically walk?

"Do you want to lie down and rest?" Caroline asked quietly.

Her mother nodded, her eyes damp and tired.

"Yes." Caroline nodded too. "That's a good idea." She helped her mother to a vinyl-upholstered bench that ran along the sunny side of the cabin. Grabbing an orange life vest to use as a makeshift pillow, she eased her mother down, the bedspread still wrapped around her like a shroud.

"Just close your eyes and rest, Mom." Caroline sat near her mother's head, tucking the bedspread around her bare shoulders and stroking the fine white hair, wishing for a miracle. Caroline took in a slow, deep breath in an attempt to calm herself so that she could think more clearly. She leaned her head back, feeling the warm sun on her face and listening to the sound of the water lapping up against the sides of the boat, the flapping flag in the breeze above her, and the haunting cries of seagulls nearby. Yes, it would be all right. Somehow it would be all right.

It wasn't long until her mother's even breathing assured Caroline she was soundly asleep. Quietly and almost reflexively, Caroline reached into her bag to retrieve her cell phone. But who to call? She wished she knew a big, strong guy—someone who could simply pick up her mother and carry her to Caroline's car—and then perhaps he'd carry Caroline away as well, off to his palace. But this was real life. She needed real friends, and there, listed first in her cell phone directory, was Abby's name. Since Abby seemed to know almost everyone in town, she would be a good choice, except Caroline was pretty sure that Abby and Paul had a marriage counseling session today. There was no way she wanted to disturb that.

Marley was a possibility, except that her house was a ways out of town, and Caroline knew that Marley was working feverishly to finish a painting in time for a special exhibit at the One-Legged Seagull. Finally, Caroline decided on Janie. Although their relationship was sometimes strained, she trusted Janie. And having been a smart New York attorney, Janie should have some brilliant ideas for how to handle this.

"It's Caroline," she said quietly after Janie answered. "I need help."

"What's wrong?" Janie sounded alarmed.

"It's my mom." Caroline gave her a quick rundown of her morning thus far and explained how she was now stuck with a naked and frightened mother on a smelly fishing boat with the police waiting nearby. "I asked them to hold off," she said finally, "but I don't know how long they'll do that. You know how police can be." Just then Caroline noticed her mother's bare feet and gasped. They were bleeding.

"What is it?" Janie asked with concern.

"Her feet—she might need medical attention too."

"Okay," Janie said crisply. "I'm on it."

"Or just some flip-flops so we can walk her to my car."

"I'm getting in my car right now."

"Hey, could you stop by McDonald's on the way?"

"What?" Janie sounded incredulous. "Are you serious?"

Caroline quickly explained that fast food somehow soothed her mother. "You know, just in case she's difficult when she wakes."

"Okay, I'll call Abby and ask her to pick up the food and to meet us at the dock, okay?"

"What about their appointment?"

"Oh, they should be done with that by now."

"We're on the wharf, out on the dock past the tuna boat. It's the fishing boat on the end with the pirate flag," Caroline said weakly. "You'll probably see a small crowd of spectators and police standing nearby."

"See you in about five minutes."

Caroline closed her phone and looked down to see that her mother was still soundly sleeping. She was probably exhausted from trekking nearly two miles with no clothes or shoes. Or had she slowly disrobed along the way, dropping clothing like Hansel and Gretel's crumbs? Was she hoping to use them to find her way back home? And why couldn't she have left her shoes on? More than these questions, Caroline wondered *why*. Why, on a day when the temperature was barely sixty degrees, would an eighty-four-year-old woman want to walk naked through town? Why would she come clear down to the docks?

Alzheimer's was a mysterious disease plagued by a long list of unanswerable whys. Caroline hated to admit it, but perhaps it was time for her to seek some serious help in caring for her mother.

Chapter 2

JANIE

The drive from Janie's house, or what was slowly becoming Janie's house, was only a few minutes from the wharf. Janie turned on the Bluetooth, then hit Abby's number on her speed dial as she drove down a back street. Abby barely said hello before Janie cut her off. "I'm on my way to the wharf right now. Caroline's mom pulled another stunt—walked down there with no clothes on and—"

"Oh my!"

"Mrs. McCann threatened to jump, then hid on a fishing boat. Caroline has her subdued, but she needs assistance in getting her off there before the police intervene."

"Paul and I were just having coffee," Abby said. "But I'm on my way."

"Can you swing by McDonald's?"

"What?"

Janie quickly explained.

"Okay, if you think it'll help."

"Caroline seems to think so." She gave Abby specifics about where to find them on the wharf.

"And I'll call Marley, too," Abby said. "Just in case she's around."

"See you in a few." As Janie set down her BlackBerry, she realized she'd gotten pale blue paint on the front of it. She'd been painting a bedroom in her house when Caroline had called, and Janie dropped everything, including a paint-soaked brush on the hardwood floor. No time to think of that now; she was already turning in to the wharf parking lot. Seeing Caroline's SUV as well as a couple of police cars, Janie pulled up and got out, hurrying past a small crowd of curious onlookers. She was stopped by the police barricade next to the wharf entrance.

"No one goes past here," a young man in uniform told her.

"I'm here to help Ruby McCann," Janie explained.

He gave her a puzzled look. "Who?"

"The naked old woman on the fishing boat," Janie said impatiently. "Mrs. McCann."

"That's right." An older male officer joined them. "Mrs. McCann is the one on the boat. But her daughter's with her. Who are you?"

"Janie Sorenson."

"And your purpose?"

"She wanted to go onto the dock," the young policeman explained.

"To see Mrs. McCann," Janie told him.

"Are you a doctor?"

"No, but Caroline McCann, Ruby's daughter, called me to come over and help."

"To help?" He looked puzzled. "How do you plan to help?"

Janie suppressed her exasperation. "I'm her attorney." Okay, maybe that was a stretch, but hopefully it would work. "Caroline called for my assistance."

"Oh, right." He peered curiously at her, as if he questioned whether she was legit. "You're an attorney?"

She glanced down at her paint-speckled overalls, then forced a smile. "Yes. I'm an attorney who happens to be painting a bedroom today. Now if you'll excuse me, I'll go find Caroline and her mother."

"Janie!"

Janie turned to see Abby just getting out of her car and waving. She had a brown paper bag in hand and was jogging toward them.

"I came as fast as I could," she huffed at Janie. "I even pushed my way to the front of the line at McDonald's—told them it was an emergency, and they put a rush on my order."

The older officer scratched his head. "What?"

"For Caroline's mom," Abby said with irritation. "Now let us past here so we can go help her."

He pointed to the McDonald's bag. "But what's in that—"

"Look, Steve." Abby put her face close to his. "We all know you're a good policeman and you've been on the force for years, but this isn't exactly a bank robbery going down here. Please, step aside and let us help our friend, and nobody gets hurt, okay?"

He shrugged, then stepped back. "Hey, you gals get that old lady safely off the boat and you'll hear no complaints from me."

"Thank you." Abby grabbed Janie by the arm now. "Let's go!"

"Nice work," Janie said as the two of them hurried down the dock.

"Yeah, I even surprised myself by taking cuts in front of a mom with two toddlers who were whining for Happy Meals."

"No, I meant nice work with the police."

"Oh, that's just Steve Pratt. He was a couple years behind us in school and I'm still pulling rank on him."

Janie started to laugh but realized they were near the boat now. "We should probably be quiet," she warned Abby. "We don't want to startle Ruby."

"Here." Abby handed her the bag. "Why don't you go first with our peace offering?"

Janie nodded and took the bag, quietly stepping onto the boat and cautiously looking around. A cheerful bit of yellow and white fabric sticking out beyond the side of the cabin seemed just a bit out of place on this crusty old fishing vessel. Tiptoeing around, she found Caroline sitting on a bench with an oversized cocoon nestled near her. A relieved smile washed over Caroline's face.

Janie pointed to the bundle. *Your mom?* she mouthed.

Caroline nodded.

Janie held up the bag, and Caroline's eyes lit up. "Thank you!"

The cocoon rustled, and Janie handed Caroline the bag before stepping back around the other side of the cabin and out of sight.

"Good morning, sunshine," Caroline said cheerfully.

"What—where am I?" growled a hoarse voice. "Who are you?"

"Here's your lunch, Mom. A cheeseburger, fries, and a vanilla shake." Caroline's voice was calm and even, as if she served her naked mother meals on strange fishing boats every day.

"Lunch?" her mom growled.

"Smell this," Caroline said sweetly. "Mmm, french fries. And they're still warm."

"Huh?" Her mom sounded interested. Janie heard sounds of paper and munching and hoped this meant they were moving in the right direction.

"Have a sip of your milkshake, too," Caroline urged. "You had a long hike out here this morning, Mom. I'm sure you've worked up an appetite."

"Apple … tight?" her mother mumbled with what sounded like a full mouth.

Janie rounded her forefinger and thumb to make an "okay" symbol for Abby, who was now sitting on a wooden crate on the dock next to the boat, looking surprisingly peaceful and relaxed considering that there were several police officers as well as a small crowd of spectators still hovering.

Janie pantomimed eating motions for Abby, pointing back to where Caroline and her mom were still presumably dining. Abby nodded, then reached into her purse to remove an emery board and promptly began filing one of her fingernails.

Janie quietly returned to the front of the cabin and leaned back against it, looking up at the sky. The morning fog had nearly burned off, and it looked like it was going to be another perfect day in the small sea town of Clifden. Once again she marveled at her decision to transplant her life back to her childhood home—such a different world from Manhattan. And yet she was deliriously happy to be here. She just hoped she wasn't experiencing some kind of honeymoon phase. It had been only a couple of weeks since she'd moved back.

The breeze blew her long hair away from her face, and she stretched her arms out wide, loosening her shoulders, which were still feeling the burn from all the painting she'd accomplished yesterday. She was restoring her parents' old ranch-style house, getting ready to live in it. She had only one more bedroom to paint, and she'd be done with the bulk of the messy work. On the inside, anyway. The outside was still waiting for a new coat of paint. Abby had assured her there was plenty of time to get to it before foul weather set in. "Don't you remember how September-October is the best time of year on the Oregon coast?" Abby had reminded her just a few days ago. "Savor it."

Janie took in a long breath of fresh sea air and decided to do just that. Really, what was so bad about being on a docked fishing boat, wearing paint-splotched overalls, and waiting for your friend's senile mother to decide it was time to go home? What was the hurry?

"My friend is here, Mom," Caroline said loudly, as if to warn Janie that she was trying to make the move to get her mother safely off the boat. "Remember Janie from grade-school days? Her family only lived a few blocks away from us. Her first name is Linda too."

"Linda?" came the gruff voice. "Linda Caroline."

"Yes," Caroline said happily. "I'm Linda Caroline. Remember me? Your little Linda Caroline." Her mom said the name again, this time with more confidence. "And my friend was Linda Jane."

"Linda Jane?"

"Yes," Caroline continued in a bubbly voice. "Linda Jane. And there was a Linda Abigail and a Linda Marlene as well. We made a club called the Four Lindas." Caroline was coming around the corner now, leading the way. "And this is Linda Jane right here," she announced.

"Hi, Mrs. McCann," Janie said gently. She pointed to the sky now. "Isn't it a pretty day?"

Caroline's mom looked up with a quizzical frown, then nodded as if she agreed. "Pretty. Pretty day."

Now Janie came along the other side of Mrs. McCann, who was still draped in a white and yellow cocoon. "Let me help you off of this boat," she said calmly.

"Yes," Caroline cooed. "We had our lunch on the boat, and now it's time to go home."

"And there is Linda Abigail," Janie continued with Caroline's list of Lindas. "That's three of the Lindas."

"Linda," Mrs. McCann said gruffly as Caroline and Janie practically lifted her from the boat and onto the dock.

Abby followed along behind them, and although Mrs. McCann was starting to resist her three-Linda escort, they continued slowly moving down the dock, walking and talking and cajoling the old woman along with each step.

By now there was an ambulance and three police cars. Janie figured a naked old woman about to leap from the dock must be a big occurrence in a small town like Clifden. In some parts of New York, such a thing would scarcely turn a head. The foursome was about halfway down the dock when Janie spotted Marley pushing past the police and coming toward them. Worried that Marley's rapid approach might unsettle Mrs. McCann, Janie attempted to tighten her grip, but the comforter made this tricky. Plus, Mrs. McCann was beginning to squirm. Her lunch must've revived her. Caroline looked at Janie with worried eyes, and Janie imagined the old woman breaking free and jumping naked into the cold bay waters.

"Want to carry her?" Janie suggested.

"Yes," Caroline agreed. "Hurry, Marley," she urged. "We're going to carry her."

And just like that, as if it had been choreographed, the four of them grabbed various parts of the squirming yellow and white comforter and wrapped Mrs. McCann securely, slowly transporting her toward the wharf entrance.

"She's not very heavy," Abby commented.

"Especially with four of us," Janie said.

"Where do we go from here?" Marley asked.

"To my SUV," Caroline instructed. "I'll take her home."

"A couple of us better come with you," Janie said. "To keep her subdued while you drive."

"Let us through," Janie commanded when they reached the police barricade. "We need to get Mrs. McCann to a safe place."

"But what about the report?" Officer Steve asked as the four women pushed past.

"Does it look like this is a good time?" Abby shot back at him.

"Come by my house, if you want," Caroline told him over her shoulder. "I need to get my mom home and into bed."

"But we have an ambulance," someone called out. "And EMTs ready to assist—"

"She doesn't need an ambulance," Caroline told them. "She just needs her own bed and some rest."

"Oh, great," Marley muttered as they toted their wriggling bundle toward Caroline's SUV.

"What?" asked Janie.

"Looks like the press is here." Marley nodded over to a short balding guy who was snapping photos like he planned to sell this to the *New York Times.*

"Oh, that's just Harold from *Clifden Weekly News,*" Abby said in a dismissive tone. "Don't worry about him."

It was a bit of a struggle, but they soon had Mrs. McCann, still fairly snug in her yellow and white cocoon, wedged between Janie and Marley in the backseat, while Abby road shotgun with Caroline at the wheel.

"I feel like we just pulled some kind of bank heist." Janie giggled as she buckled the seatbelt around Caroline's mother, pausing to smooth the fuzzy white hair a bit.

"Or kidnapped someone," Abby suggested.

"Or saved some old lady from getting locked up," Caroline said sadly. "But I appreciate it, you guys. Thanks for your help."

Janie was thinking that Mrs. McCann might be safer if she *were* locked up somewhere. In a good place. But she didn't want to say as much because she knew Caroline's mother was desperate to remain in her own home. She also knew how hard Caroline had been trying to keep her there, caring for her mother, cooking and cleaning and hoping against the odds that she could somehow bring the old woman back to her senses. Caroline's theory was that, with love and kindness and good nutrition, her mother's mental health would improve. Unfortunately, and as today proved, her theory had some holes in it. Janie thought Mrs. McCann's future looked somewhat bleak, and the sooner Caroline figured this out, the better off both she and her mother would probably be.

"Don't look now," Marley warned, "but you're being followed."

Janie glanced back to see one of the patrol cars tailing them.

"Well, at least you have your legal counsel with you," she assured Caroline.

"Do you think I'm in trouble?" Caroline asked as she turned down her street.

"I don't see why," Janie said. "No one's been arrested. And they didn't charge you or your mother with anything. Not yet anyway."

"Will they?" Caroline sounded worried.

Janie considered this. "I don't see how it would do anyone any good, but you never know which way it might go with law enforcement. Some small-town police forces seem to have a code of their own."

Mrs. McCann was mumbling something, and when Janie listened more closely, she realized the words coming from the old woman's mouth weren't of the nice variety. In fact, they would be considered rather offensive in most circles. But somehow, hearing them from a yellow and white cocoon topped by a fluffy head of white hair seemed oddly humorous.

"Mother," Caroline scolded. "Be quiet."

That only seemed to egg her mother on, and Mrs. McCann began to curse even more loudly. Janie, despite herself, started to giggle. Then Marley let out a chortle. And, although Caroline kept telling her mother to knock it off, the foul language only intensified. By the time Caroline pulled into the driveway, the old woman was swearing like a logger.

She kept it up as Janie and Marley worked to unbuckle her and extract her from the backseat of the car. Then, as the four of them began to lug the thrashing and swearing bundle toward the house, Officer Steve and his female partner got out of their cruiser and joined the women in time to witness this little ordeal.

"You ladies need a hand?" Steve asked as he followed.

"Thanks, Steve," Caroline called pleasantly through clenched teeth. "We've got it pretty much under control."

Fortunately, Mrs. McCann calmed down once she was inside her own house. They set her back on her feet, and the familiar surroundings seemed to soothe her. She looked around, taking everything in with a surprised expression, as if she had expected never to see it again. Janie wondered if the poor old woman's deluded mind had tricked her into believing it had all gone up in a puff of smoke.

"See, Mom?" Caroline took her mom's arm. "I told you we'd get you home safely."

Marley remained in the living room while Janie and Abby helped Caroline guide Mrs. McCann into her bedroom, which was cluttered and messy and smelled a bit dank. The bed, however, was clean and neatly made, probably thanks to Caroline. Nestled on a pillow was a fluffy white plush dog with a shiny black nose. Mrs. McCann stared at the toy with grateful eyes, as if it were a long-lost friend.

"I can handle Mom from here," Caroline said as she reached for a pink flannel nightgown. "Thanks for your help." Janie, not eager to see Caroline dressing her mother for bed, backed off. But Abby remained, gently setting the old woman on the edge of her bed and helping to unravel her cocoon as if she were caring for a small child, probably the way Abby would assist her young granddaughter. Of the four diverse friends, Abby seemed to have the strongest domestic side, as well as a soft nurturing way that felt slightly foreign to Janie—especially after spending most of her adult life practicing law in a city where toughness was considered a strength and softness a weakness.

Janie turned away and joined Marley in the living room, where she was absently flipping through the TV channels.

"I don't have cable at my beach house," Marley said as she set the remote down. "Not that I miss it, but sometimes I'm curious."

"I've felt a little culturally isolated here too," Janie admitted. "Not with TV so much, although I don't have cable either. But Clifden is a very small town."

"Speaking of small towns, the police are still out there waiting." Marley nodded toward the front window.

"I guess it's time for some legal consultation," Janie told her. "Care to join me?"

"Only as a witness." Marley followed Janie out, standing by her side as Janie politely inquired as to why Officer Steve had followed them.

"I realize Mrs. McCann could be charged with indecent exposure, breaking and entering, and eluding the police," Janie continued, "but did Caroline break any laws?"

"No, Caroline is okay," he admitted. "I just need to fill out my report."

"What is it you need to know?" Janie asked.

He read off some routine questions, which Janie attempted to answer. As for the ones she couldn't answer, she promised "as the McCanns' attorney" to get back to him as soon as possible. "Because Caroline's got her hands full taking care of her mother right now."

"My biggest concern is for the safety of Caroline's mother," Steve said. "She could've gotten hurt or even killed today."

"As you can see"—Janie shifted gears, using a tone reserved for convincing the jury of her case—"this is a very complicated situation.

We all know that Caroline is doing her best to care for her mother, but Alzheimer's is one of those difficult illnesses that makes it challenging to determine exactly which course is best, and when it's best. Mrs. McCann is determined to remain in her home, and Caroline is trying very hard to accommodate her wishes. I think we should respect that." She looked him in the eye now, hoping that he'd take the hint, finish his report, and be on his way.

"I understand that," he said with what seemed genuine compassion. "And this is why I've requested an evaluation from senior social services."

"I believe Caroline has already tried that," Janie explained. "Her mother would not cooperate."

"So you see that Mrs. McCann can't make these decisions for herself, and that she could get hurt. And that's why she'll probably need to be placed in a more secure situation."

"Meaning a lockdown?"

He gave her a noncommittal shrug. "It's not up to me to decide."

She nodded. "Yes. I understand. I'll inform Caroline of your concerns, although I'm sure they'll be of no surprise."

He closed his notebook and smiled. "So is Caroline just here to visit awhile, or did she move back for good?"

"She's moved back to help with her mother. As far as I know, she has no plans to return to California." Janie smiled back at him. It seemed obvious that he was interested in more than Mrs. McCann's safety. Janie noted that Officer Steve wasn't wearing a wedding band. She considered telling him that Caroline already had one guy interested in her, but then decided it wasn't her business.

He glanced over at the house. "Well, tell Caroline that I hope to see more of her, then. And if she has any questions about any of this, tell her to feel free to call."

Janie nodded. "I'll do that."

Then Steve and his partner got back into their car.

"Can you believe that?" Marley nudged Janie with her elbow as the two of them watched the cruiser slowly drive away. "That cop is interested in Caroline."

"Why should that surprise you?" Janie chuckled. "We all know that when it comes to men, Caroline is like honey to flies. And maybe Officer Steve will think twice about locking her mom up today. It's not like Caroline needs that right now."

"But she does need help with her mom," Marley said quietly.

Janie sighed. "I think you're right."

Chapter 3

MARLEY

"I'm going to walk back into town to get my car," Marley told Janie after they'd waited outside for a while. "Want to say bye to Caroline and Abby for me?"

"I think I'll join you," Janie told her. "But I'll run in and tell them first."

Marley glanced at her watch and sighed. Already it was nearly two, and she hadn't painted a single brush stroke yet. At this rate, she'd never get that painting done in time for the First Saturday Art Walk in October. It had been Marley's idea to start a monthly event like this in their town. Jack, owner of the One-Legged Seagull, had eagerly gotten on board, and the other galleries happily followed suit. This would be the first event, and everyone in town seemed enthused.

Jack wanted to feature Marley's paintings as the focal point of his gallery. But since her paintings had already been hanging a couple of weeks, his idea was for her to have a new painting to be a centerpiece. "A reason to buy new ad space in the *Clifden Weekly News*," he'd told her last week. Now she worried that Jack might be wasting his money on her.

"You look a little bummed," Janie told Marley as she came back out of the house.

Marley forced a smile. "Just thinking."

"Oh." The two of them started walking. "Having any regrets about relocating back here?" Janie asked.

Marley shook her head. "Not at all. I love it. And my beach bungalow is coming right along."

"How's the painting coming?"

"You mean on the canvas or on the walls?" Marley pointed to Janie's speckled overalls and grinned. "Looks like you were painting too."

"Yes. The last bedroom." Janie held up a hand, showing Marley a patch of pale blue. "Ocean Glass Blue."

"Pretty." Marley nodded. "Peaceful."

"It's going to be my bedroom," Janie told her. "All blue and white and very French."

"Sounds lovely." As they strolled down Second Street, Marley could imagine the room with beautiful furnishings, layers of fine French bedding, exquisite paintings (originals, of course), and expensive area carpets. Because Janie, unlike Marley, seemed to have unlimited funds when it came to redoing her house. And while Marley tried not to be envious, she couldn't help but feel a twinge now and then. It seemed that only the best was good enough for Janie. But that was probably the result of living in Manhattan for years and marrying into a very wealthy family.

Still, to be fair, Marley knew that Janie's life wasn't picture perfect. Not only had she lost the love of her life—her husband of twenty-six years—but her daughter had been battling a serious drug addiction as well. No, Marley wasn't naive. She knew that even the prettiest packages sometimes had dirt inside. Not that she considered Janie's troubles dirty—just troubles. They all had them.

"So how *is* the painting coming?" Janie persisted. "I mean on the canvas, not the walls."

Marley let out a groan.

"Oh." Janie nodded. "Is there such a thing as painter's block?"

"I think that's what I've got," Marley admitted. "I look at that blank canvas, and I just freeze up. I'm certain I can never paint anything as good as what I've already done. It's like there's no creativity left in me." She shook her head. "So I distract myself with working on my bungalow instead."

"What are you doing?"

"Oh, I found this really great deal on ceramic tiles on Craigslist," Marley began. "A small business was liquidating, and I got boxes and boxes of all these fantastic bright colors—kind of tropical-looking, you know. Lime, coral, turquoise, mango—they're so much fun. And I'm getting pretty good at putting them up, too."

"Maybe I should hire you to come do some tile work at my house," Janie suggested as they entered the wharf parking lot. "There's quite a bit to do, and the plumber is starting to complain."

"Sure." Marley nodded. "I could probably do that." Of course, even as she said this, she wasn't sure. Janie was probably a real perfectionist, and Marley's tile-laying skills were still a bit rustic.

"I won't be doing anything as lively as your bungalow," Janie continued as they crossed the lot toward their cars. "I've got some marble tiles for the bathrooms, and I really like the look of tinted glass tiles. But I wonder if they're hard to install since they're kind of clear."

"I've got some glass tiles mixed in with the ceramic ones, and I've put them up in the exact same way." Marley laughed. "Okay, I'm not sure if it was the right way. But I like the effect."

"That's what counts." Janie stopped by her car. It was a late-model silver Mercedes that she'd had shipped from the east. At first she'd been apologetic about it to her friends, as if embarrassed by her wealth. But she explained that the car had been her late husband's and still had some sentimental value.

"You should come see my bungalow sometime," Marley told Janie. "Check out my tile work and see if it would be good enough for you. Keep in mind, I'm still just learning."

"I'd love to see it." Janie pulled out her keys.

"Hey, have you had lunch yet?" Marley asked.

Janie laughed. "Not hardly. I was in the midst of painting a wall when Caroline's call for help came."

"How about if I grab us some salads or whatnot at the deli, and you can come out to my place for lunch and check it out?"

"That sounds like fun. If you don't mind, I'll swing by my place and clean up some paint things first. I took off in such a hurry that I know I left a mess behind."

"Perfect." Marley waved and got into her economy car, reminding herself that it got great gas mileage, and drove over to the deli. She selected one carton of turkey-and-apple salad and one of broccoli, cheese, and bacon, along with several garlic bread sticks and an oversized double-chocolate brownie to share. Then she drove straight home and quickly put her house in order. Sure, maybe it was small, but it was also charming. At least she thought so. Sure, it still needed work, but she'd already painted the kitchen cabinets white and replaced the hardware with a bright selection of mismatched ceramic knobs that she'd gotten online. And her colorful tile backsplash and countertops really livened the place up. All in all, it was warm and friendly and fun.

She put the salads and things into serving dishes and set out her Fiestaware plates and Mexican glasses, along with some colorful cloth napkins. She pulled out her bottle-green margarita pitcher, which she filled with water, ice, and sliced lemons. Maybe she would have all her friends over here some evening and whip up a batch of margaritas, but for now this would do. Then she opened the back door to the beach and did a quick cleanup of her deck, chairs, and tables. She was just setting the water and glasses out there when she heard Janie calling.

"Anybody home?"

Marley went back into the house to greet her. "Welcome to my humble abode," she said, glancing around the small space self-consciously. Although Janie's house was probably only three times this size, Marley knew that once it was finished, it would be much more sophisticated.

"Oh, Marley," Janie exclaimed. "This is looking fantastic. You've done so much in such a short time. I love it." Janie was in the kitchen now, running her hand over the carnival of tiles. "So cheerful and fun." She smiled at Marley. "Like you."

Marley frowned. "I'm cheerful and fun?"

"Of course."

Marley just shook her head. "Man, you could've fooled me."

Janie laughed. "You are. I always think of you as the free spirit. The hippie girl in high school. Isn't that how you see yourself?"

Marley smiled. "I guess I'm trying to find that girl again. And I have to admit, not being able to finish that painting …" She nodded over to the canvas by the south window and sighed. "Well, it's getting me down."

Janie went over to look at the barely begun seascape and, placing her hand under her chin, slowly nodded. "This is a bit different from your other work, isn't it?"

Marley joined her and peered at the painting. "Yeah. I think that's the problem. It's like I'm lost, like I don't know what I'm doing anymore."

"I love the colors you're using."

"Really? I thought maybe I'd gotten off on the wrong palette."

"They look like real beach colors to me, like the ocean right outside your back door."

Marley nodded. "That's true. But I don't usually do realistic paintings. I'm more into Impressionism. Maybe I should just chuck this and start an Impressionistic seascape. Or skip doing a seascape at all. It's not like you have to paint the ocean just because you live by it, right?"

"Maybe you should paint whatever ignites your creativity."

Marley cocked her head to one side, as though looking at her painting from a different angle might help somehow. "Unless I don't have any more creativity." She sighed. "What if I used it all up?"

"I don't think that's possible." Janie pressed her lips together. "I think creativity is like any other kind of energy. You use it, and then you refill it."

"I wonder how I can refill it."

Janie looked around the small space as if searching for a clue. "You know what, Marley?"

"What?"

Janie laughed. "I think you've been pouring all your creative energy into this little bungalow." She pointed to the arrangement of the couch and chairs, the Mexican blanket draped over the couch, the pillows that Marley had recovered from some old batik fabric she'd held onto for decades, the arrangement of sculptures and colorful candles on the mantel. "This little beach house is like your latest masterpiece."

Marley couldn't help but smile now. "You know … you could be right."

"Seriously, Marley, if you took some good photos of this place, I'll bet some magazine would use them. It's a real work of art."

"Well, thank you." Marley felt herself beaming now. "I'm glad I invited you over for lunch. Speaking of that, it's all set up."

"About this painting …" Janie was back in front of the easel.

"Yeah?"

"You don't really plan to scrap it, do you?"

Marley shrugged. "I don't know. I guess I can kind of imagine how it might turn out."

"Because if you finish it, and if it turns out okay … well, I think I'd be interested in purchasing it for my house."

"Are you serious?" Marley blinked.

"I think so." Janie nodded. "I love the colors you're working with. That sand and beach grass is so peaceful. I think it would go nicely in my house. Maybe in the dining room."

"Really?" Marley felt hopeful.

"I don't want to pressure you," Janie said quickly. "I mean, if you get inspired to do an Impressionist painting instead, I don't want to make you feel like you're committed to finishing something your heart's not into."

Marley considered this. Maybe her heart could get into a painting with a customer attached to it. Not that she wanted to admit this much to anyone. But the truth be told, finances were an issue for her. And painting, or even laying tile, for money was not below her standards at this stage of the game.

"I'll tell you what," she began carefully. "I'll keep you in mind as I work on the painting, and if it keeps going, then I'll keep going too. But even if I do finish it, I won't hold you to purchasing it. It's not like I consider this a commissioned piece."

Janie smiled. "With that said, you have to agree to let me have first right of refusal, okay?"

Marley stuck out her hand. "It's a deal."

They loaded their plates with food and went out to the deck. More fog was starting to roll in, but the combination of sun and mist created a lovely kind of fairy-dust light. "Now if only I knew how to capture this," Marley said as they sat down on the brightly colored Adirondack chairs. "Maybe in time I'll figure it out."

"It's so lovely here," Janie said almost reverently. "So peaceful … serene."

"It's a great place to rejuvenate."

"I can imagine." Janie sighed and leaned back. "I'd think in time it would fill up those creative juices and you wouldn't be able to do anything but paint."

"But I think you're right about me using my creativity on my house. It really did become my canvas. No wonder I can't paint." She pointed to a flock of tiny seabirds flying together in unison like a magic carpet. "I wish I could paint something like that," she said wistfully. "Maybe I should start by trying to photograph it first."

"You were so lucky to find this place, Marley."

"That's kind of what I thought too. Although some people who shall go unmentioned disagreed."

"You mean Paul?" Janie chuckled. "Well, Abby said it was only because he thought he'd end up being your handyman."

Marley stuck her nose up. "That has not been the situation. I would have to be very hard up to beg Paul to come over and help me."

"You don't like Paul, do you?"

Marley considered this. She hated to admit she couldn't stand one of her best friends' husbands—although Abby was the only one of them who still had a husband—but it was true. She almost thoroughly despised the man. "I think he reminds me a bit of my ex."

"Oh?"

"John was kind of married to his job too. He took me for granted. And he cheated on me."

"But Paul didn't actually cheat on Abby."

"Not that we know." Marley looked over toward Abby's mother's house, then lowered her voice. "And I'm not the only one who's suspicious."

Janie followed Marley's glance. "Doris thinks Paul was having an affair?"

"Maybe not this time. But she has her doubts about his fidelity."

Janie just shook her head. "Poor Abby."

"You won't say anything, will you?"

"Of course not. I don't know anything. Well, except that suspicion and innuendo can trick people. I like to stick to the facts."

"That's very lawyerlike."

Janie made a face. "Although I am trying to shed the lawyer cloak."

"You mean you've decided not to practice law in Oregon?"

"I'm not sure."

"Is there something else you want to pursue?" Marley broke a breadstick in half.

"At the moment, I just want to get my parents' house finished."

"You still call it your parents' house?"

Janie shrugged. "I guess I'm not ready to own it quite yet. Originally, I was only fixing it up to sell. But when I decided to leave New York, it was a handy place to land—better than the hotel. That got old fast. Although I'm still just kind of camping in the house. Not quite at home."

"Pretty nice camping if you ask me." Marley had seen some of the rooms and, while the whole thing wasn't completely done, it was all looking very nice and uptown. Especially by Clifden standards.

"Thanks, but I think I'd trade it in a heartbeat for a place like this." Janie leaned back and looked up. "The sea and the sky … does it get much better?"

"You could buy a beach house if you wanted." Marley forked her salad.

"Maybe, if my Manhattan apartment sold. But I still have to pay

Matthew's tuition. Five more years until he gets his law degree. So I want to be careful."

Marley wanted to ask whether Janie's recent reunion with Victor had anything to do with her hesitancy to make a move. Did Janie see herself marrying him someday, moving into his beach house? So far their relationship seemed to be only a friendship. But it was hard to tell. Already some were speculating about Marley and Jack. And while Jack was certainly a very nice guy, Marley didn't see them as anything more than good friends, business acquaintances, and contemporaries in the field of art. Still ... things could change ... people could change ... and none of them was getting any younger.

As Marley cleaned up after their lunch, she became slightly obsessed with the whole idea of aging. She wasn't even sure what brought it on, but she suspected that seeing Caroline's mom like that—so old and fragile, kind of cut off and alone, and really vulnerable and helpless—well, it had rattled Marley more than she cared to admit. Yet she knew that aging was inevitable. Even the ones who fought it tooth and nail eventually grew old. Well, unless one died young, which brought no comfort.

Really, Marley decided as she hung up the dish towel, she was not ready to get old or die. And she had no idea what she could do to get ready, or how long she even had to figure this all out. But it was unsettling.

—Chapter 4—

ABBY

"She's exhausted, poor thing," Abby whispered to Caroline as they tiptoed from Mrs. McCann's bedroom. They'd done their best to attend to her feet before the old woman had fallen asleep.

With the slightly worn yellow and white comforter hanging over an arm, Caroline closed her mother's door and sighed. "She's not the only one."

"You go in there and put your feet up," Abby urged her.

"In the living room?" Caroline made a face. "Did you look around in there much?"

Abby just waved her hand as if the piles and messes were no big deal. But the truth was, Abby didn't know if she'd ever seen such squalor. Not to mention the smell. She had no idea this was how Caroline was living. If Mrs. McCann had another caregiver and if Abby's marriage were more stable, she would insist that Caroline come home and live with her. As it was, she couldn't open her mouth.

"Pretty bad, isn't it?" Caroline tossed the comforter over the back of a sad-looking sofa and just shook her head. "I'm sure you're shocked."

"I'll admit I was a bit surprised." Abby looked around the cluttered room. Boxes of God-only-knew-what were piled on top of one another along the wall by what had once been a fireplace but no longer looked functional. All the furnishings looked like they'd been there since the sixties, and they weren't quality pieces, either. The Formica-topped end tables and coffee table were all piled high with old magazines, books, ashtrays, and other stuff. The walls had a dulled yellow look, probably from years of Mrs. McCann's smoking, and the general feeling of the room was dark, dismal, and depressing.

"I can tell by your face you're stunned. You can't believe I live in this kind of squalor." Caroline was starting to cry.

Abby hugged her. "I know it's not your choice to live like this." After moving some junk and the comforter from the sofa, Abby made her sit down. "You need to just chill a bit, girlfriend. I'll get you a glass of water."

"The clean glasses are in the highest cupboard right of the sink. Everything else is … well, you'll see."

Abby went into the kitchen, which was actually a bit cleaner than the living room, although it was apparent that Caroline's battle against clutter raged in here as well. She opened the cupboard right of the sink and instantly saw what Caroline meant. The highest shelf, which she could barely reach, had clean shelf paper and shiny new-looking glasses on it. The other, grimier shelves contained plastic glasses and stained cups and items that you wouldn't expect to find even at a bad yard sale. Abby's guess was that Mrs. McCann liked it that way. She turned on the faucet, but even the tap water looked dark and dingy.

"There's bottled water in the fridge," Caroline called out, but not too loudly, like she was afraid to disturb her mother. "On the bottom in back."

Abby found the jug of chilled water, filled both glasses, and returned to Caroline, who was blowing her nose. Forcing what she wanted to be a hopeful smile, Abby handed Caroline a glass.

"Sorry about falling apart like that," Caroline told Abby. "I don't like to be such a baby."

Abby moved some clothing and paper bags from an old swivel chair, then sat across from her. "I'd cry too if I had to live here," she confessed.

Caroline just nodded. "It's horrible."

"And I'm guessing you try to change things, but your mother resists."

She nodded again. "She gets so upset if I move things. I had to secretly clean out my old bedroom just so I'd have a decent place to sleep. And I tried to clean up the bathroom, but it's already looking just as bad as when I got here. It seems like the harder I try to make things nice, the harder she tries to ruin everything. I just don't get it."

"I think it's just that her mind works differently. It's like her perceptions are skewed, like she's all mixed up in her head."

"You can say that again."

"I'm no expert, but I'm guessing it's going to go steadily down-hill from here, Caroline."

"Maybe."

"Maybe?" Abby frowned. "Do you really think it can go any other direction?"

Caroline brightened. "She has good days sometimes. Okay, *days* is an exaggeration. But she has moments of clarity ... she knows who I am, and she really appreciates me, and she begs me to let her stay here, in her house. It's all she wants, to live her last days under this roof."

Abby nodded. "Yes. My mom says the same thing."

"But your mom has her wits about her."

Abby kind of laughed. "Depends on who you talk to about that. Paul sometimes wonders if she's losing it."

"Paul should count his blessings! That man just doesn't know how good he's got it."

Abby nodded sadly.

"I'm sorry," Caroline said quickly. "I didn't mean to suggest that—"

"I know what you meant, and you're right. But I'm part of the problem too."

Caroline took a sip of water, seemingly waiting for Abby to explain.

"You see, at the counselor's today...." Abby's mouth twisted to one side. "I had to admit to some things."

"Well, there are always two sides."

"Yes, and to be fair, I've probably tried to make it seem there was only one person blowing it—and it wasn't me."

"I don't know." Caroline held up a finger. "I've heard you defend Paul a number of times. I've even wondered if you let him get away with too much. Honestly, Abby, sometimes it seems like you let him walk all over you." She clamped her hand over her mouth now, as if she hadn't meant to say that. "I'm sorry. I think I'm just too tired to talk in a civilized way. I won't blame you for walking out on me right now."

Abby just laughed. "Oh, I'm not that thin-skinned. And you're right, I have let Paul walk on me at times. The counselor even said something like that today. But she used a fifty-dollar word. I think she said I was an enabler, that I do certain things that allow Paul to get away with bad behavior."

"So you're supposed to force him to be good?"

"I don't think that's quite what she meant. But I'm not supposed to put up with stuff."

Caroline nodded. "That makes sense."

"I guess so. I just hope it works."

"So how do you plan to carry it out?"

"The counselor gave us homework," Abby explained. "I'm not sure I can remember it offhand, but it's in my notes. For starters, we're supposed to list for each other five unmet needs we have, things our partner can do to improve our marriage."

"That sounds good."

Abby shrugged. "I don't know. All I can think of is the same old stuff I'm always nagging him about. Like I want him to listen to me—really listen, you know?"

Caroline nodded. "That doesn't seem too much to expect."

"Maybe for you." Abby narrowed her eyes. "You never seem to have any difficulty getting men to listen to you. Even Paul listens to you."

"That's where you're wrong." Caroline took a big sip of water.

"Just because a guy is looking attentively at you does not mean he's listening. Not with his ears anyway. It's usually a different part of anatomy that's standing up and paying attention."

Abby laughed. "Yeah, you might be right. At least in your case. That doesn't happen to me too much anymore."

"It would if you put some energy into it, Abby. You're a pretty woman, but you don't really try."

"I know, I know. I've let myself go. But the pounds just started coming on in my forties, and menopause hasn't helped any either. Besides, I'm a grandma." Abby held her arms out, looking down at her faded plaid blouse, baggy jeans, and old Earth Shoes. "Aren't grandmas supposed to look like this?"

Caroline shrugged one shoulder. "I guess. I mean, if that's what you want to look like."

"I don't know if I even care anymore."

Caroline leaned forward now, peering at Abby as if trying to see beyond her frumpy clothes and graying hair. "You don't even care?" Disbelief was written all over her face. "How can you say that? Every woman cares about her appearance. Good grief, my crazy old mom even cares. I've seen her trying to primp in front of the bathroom mirror. Unfortunately, she's clueless most of the time. But sometimes she gets it right and comes out wearing perfume on her wrists and lipstick on her mouth. And sometimes it's just the opposite, and she really doesn't care for the taste of Desert Flower." Caroline puckered her lips in an imitation.

Abby couldn't help but laugh. "You could call her Sweet Lips."

"But my point is, most women, if not all, like to look nice, Abby. And I find it hard to believe you're content to look like a grandma.

Sure, we're in our fifties, but these are the new fifties. Women our age are more like our mothers were in their thirties. And if the scientists are right, we could live to be more than a hundred years old, which means our adult lives aren't close to half over yet."

"Is this supposed to be a pep talk?" Abby frowned. "Because I do not want to live to be a hundred. Sometimes I'm so tired now that I don't care to make it to sixty."

Caroline got a concerned look. "Abby?"

Abby held up her hands in a hopeless gesture. "Sorry, I'm just being honest. There are days I feel so tired that I don't want to live to a ripe old age."

"But what about your daughters? Your granddaughter?"

Abby considered this. "Okay, I'll admit that I would miss them. Although I'm not so sure they'd miss me. Oh, maybe Lucy would. But she'd still have her other grandma. That lady is older than me but still fit and feisty." She sighed and folded her hands in her lap. "Whereas I'm just fat and flabby."

"Oh, Abby." Caroline looked seriously disappointed in her.

"I'm sorry, but it's the truth."

Caroline's brow creased. "When was the last time you had a complete checkup, Abby?"

"You mean a pap test and *mama*-gram? I go to the gynecologist about every year, give or take."

"No, I mean a complete workup with blood, cholesterol, thyroid … the works. When did you last do that?"

Abby shrugged. "That would be with my general practitioner. Well, he's about to retire, and he's kind of old-fashioned about a lot of that stuff."

"That stuff?"

"He doesn't put much stock into all those tests. He says if you go looking for trouble you'll find it. Besides, I only go to him when I'm sick."

"You need a new doctor."

Abby scowled. "Why?"

"Because you could have something wrong and not even know it."

"Maybe I don't want to know it." Abby set her water glass on a tiny bare spot on a corner of the end table, then folded her arms in front of her.

"Maybe you *need* to know it."

"Why?" She stared defiantly at Caroline. Even though Caroline's day had been relatively stressful, she looked fairly well put together in her light blue T-shirt and khaki capri pants. Tall, shapely, healthy-looking in that California-girl way, blonde and blue-eyed and tan. Who wouldn't like to look like that? Perennially young, Caroline's good looks never seemed to fade. Consequently, in Abby's opinion, Caroline made far too much over appearances.

"I'll tell you why right after I return from the little girls' room." Then Caroline stood up and flitted past Abby, almost as if she wanted to flaunt her good looks, although Abby was pretty sure that wasn't the case. Caroline wasn't really that type. Oh, she flirted with guys, but she also knew how to be a good friend. Abby was simply feeling a little out of sorts, perhaps even envious, and maybe Caroline had hit a nerve in regard to her looks. But if someone was going to chide Abby for letting herself go, did it have to be perfect Caroline?

Of course, Abby knew that Caroline had endured a double mastectomy, although she claimed her implants were superior to her previous old girls. Also, thanks to a botched abortion in the eighties, Caroline had been unable to have children. Seriously, those were high prices to pay in exchange for beauty. Not that Caroline had consciously made those choices or that they were part of any specific transaction other than fate. But in a way, Caroline's troubles were part of the package. Being childless probably preserved her figure, and the implants, well, that was obvious.

Still, Abby knew that if Caroline had been able to choose, she would've gone a different route. And despite Abby's present-day challenges (feeling tired and dowdy and consequently unsure of her marriage), she wouldn't trade her life (specifically her three daughters or sweet little granddaughter) for Caroline's unfading good looks or even for the face and body of, say, Jennifer Aniston.

"Here is why I think you need a new doctor," Caroline announced as she returned to the living room with a magazine in hand. "This is last month's issue of *O,* and I think you need to read this article." She folded the page of the periodical over as a marker, closed the magazine, and dropped it in Abby's lap. "And take that quiz in the back. Then we'll discuss whether you need to change doctors. Since I'm on the hunt for a good doctor myself—and I want it to be a woman—I'll see if she'll take you as a new patient too. Okay?"

Abby blinked. "Okay."

"If it makes you feel any better, my motives are partially selfish."

"Selfish?"

"I'd like you to be around for more than just a few years. In fact, I hope that you and me and Marley and Janie will grow old together. But if we're going to grow old, we ought to do it in style. And that means staying healthy."

A sense of realization tapped on a tiny door inside Abby's brain, like Caroline was almost making sense. "Maybe you're right," she conceded.

"Of course I'm right." She nodded toward her mom's bedroom. "Look at my mom. Now I'm not saying that she had any control over getting Alzheimer's. From what I've read, other than some genetic connections, it's pretty random. But just the same, the woman never took care of herself. For as long as I can remember, she always put my dad's needs above her own. And he treated her like trash most of the time. She ate poorly, drank way too much coffee, smoked for too many years. I mean, even if she hadn't gotten Alzheimer's, her quality of life had already been going downhill for ages. It's like Dad never respected her, and she never respected herself either."

Abby partially listened as Caroline continued to talk about her parents and their dysfunctional relationship. But another part of her was thinking about what she needed from her husband. As Caroline rambled on in a way that Abby hoped was therapeutic, Abby was mentally listing what she needed from Paul. So far they were just one-word needs, but it was a start. She could work out the specifics later: (1) respect; (2) love; (3) communication; (4) encouragement; (5) trust.

As Abby drove home that afternoon, she questioned why she'd placed respect in the number-one position. She suspected it had to do with what Caroline had been saying about her parents—how her dad had been so hard on her mom, and how her mom suffered for it her whole life. To be fair, Paul was nothing like Caroline's father. Most people who knew Paul considered him a great guy, a good old boy, a stand-up kind of fellow. But in some ways, he wasn't always quite what people thought.

Oh, he rarely if ever did anything wrong publicly, because he did so enjoy his good-guy image. He was a successful businessman, member of Kiwanis, participant in the chamber, and faithful contributor to United Way. People often went to Paul Franklin for counsel, and he was happy to disburse his wisdom.

No, for the most part, Paul kept his hands and reputation clean. Well, besides getting slightly involved with that other woman last month, which he'd tried to keep under wraps. Even now he claimed that he and Bonnie never had more than a friendly business relationship, although Abby felt fairly certain he'd considered crossing the line. Maybe he even had crossed it.

If and when Paul broke the rules, he did so in a quiet, almost subversive way. The reason Abby listed respect as her number one need had to do with those times when it felt as if he was trying to undermine her. Like he knew she was going to fail at something anyway, so why not just help the old girl get it over with by pointing out her shortcomings right from the start?

His comments zeroed in on her intelligence (or lack of it), or her hobbies (how much time and money they wasted), or her friends (who were just as nutty as she was)—and in more recent years her appearance (she was getting fat and old). As much as she tried to pretend they were okay or even humorous, those subtle putdowns not only stung, they made her question herself on every level. In a quiet yet destructive way, Paul's undermining remarks made her feel she wasn't good enough … would never be good enough. That hurt deeply and more than words could say.

=Chapter 5=

CAROLINE

Caroline had never been close to her mom. Oh, they'd never had any big fallouts or even gone through that usual teenage-girl-hates-her-mom sort of thing. Their relationship, Caroline felt, was atypical and probably her father's fault. Caroline used to blame herself for her family's dysfunction, thinking that she'd alienated her father's affections from her mother by playing her role of Little Miss Sunshine, but many sessions of counseling combined with years of life experience had convinced her otherwise. As her counselor used to tell her, Caroline's dad was supposed to be the parent. It was his choice, and a bad one, to place his pretty daughter over his browbeaten wife.

Caroline knew this was all water under the bridge now, not to mention hopeless, but she still longed for a good relationship with her mother. As she swept the kitchen, wiped down the cluttered countertops, and scrubbed the sink, she wished she could say the magic words and have her mother appear fully dressed and in her right mind. Then the two of them could sit down for coffee and discuss this fine little mess that they seemed to have gotten themselves into. Maybe they would even laugh over it. Her mother would make light of the fact that she'd gone streaking through the sleepy town of Clifden. Caroline could joke over the way she and her friends had carted the wiggling cocoon off the dock. And then her mother could tell Caroline the sensible thing to do in this situation.

Caroline was just closing the dishwasher when the phone jangled loudly. Not her cell phone, but the landline, which could only mean one of two things—telemarketers or social services—and Caroline bet it was the second. She braced herself and answered in the same way her father had taught her decades ago. "McCann residence."

"This is Beverly Miller of senior social services," a pleasant voice chirped in an automated way. "Is this Caroline McCann?"

"Yes." Caroline forced cheer into her voice. "How are you doing, Beverly?"

"Very well, thank you. But my question is, how are you doing?"

Caroline could tell by Beverly's voice that she had heard the whole story, which didn't matter. Caroline had nothing to hide. Beverly had already been out to the house. She knew what Caroline was up against. "To be honest, I'm feeling pretty frustrated."

"I can imagine."

"And I know what you're going to tell me."

"You do?"

"That my mother needs round-the-clock care ... that she should be locked up ... that she'll probably hurt herself if I keep her here."

"Actually I was going to ask you if you'd gone to that support group I told you about last time we talked."

"Oh." Caroline stood in front of the kitchen sink. "Actually, I have a pretty good support group of old friends."

"Oh, well, that's good. But do any of them understand Alzheimer's?"

"Not specifically, but they understand me."

"Yes, well, that's fortunate. Now let's discuss your mother."

Caroline sighed. "Feel free."

"Did you file for guardianship, and did you get her on any of the nursing home waiting lists that I gave you?"

"I did file for guardianship, and I rearranged her banking as you suggested, but no, I don't want to place her in a nursing home. Not yet. I decided to relocate back here in Clifden. I want to care for Mom myself."

There was a long pause.

"I know you disapprove. But this house—even though it seems like a wreck—is like Mom's security blanket. She feels safe here." Caroline pushed back a shabby curtain, peering out the window over the sink. She doubted that Beverly had even seen how bad the backyard looked. What would she say if she could see all the junk and debris that Caroline's mother had heaped back there over the years?

"I understand that's been the case in the past, Caroline, but your mother may be reaching a stage where no place feels safe and everything will soon become unfamiliar, even her own home."

"But she's not there yet."

"Then why did she leave the house and remove her clothes and hide out on a fishing boat and threaten to jump into the bay, Caroline?"

Caroline was stumped. Why would anyone do that?

"Because she is in the *final stages* of this illness. She is not going to get better. And this is the stage where she needs constant care and supervision—I'm talking twenty-four/seven, Caroline. It's too much for just one person to do. I admire your dedication and energy, but you are setting yourself up to fail."

Well, if there was one thing Caroline did not like to hear, it was someone predicting she would fail. That was an invitation to simply try harder. "I respect your opinion," Caroline said firmly. "But I must also respect my mother's wishes. And she does not want to be removed from her home."

Beverly let out what sounded like an exasperated sigh. "Then will you at least go to the support group?"

"If I need to be with Mom twenty-four/seven, I don't see how."

"We can arrange for some respite care."

"Respite care?"

"I can schedule someone to come over and relieve you from time to time. Would you like that?"

"Sure." Caroline brightened. "That'd be great."

"I have a volunteer available on Monday, Wednesday, and Friday mornings at ten for two hours. I will assign her to you on the condition that you attend a support group on Friday mornings at ten thirty. Are you agreeable to that?"

Caroline could think of things she'd rather do, but the idea of having some help with her mom was appealing. "Okay."

"And we'll look into getting a nurse's aide to visit once a week just to check on her and perform simple health and hygiene tasks, if you don't mind."

"I don't mind a bit." Caroline just hoped her mom wouldn't mind. She knew how much she hated strangers. But a lot of the time she thought Caroline was a stranger too, so what difference would it make? "Will a nurse's aide be expensive?"

"Some of it will be covered by your mother's Medicare. But eventually we'll need to decide about hospice, and at that point, a nurse's aide and other kinds of medical assistance will be completely covered."

"Hospice?" Caroline's understanding was that hospice was for terminal cases. "Do you think she's dying?"

"It's hard to say. A final-stage Alzheimer's patient can last for years ... or be gone within months. It just depends."

Depends.... That reminded Caroline she'd run out of her mother's adult diapers and had forgotten to grab some when she went to the store this morning. "Uh, Beverly, you say my mom needs constant supervision, but isn't it okay for me to slip out to the store or whatnot while she's asleep or watching TV? I mean, it's not like I'm supposed to sit in this house and just watch her round the clock, right?"

"Isn't that what happened this morning? You slipped out to do something, thinking your mother was safe, and when you returned she was gone."

Caroline sighed. She wasn't about to admit that it hadn't been the first time, either.

"Caring for a stage-seven Alzheimer's patient is demanding work for a trained staff in a professional care facility, but it's nearly impossible for a relative in the home, and I suspect it won't be long until you figure that out."

"Yes, you're probably right. In the meantime I'll just muddle along."

"Darlene will be by tomorrow at ten to relieve you."

"Thanks."

"Hang in there."

"I'll try." Caroline hung up with a mixed feeling of relief and fear. On one hand, she was thrilled with the idea of having some respite care. On the other hand, she was fairly sure that Beverly was right. Caroline was navigating an impossible course. And yet she knew she had to give it her best shot.

She peeked in on her mother, relieved to see that she was still sleeping. This morning's activity had really worn her out. So much so that Caroline wished she could set up some kind of physical exercise program on a daily basis. Not that her mom would cooperate. Her favorite pastime was to sit in her recliner and stare blankly at the TV, yet even that seemed to be losing its appeal of late.

Caroline had already tried various activities to engage her mother's mind—simple card games, coloring books, picture books. She'd even brought Play-Doh home from the store once. It seemed to work until her mom tried to eat some and got so angry that she wouldn't even touch it after that. Food was a challenge too. Often Caroline would discover something her mom enjoyed, like applesauce, flavored yogurt, or even Ritz crackers. Caroline would stock up on this item, but the next thing she knew, her mom would change the rules and refuse to even look at it. Caroline had never had children, but this seemed to her a bit like what parenting a toddler must feel like. Except that you could count on a toddler outgrowing tantrums and potty training.

Caroline paced back and forth in the kitchen. She felt trapped. Seriously trapped. Until her conversation with Beverly, Caroline had believed she could come and go as needed. Oh, sure, her mom might make a mess while she was gone. Or go outside and yell obscenities at the neighbors. Or even wander down the street. But Caroline hadn't been terribly worried. After all, her mother had been living on her own and doing these things for some time already.

But now Caroline felt as if everything and anything her mother did was Caroline's personal responsibility. If her mother ran off or fell down or robbed a convenience store, Caroline would be held accountable. After all, Caroline did have guardianship now. That meant full responsibility. Maybe Beverly was right … it was too much to expect of one person. For the second time today, Caroline prayed for help, asking God to please lead her through this messy maze of her mother's mental illness.

Just as she murmured, "Amen," Caroline heard a whimpering sound coming from her mom's room. She hurried down the hallway in time to find her mother standing next to her bed with her pink nightgown pulled up to her waist and her last pair of Depends hanging down around her ankles in an ugly mess.

Caroline let out an involuntary groan. Of all parts of caring for her mother, the toileting challenge was by far the worst. It had only been the last couple of weeks that her mom seemed to give up using the toilet altogether. Before that, Caroline faced only the occasional accident. Now it seemed to be an accident if Ruby made it to the bathroom on time.

"Oh-oh-oh," her mom was saying in a childish voice. Tears began to fall down her cheeks, and she was sobbing.

"It's okay," Caroline said soothingly. "Just stay there while I get something to clean this up."

"Hurts," her mom whined loudly. "It hurts."

Caroline frowned. "Just don't move, okay? I'll be right back." Now she made a dash for the kitchen, grabbing the lifesaving "cleanup kit" she'd put together a few days ago: moist baby wipes, toilet paper, paper towels, disinfectant spray, and plastic bags all tucked into a reusable Safeway shopping bag. The only thing missing was a fresh Depends, and she hoped her mom wouldn't need it right away.

Caroline dashed back to the bedroom to find that her mom had sat back down on the bed, which meant Caroline would now need to change and wash the sheets—for the second time today.

"Oh, Mom," she said in disappointment. "I asked you not to move. Couldn't you have just waited a—"

Her mom let out a loud howl. "Quiet, Mom," Caroline said sternly. She bent down to begin attacking the horrid mess, which stank so badly Caroline felt her gag reflex kicking in.

Her mom let out another howl, even louder this time. "Hurts! Hurts!"

Caroline had the diaper and floor nearly cleaned up and was about to lose her patience or her lunch … or maybe both. "Mom!" she snapped. "Be quiet. A dirty diaper never hurt anyone." Caroline sprayed some disinfectant on the soiled floor, wiping it clean and depositing the gross items into the plastic bag, then setting it aside.

Her mom was still crying. But now she was pointing at her feet. "Hurts! Hurts!" she cried like a little child who had stubbed her toe. Then Caroline remembered her mom's bare feet and how bad they had looked on the boat earlier today.

"Oh, your feet? Do they hurt?"

Ruby nodded with tears streaming down her cheeks. "Hurts! Hurts!"

Caroline gently examined one of her mom's feet and cringed. "Oh, Mom," she said gently. "I'm sorry. Your feet must really hurt."

Her mother nodded again but seemed slightly relieved that Caroline understood.

"Stay here," Caroline said. "I'll get something to help your feet, okay?"

"Okay," she muttered.

Leaving her mom still sitting in a stinky nightgown and soiled bed, Caroline went off in search of something to soak her mom's feet in. She quickly gathered a tub of warm soapy water, a couple of towels, and a kitchen chair, and before long her mother was settled on the chair next to her bed with a makeshift towel diaper folded beneath her bottom. After some coaxing from Caroline, her mother had consented to soak her feet in the tub. Caroline opened the window to let some fresh air into the room, stripped the dirty sheets from the bed and rushed them directly to the washing machine, then returned with a fresh can of grapefruit-scented aerosol and clean sheets.

It was close to five by the time Caroline had her mom's feet cleaned up and bandaged. Despite her mom's complaints, she carefully slipped a pair of bed socks over the bandages to hold them in place; then, because her mom couldn't bear to walk, Caroline helped her back into the fresh-smelling bed. Judging by her mom's expression, she appreciated it. And that was something. Caroline's only problem now was that a bath towel could not take the place of an adult diaper, and Caroline did not want to change the sheets one more time today.

She gave her mom a kiddie-sized box of Cranapple juice, her drink of choice this week (although that could change at any moment), then got her phone out. She already knew the drugstore wouldn't deliver and the grocery store would only if she placed her order hours ahead. Tempted as she was, she was not going to ask her young friend and errand boy, Jacob, to go fetch a big green box of Depends and risk being seen by friends. That was above and beyond what any twelve-year-old boy should be expected to do. So that left her own friends. Because Janie lived closest, Caroline called her first.

"Oh, Caroline, I'd be happy to do a favor for you," Janie said pleasantly. "Except that right now I'm in the middle of the bay."

"The middle of the bay?" Caroline imagined Janie having plunged over the side of a fishing boat. "What on earth happened?"

Janie laughed. "Sorry to be unclear. I'm out on the bay with Victor. He just got the sweetest little sailboat this morning, and he invited me to try it out. I haven't sailed in years, but it's all coming back to me. Victor says to tell you hello."

"Tell him hi for me too."

"Is it something I can help you with when we're done? We'll probably only be out a couple more hours. Sunset's around seven thirty."

Caroline imagined sunset on a sailboat on the bay and controlled the urge to howl like her mom had been doing earlier. "Thanks anyway, Janie. I'll take care of it before that."

"I'm sorry, Caroline. How's your mother doing?"

"She's okay. Worn out. But fine."

"Oh, good."

"I'll talk to you later … and … have fun." Caroline sank down into the couch and let out a low moan. It was hard to imagine that her friends were out having a good time while she was trapped in what felt like a torture chamber. She knew it was childish to be jealous, and it wasn't that she wanted to spoil Janie's fun. Even though Caroline had been interested in Victor—or maybe it was just his beach house and money—she wasn't really longing to trade places with Janie. Not exactly, anyway. She just wondered when, if ever, she would have a life again.

Caroline thought about Mitch—specifically about their last conversation when he'd flown up for Labor Day. They had a great time together, and he encouraged her to move back to California. Not LA, but the Bay Area. He thought maybe they could pick up where they'd left off more than twenty years ago, but, as tempting as that sounded, Caroline knew that her first responsibility was with her mother.

"I'm all she has," Caroline had explained. "She's the reason I moved back here." Then he suggested she relocate her mother to the Bay Area as well, and Caroline had just laughed. "If you knew my mother—the condition she's in, I mean, mentally—you would realize how totally unrealistic that is."

His brown eyes grew sad. "Long-distance relationships aren't easy."

At first she'd felt encouraged that he was even interested in a long-distance relationship, and for several days they had talked on the phone each evening before bed. Then a day slipped between calls … and now he was in the Philippines working on some kind of software deal. They'd exchanged some brief emails, and he'd promised to fly up to Oregon when he returned, but Caroline was getting it ... long-distance relationships were not easy. Nothing about Caroline's life was easy.

In fact, despite her usual optimism, nothing about her life had turned out like she dreamed it would. Caroline hated to admit it, but the truth was she still suffered from Princess Syndrome, the longing to be rescued by a knight on a white horse. More than ever, Caroline longed for someone to sweep her away, to take care of her, and to ensure that she lived happily ever after. Did Mitch fit that description? Probably not. Besides, considering Caroline's track record with men, she knew better than to hope for as much.

She checked on her mom, who appeared to be snoozing, and decided to risk going out. One fast trip to the nearest store to grab a package of Depends should take less than twenty minutes. What could happen in twenty minutes, especially with her mother's feet in such bad shape?

But as Caroline drove, she felt her blood pressure rising. She imagined her mother sneaking out of the house, stripping off her nightie and running naked through the streets again. Knowing she could get a ticket, Caroline snagged one of the handicap-parking spaces, ran through the store, snatched up a package of Depends, and ran back to the cash register. An elderly man turned and smiled at her, then, seeing what she was about to purchase, just turned away.

"They're for my mom," she snapped at him. "I just hope it's not too late."

His eyes widened, and he stepped back, waving his arm forward. "Go on ahead of me if you like, young lady."

Caroline rewarded him with a golden smile. "God bless you!" Then she paid for the granny diapers, dashed out, and was relieved to see that no one had cited her car.

On her way home, while stopped at a traffic light, she looked longingly out toward the bay, wondering if she might possibly spot Victor's new sailboat out there. Then the light turned green, and she quickly pulled away. But as she turned to drive west, she glanced at the way the clouds were gathering along the horizon of the ocean. It promised to be a gorgeous sunset this evening. Not that she'd be watching.

====Chapter 6====

JANIE

"There's one thing I can be thankful for ... during all those years working in Chicago ..." Victor paused as he lowered the mainsail.

"What's that?" Janie helped him to secure it.

"Lake Michigan. It's where I learned to sail."

"Really?"

He nodded as he checked the anchor. "Marcus talked me into getting a boat when he was about fourteen. Some of his friends' families had boats, and Marcus has always been one to keep up with the Joneses." He chuckled. "Turned out that Marcus was prone to seasickness and after several attempts at sailing decided it wasn't so great. But Ben, who was ten at the time, absolutely loved it. He begged me to keep the boat, and so for years Ben and I would go out whenever weather and time allowed."

"Your wife didn't sail?" Other than Victor's admission that he was partially to blame for the divorce, Janie knew very little about his ex. But she was under the impression he didn't like to talk about it. And so Janie had never brought it up.

"She and Marcus seemed to have the same problem." His brow creased. "Guess it was genetic. But it was about the same time I got the boat that Donna moved out."

Janie felt her eyebrows lifting but tried not to act surprised. "Because of the boat?" she asked.

He laughed. "No. Because of Larry."

"Larry?"

Victor reached for her hand, guiding her back over to the cockpit to sit. He had anchored the boat in a quiet cove, and the plan was to eat a picnic dinner, which he had packed, and then sail back to the wharf before dark. "Larry was Donna's boss as well as her romantic interest. They're married now."

"Oh." Janie nodded as she sat on a vinyl-covered cushion. "I wasn't trying to be nosy."

"I know." Victor handed her a paper bag with packages of paper plates, napkins, plastic cups, plastic forks, and several bottles of water. "I haven't had a chance to outfit the galley yet, so we have to make do, okay?"

"If this is called making do, count me in." She looked over the calm blue water out toward the bay bridge and beyond to the ocean. So peaceful … beautiful. A sight better than this morning's nautical experience when they'd rescued Ruby McCann from the fishing boat.

"My caterer was the Safeway deli section," Victor admitted as he opened another bag, pulling out packages of specialty cheeses, olives, smoked salmon, and even some pasta salad. "Do you think we can make a meal of this?"

"Absolutely." She opened the carton of olives, popping one into her mouth. "Delicious!"

Next he pulled out a loaf of French bread and bottle of cabernet. "I wasn't trying to wax poetic, but a loaf of bread and jug of wine sounded awfully sweet for the maiden voyage of my new craft."

"It's perfect."

He glanced around. "Except that I forgot a corkscrew."

"Do you think there's one in the galley?" she asked.

He looked doubtful. "The owners took pretty much everything with them to outfit their new boat—a forty-footer, which I think might've tapped their budget a bit." He held up the bread. "And no knife either."

"I know." Janie held up her purse with a sly smile.

"Your Gucci comes equipped with kitchen utensils?"

She laughed as she dug down deep to retrieve a red pocketknife.

Victor looked impressed. "You travel with a Swiss Army Knife? Must be tough sneaking it through airport security."

"It was my dad's," she confessed. "I found it in his old rolltop desk. I'm not even sure my dad would approve."

"Wouldn't approve of you going through his things?" Victor chuckled. "Or did he think you were dangerous with a knife?"

"Probably both."

"So you and your dad had some issues?"

"Didn't everyone have issues with their parents?" She looked away, unsure of how much to say.

"Some worse than others." He set the wine bottle aside. "What was it like with yours?"

"My father was a very private man. He sort of kept a distance."

"My grandfather was like that."

"My father always seemed to push me away, to hold me at arm's length. I knew he loved me, but a lot of times I felt that he disapproved of me. I always wanted to make him proud."

"I can't imagine any father who wouldn't have been proud to have a daughter like you, Janie. I don't really get that."

"I don't really get it myself. It's hard to explain. Anyway, I thought this knife was worth saving … that it might come in handy." She held it out to him and watched as he fiddled with it until he did, indeed, discover a corkscrew.

"I'll bet your dad would be proud to think he raised such a good Boy Scout," he grinned at her. "Always prepared."

She chatted about other things as she opened the packages and arranged their deli feast on the small table in the middle of the cockpit. She wanted to push unhappy thoughts away from her. They were not welcome on this little cruise. Then she and Victor used their hands to load their paper plates, and finally Janie lifted her plastic cup in a toast.

"To your wonderful new sailboat," Janie proclaimed.

"To many happy miles and good friends and beautiful sunsets." He clicked his cup against hers.

"Heavenly." Janie leaned back and sighed with contentment.

"That's it," he said suddenly.

She sat up straight. "What?"

"The name for the boat."

"I thought her name was *Mona Lisa*." Janie was confused. "That's what it says on the back of the boat."

"The owners wanted to keep the name, too. It's after their daughters, Monique and Elizabeth—Mona Lisa for short."

"Oh … cute."

"So I need to rename her. And you just picked it."

"Heavenly?"

He nodded, lifting his cup again. "To the *Heavenly*."

She smiled and followed suit. "To the *Heavenly*. Nice."

After dinner, Janie offered to stow the leftovers below while Victor straightened out some ropes. The galley was compact, but in the fashion of good nautical design, the area wasted no space. As Victor said, it had been stripped pretty clean. She stuck the paper plates and things in an empty cupboard above the tiny stainless-steel sink, then, seeing that the refrigerator was running, she went ahead and put the remaining food in it, folded the paper bags, and stowed them in a drawer. She was curious as to how Victor would outfit the *Heavenly*, but if it was anything like his house, it would be nice.

He'd already given her the full five-minute tour, but she decided to snoop around a bit more. She peeked into the sleeping cabin to see the captain's bed with drawers beneath, mahogany bookshelves lining the walls, and two nicely placed portholes. Very cozy. With the right accoutrements it could be very comfy, too. Not that she planned to spend any time in here. She closed the door and peeked into the bathroom, which was extremely compact, so tight that the space for the toilet and sink doubled as the shower as well. In a way, that made it self-cleaning. She chuckled as she closed the door, then went back up. The sky was just starting to turn shades of gold and pink.

"The *Heavenly* really is heavenly," she said as Victor was pulling up the anchor. "It's like a little dollhouse."

He frowned. "A dollhouse?"

"Oh, you know. Everything is so small. I guess I meant a play-house. You're going to have fun outfitting it."

He set the anchor into place, then wiped his damp hands on the back of his jeans. "You think that would be fun?" He looked skeptical.

"Of course. Don't you? Think about it—you'll need dishes and linens and books for your shelves, and all those personal touches that make the *Heavenly* your own."

"Well ... now that you put it like that ... I suppose it might be fun."

"Of course it will be fun. And if it turns out half as lovely as your home, it'll be one sweet little boat."

He laughed. "You don't think I was in charge of the interior design of my home, do you?"

"I just assumed."

He shook his head. "I bought it furnished. Right down to the forks and spoons and bottle openers."

"Oh." She studied him. "So you really don't know how to do that sort of thing?"

"You could say that again. Donna, my ex, well, she was pretty territorial in the house. She knew what she liked, and my suggestions were, shall we say, unwelcome."

Janie was surprised by this. She and Phil had always made these kinds of decisions together, whether about an expensive piece of art or a mere lamp. They always made sure they both liked it before bringing it home. She wouldn't have dreamed of forcing her own tastes upon him. In fact, because he'd grown up wealthy and surrounded by quality things, she had always trusted his sense of style more than her own.

"Maybe you'd like to help me with outfitting the boat," he suggested hopefully.

She considered this. "Well, I don't consider myself an expert in interior design, but I have enjoyed putting my parents'—I mean my house together."

"And so far it looks great," he reminded her. "I think you've got great taste."

"But I wouldn't be comfortable making decisions for you," she admitted. "You see, Phil and I always worked together on things like that … so we were both happy." Janie felt her cheeks growing warm, as if she were propositioning him, like she thought they were going to share this boat. "What I'm saying is that I don't have the confidence to make choices like that … because it's your boat. I think you should have a say."

"Here's a thought." He nodded as he began hoisting the mainsail. "Maybe we can work on it together." He glanced at her as if gauging her response. "And we can make this a job if you like. I'll hire you as my interior designer."

She laughed. "No way. I'm not ready for that. But, as your friend, I'd be happy to help you."

He grinned. "So, help me now, will you? Let's get that jib up and get ourselves out on the water while the sun is setting."

Together they got both the main and jib sails up, and within minutes they were gracefully cutting across the bay, enjoying the beautiful colors as the sun and the clouds painted the sky and the sea.

It was after eight o'clock by the time they finished docking the boat and getting her safely tied down for the night.

"Would you ever spend the night here?" Janie asked as he helped her from the boat.

"Here on this wharf, you mean?" He glanced curiously at her.

"I mean in your boat." She giggled. "As a girl I always thought it would be fun to sleep on a boat docked out here. I'd see other people coming and going on their boats, and, well, I wondered what it would be like."

"You never slept on a boat before?"

She shook her head. "When we sailed with my husband's family, we only took day trips."

He chuckled. "Well, if you ever get the hankering to sleep on a boat, you feel free to come on down here. I'll even give you a key of your own."

"Really?"

"Just make sure you're safe about it. Lock the cabin door and have your cell phone with you. Not that I've heard of much crime down here, but you never know … and a woman alone."

"I bet it would be peaceful," she said as they walked across the gravel lot to where they'd parked their cars. "The gentle lapping of the waves against the boat."

"Oh, yeah, it's peaceful all right."

"So you've slept on a boat then?"

He jingled his car keys in his hand. "Sure … more times than I care to remember."

She stopped next to her car and looked up at his face. His expression, illuminated in the streetlights, was hard to read. "What do you mean? Did you used to be in the navy?"

"No. I just spent quite a few nights on my boat after Donna and I split up."

"I thought you said she left you?"

He nodded. "She did. But then she came back."

"You got back together?"

"No. She came back and told me to leave."

"But wasn't she the one with the lover?"

He nodded again. "But the boys were in school and I was working long hours and she didn't want to disrupt their lives. All in all, it made a lot of sense."

"So you stayed on your boat?"

"Well, it was late spring going into summer, and the marina was pretty close to work, so it was convenient. I actually kind of enjoyed it at first. But after a few months and when the weather started to get cold, the enjoyment factor dimmed considerably."

"I can imagine."

"But, you're right, it was fun." He touched her cheek. "You should try it sometime."

An unexpected tingle went down her spine, and she reached up to put her hand on his. "Thanks for showing me your boat, Victor."

"Thanks for naming her." He leaned down and kissed Janie gently on the mouth, then straightened back up. "And thanks for the offer to help fix her up with me."

"Thank you." She took in a quick breath and steadied herself. So far, this was as far as the romantic side of their relationship had gone—at her request. She had asked Victor to take this thing slowly. Yes, more than two years had passed since Phil's death, but they'd been married twenty-six years, and letting go wasn't exactly easy. Fortunately, Victor respected that, and he hadn't been pushing her. But sometimes, like right now, she considered changing the rules. "Well, I should go," she said nervously. "I promised Caroline I'd check in with her. She had a hard day with her mom."

He nodded. "Give her my best. Poor Caroline … she's got her work cut out for her."

Then they got in their cars and drove their separate ways. Victor headed for the beach and to his lovely new home, and Janie headed back to the same sixties housing development that she'd grown up in, just a few blocks from Caroline. It was ironic—both Caroline and her living in their childhood homes at this stage of life. At least Janie had control over the state of her home, whereas poor Caroline was stuck.

As soon as she got in the house, Janie called Caroline. "Is there anything I can do to help?" she asked.

"No, that's okay," Caroline answered in a tired voice. "I'd gotten Mom cleaned up after another accident only to realize she was out of her adult diapers. And that was after social services told me I couldn't leave Mom unattended."

"Oh, I'm sorry, Caroline. If I'd been on dry land, I would've gladly run and got them." Janie considered this—maybe it wouldn't have been too gladly. She had never even been that comfortable purchasing her own feminine hygiene products and had eventually got into the habit of ordering them online. Going into a local store for adult diapers? Well, that would've been a sacrifice of love. "Hey, why don't you order them online?" she said.

"Online?" Caroline questioned. "You can do that?"

"Absolutely." So Janie explained online drugstores and told Caroline which was her favorite one and how she might even find coupons and such.

"Wow, that's a great idea."

"You can even get groceries online," Janie continued. "I think you can get almost anything online."

"Yes, according to my spam, you can get the perfect man online too." Caroline laughed. "But I guess you don't need that."

Janie thought she heard a trace of jealousy in that last comment. Although it didn't really make sense. "I thought you found a pretty good guy yourself," Janie said cautiously. "Aren't you and Mitch still together?"

Caroline made a loud sigh. "Yes. I suppose we are. But Mitch was right. A long-distance relationship is hard. Especially for me. I'm at a place in life where I could use a good man close by." She laughed. "And I don't mean in a sexual way."

"What do you mean then?"

"For friendship ... companionship ... a shoulder to cry on. Especially today." Caroline sounded like she was crying.

"Oh, Caroline," Janie said quickly. "Do you want me to come over and keep you company for a while?"

"You—you would do that?"

"Sure. You know I'm just blocks away."

"Well, yeah, sure. That would be nice. It's been a rough day. And it's kind of lonely. Yeah, if you wanted to come by, that would be great."

Janie looked around her unfinished kitchen, wondering what she might be able to take to cheer up Caroline. She remembered the time Caroline had brought a piña colada when Janie was feeling low. But other than a bottle of champagne that Abby had put into a welcome-back basket, Janie's wet bar was dry. She opened her freezer and spied an unopened carton of mocha-almond-fudge ice cream. After grabbing it, she was on her way.

It was such a balmy evening that Janie decided to walk the few blocks. Although it was dark, Janie felt completely safe and was reminded of when she walked to Caroline's as a kid. Not that she'd spent so much time at Caroline's house, because, thanks to a cantankerous father, Caroline usually wanted to get away from there herself. In fact, right from the start, that had been one of the commonalities between the two girls. Neither of them ever felt comfortable in her own home. Although Janie's father wasn't as mean as Caroline's, he was cold and unbending. It was his way or the highway, and as soon as Janie was old enough to leave home, she had. In grade school, though, she escaped to her friends' houses. She couldn't even imagine how many times she must've walked over to meet Caroline before together walking over to Abby's or Marley's. Both of those friends had the kind of home where all four girls felt welcome and comfortable, where hanging out was encouraged, and where it seemed that voices were only raised in laughter.

Abby's house had been in what was now called the historic neighborhood. It was a big old Victorian with a basement, where the four girls could do pretty much as they pleased for hours on end. Plus, there was always something good to eat there because Abby's mom loved to cook. And Marley's house was a very cool modern design up on the bluff overlooking the bay, a house that even now Janie wouldn't mind owning. Marley's parents, although older like Janie's, were laid-back and cool. They always had jazz or blues playing on the stereo, with martinis in real martini glasses, and Marley's mom was usually working on something creative like macramé or pottery or beads or candles—whatever the latest craft craze was. It was no wonder Marley became an artist.

What times the Four Lindas had enjoyed during their preadolescent years! But then they entered their teens and began to drift apart.

═Chapter 7═

ABBY

Abby wasn't sure what made her feel most lonely tonight. Was it the sound of the sea? Or living in this recently built house that was slightly isolated from neighbors? Or the fact that it was after nine and Paul was still not home from his chamber of commerce meeting? Or maybe she was simply hormonal—it was certainly an excuse she'd been using for the past couple of years. But someday she would be past the perimenopausal stage. And what would she use for an excuse then? Mental instability? Perhaps the early onset of Alzheimer's? She thought of Ruby McCann and shuddered. No, definitely not that.

As Abby paced in the kitchen, she thought about the article she'd just read and what Caroline had told her about getting a new doctor. The more she thought about it, the more it made sense. Abby was chemically, not mentally, imbalanced. And the sooner she figured it out, the better things would be. For Abby and Paul both. She looked at the clock. Why was he so late? Chamber meetings, unless they were planning some big event, usually ended by eight.

Abby picked up the phone. Jackie Day, an old school friend who ran a bed-and-breakfast in town, usually went to the chamber meetings. Maybe Abby could extract some information from Jackie about Paul's whereabouts. Sneaky, perhaps, but Abby was tired and wanted to go to bed without worrying that Paul was involved in a bad car wreck or up to no good.

"Hi, Jackie," Abby said cheerfully. "Sorry to call so late."

"Oh, that's okay. I was just getting some things set up for breakfast. What's up?"

"Well …" Abby didn't really like to lie, but she also didn't like to be obviously checking up on her husband either. "I was thinking about your bed-and-breakfast, and I wanted to ask you some questions."

"Questions?" Now Jackie sounded slightly suspicious. "Do you think I'm doing something wrong over here?"

"No, nothing like that, Jackie. Now, don't get worried, but I've been considering starting a bed-and-breakfast myself. I'm sure I've mentioned that to you before."

"Oh, yeah, of course. Really, are you getting serious about it now?"

"Maybe. I'm curious as to how much work it really is. For instance, here it is after nine and you're still working at it, and that has me concerned."

"Oh, I'm only working at it because I was at a chamber meeting tonight. Normally, I'd have things set up long before now."

"Oh, right, the chamber meeting. Paul had that too. I forgot. It must've run late tonight."

"Well, we started talking about First Saturday Art Walk, and I suppose that dragged it out a bit."

"Marley told me about that. It seems like a good idea."

"So, back to B and Bs. What do you want to know?"

Abby thought hard. "Well, do you think our town has room for another one? I wouldn't want to encroach on your business."

Jackie laughed. "Oh, I'm not too worried. A lot of my guests are regulars. I think they'd be loyal. But you know, I've dreamed about having someone setting up another B and B—and the possibility of running them together."

"Together?"

"You know, we could share advertising and booking, and if one of us had to close for some reason, perhaps the other one could pick up the slack so we wouldn't lose business."

"That's a good idea, Jackie. Kind of like a co-op."

"Exactly."

Abby was no longer pretending. "You know, I've always regretted selling our old Victorian house in town and—"

"I heard it's going back on the market."

"Are you kidding?"

"No. Don't say you heard it from me, but Marsha at the bank told me that it's probably going to be a short sale. I guess the owners got in over their heads financially."

"Really?" Abby's heart began to beat a little faster.

"That's what I heard."

"Don't you think that would make a great bed-and-breakfast?"

"Of course. And I like that it wouldn't be in direct competition with me in regard to location."

"Well, no one can beat your waterfront location near the wharf, Jackie. It's really just about perfect."

"But your location is perfect for walking to the park or the library or town."

"Believe me, I know it. I still wake up some mornings and think that I'll get up and walk to the post office and mail something."

Jackie laughed. "Well, it would be a long walk, but you could probably do it."

"Not if I had to walk back."

"So are you going to look into it?"

"Walking to town?"

"No. Buying the old Victorian again."

Abby thought hard. "Well, I just don't know for sure. But I might give it some thought."

"Keep what I said in mind—about the possibility of partnering."

"I will." Abby's mind was already running ahead, wondering how she could do something like this and what Paul might say. "But please, Jackie, don't mention our conversation with anyone, okay?"

"Mum's the word. You can count on it, Abby. Partly out of self-ishness, because I'd rather have you buy that house for a B and B than anyone else. I'll be keeping my fingers crossed and sending up some prayers."

"Thanks, Jackie! I appreciate it." Abby hung up, and instead of obsessing over Paul's lateness, she got out a notepad and a calculator and started to do some quick mathematical figuring. Math had never been her forte, but she did know how to balance a checkbook. How much different could this be?

She could only guess on the price of the house, but if it was a short sale, it would probably be reasonable and hopefully below market value, so she listed it at just a bit less than what they'd sold it for back before the real estate market took a dive. She knew how much she had in her savings, which might barely make a 10 percent down payment, but then she would have nothing left to run the business with, and she knew it would take cash to get the place set up.

She wondered if her mom might want to get involved, then penned in a number that she thought her mom might be comfortable investing, just to get Abby started. Actually, that seemed reasonable, considering how her mom was always telling her to get a hobby or interest to take her mind off herself and her troubles. Then she estimated what the monthly payments and expenses would be, countering that with what she could make if all six bedrooms were rented most of the time. Suddenly she was amazed. She had no idea that a B and B could make so much money. She'd be rich in no time!

"Sorry to be so late," Paul said from behind her, making her jump and drop her pen.

"Oh!" She took off her reading glasses and looked up. "You scared me. I didn't even hear you come in."

"Sorry." He leaned over and pecked her on the cheek. "Just wanted to say good night before I head for bed. I'm beat."

"Good night." She picked up her pen and looked back down at the notepad.

"Doing your homework?" He leaned over to see.

She covered it with her hand and smiled coyly. "No, just doing some figuring."

"Figuring?"

"Just dreaming about something … doing the math to see if it could even work."

"Does it work?"

"Oh, yeah." She nodded happily.

"So what is it you're dreaming about? A vacation in Europe perhaps?"

"Maybe something that could lead to a European vacation. Now that Nicole seems determined to stay there, I might want to go visit her sometime. To do that, I'll need some cash."

Phil pulled out a stool and sat down at the breakfast bar with her. "What exactly are you planning here? Not some crazy get-rich scheme."

"No. If you must know, I was thinking about starting my own business."

He frowned. "Your own business?"

She nodded firmly. "Yes. And according to my calculations it could be quite a lucrative one too."

Now he looked both skeptical and curious. "Tell me about it."

"Thought you were tired ... wanted to go to bed."

"Suddenly I find myself wide awake." He smiled, but it looked a bit stiff around the edges.

"We can talk about it in the morning."

"I'm playing golf in the morning."

"Golf on a Wednesday?"

"Shore Links is offering a cheap midweek rate. It was just announced at the chamber meeting tonight. Some of us promised to give it a try at seven tomorrow."

"Oh. Maybe you should get to bed if you have an early morning."

"Not until you tell me exactly what kind of business venture I'm going to get stuck with."

"You?" She peered at him. "Who said you would be part of it, Paul? This is going to be *my* business."

He laughed. "Right. You're going to run a business on your own, Abby? With no help from me? You honestly expect me to believe that?"

"Yes. As a matter of fact, I do."

"And what are you going to use to finance this little business venture?"

"My savings." She held her chin up and wished he'd quit using the word *venture* as if her dream was some kind of a recreational idea and not a legitimate business.

He scowled, then stood and went to the fridge to get a bottle of water. He took a long slow swig. Paul had never liked that Abby kept her own savings account. But it was something Abby's mother had encouraged her to do and even helped her get started when finances were tight. Her mom called it Abby's "just-in-case account," confessing that Abby's father had briefly stepped out on their marriage when Abby was a teenager.

"It's your insurance policy," Mom had explained. "The idea is to have it and never need it, which is better than not having it and needing it."

Over the course of more than thirty years, Abby's just-in-case account had grown considerably, although most of the time Abby never really thought about it.

"So what kind of business venture are you planning to embark upon?" He set the water bottle on the countertop with a thud. "If I may ask."

"Well, since you probably won't leave me alone until I tell you, it's a bed-and-breakfast."

He let out a groan. "Oh, not again."

"I was talking to Jackie Day about it and—"

"And I'm sure Jackie Day is just over the moon about you starting up some competition for—"

"As a matter of fact, Jackie is supportive. She would like to have another B and B in town, sort of as a co-op. We could share advertising and business and—"

"And did Jackie tell you that running a B and B is a full-time, seven-days-a-week, three-hundred-and-sixty-five-days-a-year job? Or that you'd have to live on the premises?"

"There might be more than one—"

"And where, if I may ask, do you plan to operate this B and B?" He looked around the kitchen. "Certainly not here, since we have only two spare bedrooms."

"I'm going to buy our old house."

Now Paul laughed. "Sure. You're going to go up and knock on the front door and ask the owners to sell it back to you, right?"

"I have it from a good source that it'll be for sale soon."

Paul looked surprised. "Well, even if that's true, how would you possibly afford it? I don't know for sure, but I doubt there's that much in your savings account."

"I will use my savings as a down payment and get a loan."

"A loan?" Paul was pacing in the kitchen now. "And what will you secure your loan with? What kind of collateral?"

She considered this. "I'm not sure. I figured the bed-and-breakfast would secure it. Maybe I'll get a business loan."

"Oh, yes, I can see you've given this idea of yours lots of careful thought, Abby." Now he smiled and patted her head. "Why don't you just give that brain of yours a little rest and think about this tomorrow."

"Because I want to think about it now, Paul. And if it's not too much to ask, I want some respect from you."

"Respect?" He looked confused.

She slammed her fist on the table. "Respect! R-E-S-P-E-C-T!" She refrained from singing, "Sock it to me, sock it to me."

He held up his hands, looking at her like she'd totally lost her senses, as if maybe he was the victim. "What is going on with you, Abby? What brought all this on? Is it something I said or did? Something the counselor suggested? Or are your hormones running amok again?"

"You make it sound like it's crazy for me to want to run my own business," she said as calmly as she was able. "Like you think I don't have what it takes to succeed at something. Is that what you think?"

He pressed his lips together and just looked at her.

"I want to do this, Paul. And it would be a lot nicer if you believed in me instead of treating me like I'm a child or an imbecile."

He actually looked like he was taking this in.

"Remember our assignment today?"

He just nodded.

She flipped back some pages on her notepad. "Well, I did mine. Did you do yours?"

He made a tired-looking half smile. "It's been a long day, Abby."

"So long that you don't have time to hear my five needs?"

He shrugged. "Go ahead."

She looked at the page. "Respect, love, communication, encouragement, and trust."

He nodded. "Good list. I think mine would be nearly the same."

She wasn't sure whether to be encouraged that he agreed or concerned that he was copying her homework, just like he used to do back in high school. "You said *nearly*." She held up the list. "What would be different on your list?"

"I guess I'd replace the last one with affection."

She looked back at her list. "You'd take out trust?"

He scowled. "I didn't mean it like that, Abby. I just meant I'd put affection on my list."

"In *place* of trust?" She scowled back at him.

"Not in place of. I guess I'd just have to have six things on my list." He looked at her list again. "Or maybe I'd take out communication."

"You'd take out communication?" She stared at him. "You don't want to talk to me?"

"Sometimes you talk too much."

"And most of the time you don't talk enough," she shot back. "Or when you're talking you're putting me down."

"Look, it's obvious we're both tired. And the counselor said not to start these conversations when it's getting late or we'll end—"

"And why are we having this conversation when it's so late?" She stood and locked eyes with him. "Especially when I know that the chamber meeting ended a long time ago?"

"What are you doing?" He glared at her. "Checking up on me?"

"Where did you go after the meeting, Paul?" Now her heart was pounding, and she realized she had just entered some territory where she did not intend to go. But how to turn back?

"I went to have coffee with some guys from the chamber."

"Which guys, Paul? Exactly who was there?"

He looked caught off guard. "So do you have spies on me now, Abby? What about item five on your list? You have no trust?"

"I want to have someone I *can* trust." She kept her voice quiet but intense. "Now tell me, Paul, who did you have coffee with tonight? Surely you can remember."

He looked like he was thinking. Was he about to make up some names?

"I want the truth, Paul. Trust me, I *will* know if you're lying." Okay, this was a bluff, but who could blame her?

Paul looked like a kid with his hand in the cookie jar. Abby was getting seriously worried, not to mention mad.

"Fine." He held up one finger. "Craig from Coastal Excursions was there." A second finger popped up. "And Drew from Shore Links." Now he looked like he was trying to recall, but then he just shrugged, almost as if he was surrendering, and a third finger went up. "And Bonnie Boxwell was there too." He looked down at the list still lying on the breakfast bar.

Abby wasn't sure how to react to this bit of news. On one hand it was exactly what she'd been fishing for. On the other, she didn't think she was ready to hear it. She took in a careful breath. "Why was Bonnie Boxwell there?"

"To have coffee," he answered rather stupidly.

"With the guys from the chamber?" she persisted.

"Bonnie joined the chamber."

"Bonnie joined the chamber." Abby shook her head with a frown. "Why?"

"Because she opened a store. Bridgeport Interiors. Haven't you seen it?"

Abby thought for a moment. "I saw an ad for it last week, but I haven't been in. *That's* Bonnie's store?"

He nodded. "So it made sense she should join."

"Don't you have to be invited to join?"

He nodded again.

"Let me guess, Paul? You invited her, right?"

Again with the nod. Did he have any idea how guilty and stupid that made him look?

"And that's why you've been faithfully going to chamber meetings all of a sudden?"

"Hey, I've always gone to chamber meetings. Not all of them, of course, but I try to stay involved. I had to be there to nominate Bonnie at the last meeting and to introduce her today. And if it makes you feel any better, she asked me to do this for her weeks ago. I couldn't exactly back out now, could I?"

She shrugged.

"So don't go making this into something it's not. I can't help it if Bonnie wants to be part of the chamber, can I?"

"And have coffee with you afterward?"

"Not just me, Abby. I told you who was there. And I'm sure your spies told you as well."

"Spies?" She looked askance at him. "Really, Paul, are you suffering from paranoia or just a guilt complex?"

Paul picked up the water bottle from the counter and shook his head. "Good night, Abby. The next time you want to interrogate me, why don't you start earlier in the evening?"

"Why don't you come home earlier in the evening?" she yelled to his back as he walked away. And then she turned off the lights and went to the guest room to sleep. At least she tried to sleep.

Chapter 8

MARLEY

"Are you feeling okay?" Marley asked Abby as they sat down with their coffee and pastries. She didn't want to make Abby feel bad, but she could've sworn that her friend had aged by several years since just yesterday.

"Do I look that awful?" Abby frowned and blew on the surface of her latte.

"I wouldn't say awful, just a little frazzled maybe."

Abby sighed. "Paul and I had a great big fight last night."

"Oh." Marley nodded. "Well, that explains a lot."

Abby looked close to tears now. "I just don't know, Marley. Sometimes, like now, it feels like a lost cause."

"Your marriage, you mean?"

She picked up her napkin and used it to dab the edges of her eyes, then nodded.

"Well, I know what that's like." Marley took a sip of her Americano. "And I have to say that nothing or nobody could make me want to go back there."

"Not even if John changed?"

Marley laughed. "Short of a serious head injury or lobotomy—and I wish neither upon him—I don't think that's possible."

"So how did you know it was over?"

"To be honest, I knew it was over long before I decided to end it. I just didn't have the nerve earlier on. I kept telling myself that I'd wait until Ashton got older. First it was until he was old enough to drive. For some reason I thought that would be a good time. Then it was until Ashton graduated high school. Then when Ashton was in college I realized I had no more excuses. I made a plan, and I left."

"Was it hard?"

Marley considered this. "In some ways it was excruciatingly hard. For starters, I was totally unprepared to support myself. I had depended on John for all those years, allowing him to make all the decisions, take care of the finances, everything."

Abby looked confused. "You don't seem like that kind of a person to me, Marley. I always got the impression you were a go-getter and no one pushed you around."

"But I've told you about John before."

"Maybe it never really sank in. Or I thought you were exaggerating."

"Probably the opposite. If anything, over the years, I learned to play things down, tried to convince myself that it wasn't so bad."

Abby nodded. "Yeah, I do that sometimes."

Marley wanted to protest, to say that Abby's situation was nothing like what Marley had endured, but she stopped herself. "But it was bad," she confessed. "John was controlling and mean. And I became so emotionally exhausted from all those years of verbal abuse and mental bullying that I didn't even know how to live once I was on my own. I got counseling and that helped. But I was kind of broken, you know?"

Abby nodded, but her expression suggested that she didn't know. Not really. Not deeply.

"Don't get me wrong," Marley told her. "I'm not saying I know Paul that well. And you know that Paul and I don't exactly get along, but I've seen you two together, Abby. And it seems like there's more hope for your marriage than I ever had for mine."

"But that's seeing us when we're with you," Abby pointed out. "You don't know what it's like when no one's watching."

"Is Paul abusive?" Marley leaned closer.

Abby seemed to think about this. "Not physically, of course. But he belittles me. And a lot of times, like last night, it feels like he's trying to undermine me. Do you know what I mean?"

Marley nodded. "Oh, yeah. I've had lots of experience having the rug ripped out from under me. John was extremely passive-aggressive."

"I've heard the term, but I'm not totally sure what it means."

"I'll give you my definition. It's not exactly clinical, but it works for me. A passive-aggressive person is someone who acts like they like you but gets a real kick out of watching you fall flat on your face."

Abby's eyes lit up. "That sounds like Paul."

Marley grimaced. "Oh, I don't know, Abby. Certainly, Paul's got his problems, but he's probably not that—"

"Wait, hear me out." Abby explained how she wanted to start a bed-and-breakfast, and how Paul had put her down. "He was so certain I would fail at it. It's like he gave up on me before I even had a chance."

Marley thought about it. Though Paul's behavior sounded unfair, Marley was inclined to agree with him. Starting a bed-and-breakfast did seem a huge undertaking. "So that's what you fought about?"

"That and the fact he had coffee with Bonnie Boxwell last night." Marley slowly shook her head. "Okay, now *that's* something to fight about. What does he think he's doing—marriage counseling with you in the morning and coffee with Bonnie at night?"

"He made it sound like it was nothing, like it was just some people from the chamber getting together for coffee after the meeting, but I know—"

"You mean he wasn't alone with Bonnie?"

"No, according to him a couple other guys were there too."

"So maybe they *were* just having coffee." Marley studied Abby. Was it possible she was blowing this thing with Bonnie out of proportion?

Abby clenched her fists and scowled. "I don't know. The way he reacts when I question.... It just doesn't feel right."

"But as far as you know, nothing has happened between them, right?"

Abby nodded. "Right."

"And he's doing the marriage counseling with you, right?"

"Yes."

"So it sounds to me like he's still committed to your marriage, Abby."

"I guess."

Marley felt she was in over her head. Of all Abby's friends, Marley was the least equipped to dish out marriage advice. Part of her had no tolerance for a husband who treated his wife poorly, and if Abby pushed for a verdict, Marley would probably just tell her to kick the jerk to the curb and move on. And yet Marley knew people who had worked through bigger problems than Abby's, saved their marriages, and seemed to be living happily ever after. Or mostly. "I'm not the best person to talk to about marital troubles," she admitted. "Sure, I can listen, but I'm not terribly objective if you know what I mean. And I don't want to project my negativity about marriage onto you. Personal feelings about Paul aside, I still haven't gotten past how he said my beach house was a scrapper. I have to admit he's got some good qualities, and I think he loves you, Abby. You should be taking your concerns to the marriage counselor … and to Paul."

"I know. I guess I just wanted to vent."

Marley smiled. "Venting I can handle. It's just the dispensing of advice that worries me."

"Did you have someone to vent to about your marriage?"

"I went to a counselor for a while, and she kept telling me the only hope for my marriage was to get John in there with me, but he refused. She never said as much, but I think she got fed up with me for putting up with him." Marley sighed. "So the fact that Paul is willing to go with you is worth a lot."

"What attracted you to John in the first place, Marley?"

"It's embarrassing to admit, but it was actually his Air Force uniform that caught my eye. And I was a confirmed hippie. Go figure." Marley laughed. "Also, I was young. John started pursuing me—relentlessly. I was flattered, and I eventually gave in. He was being stationed in Germany … and then I was pregnant … getting married just seemed to be the answer."

Abby nodded. "Sometimes I regret marrying so young."

"You were *really* young." Marley recalled her surprise when Abby and Paul married right out of high school. "In fact, I remember thinking your marriage wouldn't last. And here you are all these years later, still together."

"Barely." Abby stirred her latte. "So does Ashton have a good relationship with his father?"

Marley wasn't sure how much she wanted to say. She'd spent so many years covering things up, but why should she continue? Was she still letting John control her? "Actually, John and Ashton have no relationship," she confessed. "John disowned his only son when Ashton told him he was gay."

Abby looked surprised but nodded like she understood … or was trying to understand. "And how's your relationship with Ashton?"

Marley smiled. "Pretty good. I'm hoping it'll get even better now that I live so much closer to him. It was hard being six hours away in Seattle. But Ashton is a good boy." She laughed. "Good grief, he's almost thirty-two, and I'm still calling him a boy. He's a good man. And I like his partner, Leo. They have a successful business and are quite happy together."

"I've wondered about my daughter Laurie in, uh, that regard." Abby looked uncomfortable now.

"What regard?" Marley questioned. "You mean you think she's a lesbian?"

Abby twisted the napkin in her hands. "I don't have any real reason, but she's so distant from her family and kind of defensive, you know?"

Marley nodded as if she knew, although this didn't really sound like Ashton.

"And she works for the city in … San Francisco."

Marley laughed. "So you think because she's a little defensive and lives in San Francisco she might be a lesbian?"

Abby made an embarrassed face. "I know that sounds silly."

"And what if she was?" Marley watched Abby's reaction.

"Well, I honestly wouldn't wish that on any of my daughters. But I hope that I'd be able to get past it." Abby's brow creased. "I actually think it would be harder on Paul than me, but I don't think he'd disown her. I can't imagine disowning any of my children for any reason."

"Good for you. Trust me, it gets easier once you get over the initial shock. If it wasn't for John's negative influence early on, which I'm still trying to shake off, I would probably go around telling everyone that my son's gay." She grinned. "Maybe I will. I'm proud of Ashton. He's doing some very cool things with his life. And having a gay child is nothing to be ashamed of." She laughed. "Maybe it's the parents who should come out of the closet."

Now Abby looked nervous, as if Marley had taken this too far. "I could be wrong about Laurie," Abby said quickly. "After all, she's a middle child, and she's always been a little difficult and overly sensitive. I don't think she got enough attention growing up. At least that's what she told me once when she was pointing out all the things I did wrong in raising her. Although her sisters don't agree. Anyway, she might not really be a lesbian."

"But if she is," Marley persisted, "you'll get over it. You'll still love her."

"Of course." Abby blinked, then picked up her coffee.

"The hardest part for me is that I won't have grandchildren." Marley sighed. "I'll miss that."

"Couldn't they adopt?"

"Ashton has said he would never do that. He thinks it's unfair to the child."

Abby nodded. "He sounds like a mature young man."

"I've told myself I could probably adopt some grandchildren if I wanted. I still remember an older couple who played grandparents to Ashton while we were stationed in Germany. They came over for birthdays and holidays and really made a difference while he was in preschool."

"Sometimes nonrelatives are less complicated than the real thing. I know there were times when I wanted to disown my mother." Abby chuckled. "But I have to admit she's been a good grandmother to the girls."

Marley imagined what it would be like to have a little one around just long enough to spoil and then send home. "Surely there must be a child somewhere in Clifden who needs a doting grandma."

"Doesn't Jack have grandchildren?" Abby asked.

Marley cocked her head to one side. "Yes, but why should that have anything to do with me?"

"Well, I just thought maybe you and Jack …" Abby smiled sheepishly. "I thought maybe Jack would like to share his grandchildren with you."

Marley chuckled. "Yes, he's a generous guy; he probably would. If I was interested that is."

Abby leaned forward and lowered her voice. "So are you telling me you're *not* interested? In Jack, I mean."

"I'm interested in his friendship. And I'm interested in having my art in his gallery." Marley shrugged.

Abby looked disappointed. "And that's it?"

"I can't predict the future, Abby."

"But you're saying you're not attracted to him?"

"I don't know. I guess I haven't really let myself go there yet. I keep telling myself that Jack's a lot older than me."

"How old is he?"

Marley laughed. "I don't even know. But I think he's in his sixties."

"Sorry to dampen your youthful spirits, but he's not *that* much older."

"Maybe not." Marley watched some young women coming into the coffeehouse and wondered why she didn't feel that much older than they looked. Was she really in her fifties? Where had the years gone?

"Jack seems like a good guy to me. I think he'd be a good catch."

"He is a nice guy. But I don't know that I'm ready for a serious relationship right now. I spent so many years in a really bad marriage. And then, even after I got out, I was kind of stuck for a while, like I had arrested development or shell shock or something. But it was like I had to decompress for a couple of years. I had to learn how to live, how to breathe and walk on my own two feet. I feel like I've just moved beyond that stuck place. Moving back to Clifden and buying my beach house is a huge step for me. And maybe, now that I'm feeling stronger and more independent, I think I'd like to spread my wings and fly a bit."

Abby sighed, looking longingly out across the bay. "That sounds lovely. I wish I could fly too."

"Why can't you?" Marley smiled hopefully. "So, tell me more about your bed-and-breakfast idea."

Abby's eyes lit up. "I want to keep this news under my hat, but I heard that our old house, the Victorian that Paul and I lived in for all those years, may come up for sale soon. I'd always dreamed of turning it into an inn after the girls were grown and moved on. Operating a bed-and-breakfast sounds like fun to me. You know how I love to cook and play hostess and decorate and just basically take care of people. Why wouldn't I make a good B and B owner?"

Marley thought about it. "You know, you probably would, Abby. So what was Paul's biggest worry?"

Abby rolled her eyes. "Money, of course. First of all, he doesn't like the idea of me using my savings for a down payment. Then he questioned what I'd use for collateral for the loan, and he was worried that I'd have to live at the B and B."

Marley nodded. "Those seem like legitimate concerns. Money and loans are a big deal and something you two need to discuss. And if he's worried about you living at the B and B, it sounds like he wants to keep you around."

"To clean his house and cook his food. Sometimes I think that's all he cares about."

"Sounds like this is something you should talk about with your counselor next time you meet."

"Yeah. Sorry to keep dumping on you."

"Sorry for not having more answers." Marley looked at her watch. "And now my time is up. I'm on my bike today, and I promised myself to be back home by ten to work on my painting, so I should probably get moving."

"How's the painting coming?"

Marley forced a smile. "I made a few new brushstrokes yesterday, thanks to Janie, since she really likes it. She said she might even want to buy it for her house when I'm done. But I'm not holding my breath. Anyway, my plan is to stick a stack of old jazz albums on the stereo and force myself to paint until noon. If I put in two productive hours, my reward is to have lunch, then walk on the beach afterward. After that, I'll try to paint for two more hours before I allow myself to break for dinner."

"What discipline."

Marley frowned as she stood. "It seems like I shouldn't need discipline to do something I enjoy, but I've kind of had a case of painter's block."

"Well, good luck." Abby stood and picked up her purse. "I've got a busy day too. I plan to do some more investigation in regard to my bed-and-breakfast idea. I want to find out when the house will be for sale. I'm going to meet with Jackie Day and learn some of the nuts and bolts about running an inn, and then I have an appointment with a loan officer this afternoon."

"Let me know how it goes," Marley told her as they walked outside. They hugged good-bye and parted ways. As Marley unlocked her bike, she wondered if Paul knew about Abby's bank appointment. She suspected he didn't, and she could imagine what he would think when he found out.

Once again, Marley was exceedingly thankful for her single status. As she rode her retro-style Schwinn—complete with fat tires, padded seat, and wicker basket—along the old beach road, with the wind blowing her short hair, she imagined she was flying, that she truly did have wings. And it felt good.

═══Chapter 9═══

CAROLINE

Trying to rebandage her mother's feet was a bit like bull wrestling. Not that Caroline had ever wrestled a bull, but she'd been to a few rodeos in her time. In fact, she'd gone through a phase the summer before high school when she actually cleaned stalls in exchange for Western riding lessons. She'd taken this route shortly after admiring the rodeo queen in the Clifden Memorial Day parade. Astride a gorgeous palomino stallion and dressed in a pink-fringed rhinestone ensemble, Glenda Gordon looked like she was a real celebrity. Caroline's new goal became to run for rodeo princess when she turned sixteen. She actually got pretty good at riding and even attempted barrel racing in a small rodeo up north, but eventually the smell of ripe manure, combined with the demands of cheerleading practice and the distraction of boys, tempted Caroline away from her cowgirl dreams.

"Please … hold … still," Caroline hissed between her clenched teeth as she tried once again to get the ointment on the sole of her mother's right foot. But Ruby kicked again, and the ointment landed on the sheet.

"Hurts—hurts—hurts!" her mother yelled so loudly that the neighbors probably thought Caroline was torturing her.

"Fine." Caroline stood. "I give up. But if you get an infection, you'll have to go to the doctor."

Her mom whimpered as she pulled away, looking up at Caroline with the eyes of a wounded animal, as if she thought Caroline were responsible for her pain.

"And you won't be able to walk," Caroline pointed out. "You'll be stuck in bed all day."

Her mother turned from her now, facing the wall and still whimpering. Caroline looked at her watch. Well, at least the respite caregiver would arrive soon. Maybe Ruby would allow her to touch her feet. Frustrated, Caroline picked up the breakfast tray, which was mostly untouched, and carried it back to the kitchen. Maybe the professional could coax her mom to eat something too. Despite Caroline's brave talk to Beverly yesterday, she was having some serious doubts today about her ability to care for her mom. How could she care for someone who did not want to be cared for? Perhaps it really was time for that Alzheimer's support group after all. Too bad it wasn't until Friday.

Caroline was just finishing cleaning the kitchen when the doorbell rang. Of course, the sound of the doorbell made her mother start calling out too, yelling, "Go away! Go away!"

Caroline opened the door to see a stocky older woman. Her hair was various shades of gray and pulled into a tight, unattractive ponytail, but her brown eyes looked kind. "I'm Darlene Kinsey." She held out what appeared to be an ID card. "Here to give you a break."

Caroline let out a relieved sigh as she introduced herself. "I'm so glad to see you. Come in."

"Beverly said that your mother is probably in the final stage of Alzheimer's." Darlene put her ID card back in her oversized canvas bag as she followed Caroline into the kitchen.

"Yes. That's what Beverly told me, too."

"That's a lot to take on." Darlene eyed Caroline with a questioning look. "It must be exhausting."

Caroline nodded sadly. "Yes. And this morning I'm wondering if Beverly is right. Maybe I do need to find a nursing home."

"Maybe you do, or maybe you just need a break. This will be your first experience with additional help. It might be a way to buy some time … to figure things out."

"And you're experienced in working with people like my mom, right?" Caroline studied Darlene, wondering what kind of person would actually volunteer to do something like this. Was she a masochist or a saint? Or perhaps, like Caroline's mom, Darlene wasn't in her right mind either. What if she was some kind of sadistic elder abuser? Not that she looked mean.

"My first experience was with my own mom." Darlene set her bag on a kitchen chair. "She passed on about twelve years ago. At the time I cared for her, there wasn't a lot of help or resources for in-home caregivers. No support groups. After Mom died, after I'd spent all that time learning things the hard way, I decided to get involved with senior services … hoping I could make a difference."

"That's generous of you."

"I think God wants us to use our difficult times to help others."

"Maybe someday I'll want to do that too." Caroline sighed and wondered if that was a gross exaggeration or just a downright lie. "But right now I mostly want to run screaming in the opposite direction." Darlene chuckled. "Yes. I remember that feeling."

Caroline explained about her mom's messed-up feet and how she didn't eat much breakfast. "Maybe she'll respond to you better than she did to me." But as much as she hoped it would be true, she was doubtful. Her mom rarely took to strangers, even long before Alzheimer's kicked in. "Thanks to her feet, she's pretty much confined to bed," Caroline said as she led Darlene down the hallway. "If you have any suggestions, I'm more than open." Caroline slowly opened the door, calling out to her mom as she entered the bedroom. "I have someone for you to meet, Mom," she said in a cheerful voice.

Her mom looked up with suspicious eyes, and then upon seeing Darlene she began to glare, pulling her curled fists into her chest in a defensive manner. "Go away!" she growled.

"Darlene is here to help take care of you," Caroline explained, although judging by her mom's reaction, tightly shut eyes, and downturned head, she might as well have been speaking to the chair. "She's a very nice woman, and if you get to know her, I'm sure you'll like her."

"I'm happy to meet you, Mrs. McCann," Darlene said in a friendly but not childish voice. "Don't worry, I know it takes time to get to know new people." She sat down on the chair by the bed now. "I took care of my own mother. She was a lot like you. She didn't like meeting new people either." Darlene waved to Caroline now, motioning that it was okay for her to leave. Then she continued rambling on in a gentle, soothing tone that almost made Caroline want to fall asleep. Instead, she backed away and, while her mother's eyes were still shut, slipped out of the room. Feeling like a runaway child, she grabbed up her purse and darted out the front door, got into her car, and just drove.

She didn't even know where she was going or what she would do. All she knew was that she was getting away. For two glorious hours, she was free to do whatever she pleased! Of course, she was only a few blocks from home when guilt set in. What if her mom threw a fit? Or what if she needed a diaper change and Darlene couldn't find the bag? Why hadn't she showed Darlene where things were? Or what if there was some medical emergency? Caroline hadn't even left her cell-phone number for Darlene. Maybe she should go back and take care of these things. Or maybe she should just call. But that might make things worse—especially if by some miracle her mother was actually getting used to Darlene and her soothing voice.

Caroline turned onto a side street and pulled over. She tried to think. What should she do? What should she do? Was this how a mother felt the first time she left her infant with the babysitter? Or was this a twisted case of Stockholm syndrome? Caroline looked at the intersection sign and realized she was on Janie's street. Maybe she should stop by there, check the progress of Janie's redecorating efforts, and see if she had any more advice.

But only the plumber was there, and he told Caroline that Janie had gone out to shop for tiles. So Caroline called Abby, trying her home phone first since Abby didn't always keep her cell on. When no one answered, she tried the cell phone, and that went straight to voice mail. Caroline hung up and considered calling Marley, except Janie had told her of Marley's plan to dedicate this part of the morning to painting. Caroline hated to disturb her. And, really, Caroline wasn't a baby. She could handle this without running crying to her friends.

And yet Caroline continued cruising through town in the hope she might spy Janie or Abby and talk them into getting coffee or an early lunch with her. But with no luck, she decided she could at least make use of this time by going to the store to pick up a few things. This would be her last chance at freedom until Friday, and that wouldn't really be freedom since she'd promised to attend the support group, which she was actually looking forward to. That only showed how truly pathetic her life had become, but it also meant her next chance at *freedom* freedom wouldn't be until Monday—five days away!

On her way to the grocery store, she took a backstreet that ran right past Mulberry Manor. The nursing home had been around for as long as Caroline could remember. In fact, while Caroline was living in California, her grandmother had spent her final days there. And yet Caroline had never been inside those brick walls. Without really thinking, she turned in, parked in a guest space, and got out.

Caroline knew that her mom had been the one to place Grandma here, because at the time Caroline had questioned the decision. Grandma suffered a stroke and needed assistance, but Caroline was surprised that her mom didn't try to care for her. Of course, that might've had to do with Dad, since he didn't get along with his mother-in-law any better than he got along with his wife. As Caroline walked through the door, she thought, *If this place was good enough for Grandma, why wouldn't it be good enough for Mom?*

"Can I help you?" a serious-faced young woman at the reception desk asked.

Caroline felt a wave of guilt, as if she were about to betray her mother by having her locked up. "I, uh, I've been caring for my mom," she began nervously. "She has Alzheimer's, and I was wondering about putting her into a care facility. Not that I've made up my mind yet. I mean, I haven't. I'm just curious, and I thought it might help to check this place out. If that's okay?"

"Are you on our waiting list?"

Caroline shook her head. "But it's because I'm not sure. I mean, whether it's a good idea or not. It's a hard decision."

"Would you like to talk to someone?"

"I don't know. I guess I was hoping maybe I could just look around a little. You know, to decide whether my mom would fit in here."

The woman picked up the phone. "How about if I let our manager talk to you? I don't think she's too busy this morning."

Caroline just nodded and waited, feeling even guiltier now. What was she doing here? Really, maybe she should just turn and make a run for it before the manager came out.

"I'm Marybeth Brimley." A short brunette stuck out her hand and smiled. "How can I help you?"

Caroline introduced herself and explained her dilemma and Beverly's recommendation to look into nursing-home care. "But I might be premature," she explained. "I just thought if I could look around it might help with my decision."

Marybeth nodded. "How about if I give you a quick tour of our facility?"

"Thanks, I'd appreciate it."

Caroline wasn't sure what she thought as Marybeth led her

around. Certainly, it seemed fairly clean, probably cleaner than Caroline's mom's house, although Caroline didn't blame herself for her mother's pack-rat habit. And the "residents" seemed to be fairly normal. Just old. Many were in wheelchairs, and some looked a little spaced out, not unlike her mom at times, but no one appeared neglected or particularly unhappy or even crazy.

A number of them were in the activity room, mostly gathered around the big-screen TV where *The Price Is Right* was playing. But there seemed to be games and other activities available. The dining room was cheerfully decorated in an aquatic theme with an interesting ocean mural on one wall. The rooms didn't even seem institutional with their individual decor and furnishings, and they even had TVs. All in all, the place seemed okay, and yet something felt amiss. She felt slightly like she was being tricked, or maybe that was just her guilty imagination.

Back in the lobby, Caroline looked toward what appeared to be another wing. "What's over there?"

"Just more of the same," Marybeth told her. "So, would you like to put your mother on our waiting list? It's not as if you're making a commitment to have her here, you merely increase your chance of getting a room should you eventually decide she needs some additional care and supervision."

Caroline nodded. "Yes, I'm sure you're right. I should put her on the list."

Marybeth led Caroline back to an office and handed her a folder. "Just fill out this paperwork and we'll put you down." She stood. "Feel free to stay here to do it. I have to go see to something in the kitchen."

And so Caroline sat there and filled out the preliminary information forms. Really, it was all fairly simple and straightforward, and like Marybeth had said, it wasn't as if Caroline were making any legal commitment. She was simply securing a room … just in case. Feeling a bit less like a traitor, she left the folder on Marybeth's desk, exited the building, and got into her car. Then she sat there looking at the long, low brick building.

Caroline tried to imagine she were in her mother's shoes. Would she want to be placed here if the tables were turned? She thought of the smell, that unpleasant mix of overcooked food and, well, other things. She thought of the confinement, the lack of windows, and come to think of it, she hadn't noticed any outdoor areas. Caroline wasn't sure about her mother, but she herself would not want to be cut off from daylight and fresh air. Although, she hadn't seen the whole building. Perhaps there was a courtyard somewhere in back.

As Caroline drove away, she knew the truth. She would rather be stuck in her mom's old, decrepit, and overly crowded house with its small backyard than be locked up in Mulberry Manor.

But what if her mother became so out of touch with reality that she didn't know where she was anyway? What if she couldn't tell the difference between a room at Mulberry Manor and her own bedroom? Or what if her mother became seriously dangerous to herself or others? What if she started a fire? Or what if she ran out into traffic and some driver suffered a fatal accident to avoid hitting her?

Or what if, with the proper health care and nutrition that Marybeth described, her mother's quality of life did improve? Perhaps even her memory would improve. What if Caroline, with her lack of caregiving skills, was keeping her mother from receiving what she really needed? Or what if Caroline reached her breaking point and could no longer provide care? Really, she decided, it was the right thing to put her mom on the list.

Feeling relieved, she decided to loop around the back of the facility in the hopes of spotting a cheerful courtyard with residents out enjoying the sunshine and flowers. But the only thing back there seemed to be an employee parking lot and trash bins. As she turned her car around, she noticed an open door, probably to the wing that she hadn't toured. Out of curiosity, she took a long look down the corridor. Unlike the other side of the building, this hallway was completely empty. Was this half of the building vacant? And, if so, what was up with the waiting list?

She parked her car and walked to the open door to peek in, but the first thing that met her was the stench. She hadn't cared for the odor on the other side of the nursing home, but this was far worse. With no one to stop her, she ventured in. Tiptoeing down the hallway, she glanced into the first room to see that it looked nothing like the rooms on the other side of the facility. This very clinical-looking room had three hospital beds, all occupied. Two of the residents were being held by restraints, and the other appeared to be comatose with IV bottles dangling above him. The two restrained people looked her way with glazed expressions that made Caroline suspect they were sedated as well.

"What are you doing in here?" someone from behind snapped.

Caroline turned around to see a woman in a nurse's uniform. "I, uh, I was having a tour of Mulberry Manor," she said.

"Not in this wing, you're not," the woman said.

"I must've gotten lost."

The woman rolled her eyes as she took Caroline by the elbow. "More like spying if you ask me. I think I'll call for the manager."

"No need," Caroline said crisply. "I'll speak to Marybeth myself."

The nurse released her arm. Perhaps the name of her boss carried some weight. "I assume you can find your way out?"

"No problem." But instead of using the back door, Caroline headed the other direction, toward the lobby. She passed more rooms with more residents who looked frighteningly similar to what she'd just seen. Then she walked through the lobby and into Marybeth's office, where she snatched up the folder with her mother's information in it. As she was leaving she ran into Marybeth.

"Something wrong?"

Caroline nodded crisply. "Yes. I just saw the other side of the nursing home, where your so-called residents are shackled to their beds and look as if they've been drugged. This is *not* the kind of place I want my mother to—"

"You don't understand. Those are patients who need to be restrained for their own safety and—"

"Or for the convenience of your staff." Caroline glared at her.

"We have only the very extreme cases in that wing. I doubt that your mother would—"

"You don't *know* my mother," Caroline told her with tears in her eyes. "And you never will either. Thank you for your time." Then she turned on her heel and left.

Caroline had only an hour of respite time left now, but she knew what she was going to do. She drove to Clifden's biggest one-stop-shopping store and headed straight to the pharmacy, where she'd noticed a good selection of home-health products before.

With the help of a savvy pharmacist, Caroline selected a number of what she hoped would be helpful items, including a special massaging footbath, a wheelchair, a bedside toilet, and some other things that the pharmacist recommended.

"My aunt cares for my grandmother," she told Caroline. "These are some of the things she finds useful."

"I don't think everything will fit in my car," Caroline said as she waited at the cash register. "It's just a small SUV."

"We can deliver them if you like," the pharmacist told her. "We're just starting a special service for our shut-ins, and since you're caring for one, I think we can apply it to you as well."

"Thank you so much." Caroline filled in the check and was thankful it wasn't drawing from her own funds, which would remain limited until her condo in California sold. She'd set this account up when she got guardianship of her mom. Thanks to a reverse mortgage that Caroline had helped her mom secure a few years ago, her mother wasn't dependent on Social Security to survive.

"I think our delivery guy will be going out later this afternoon. Will that work?" the pharmacist asked.

"Perfect." Caroline thanked her again. Then, as she was about to leave the store, Caroline noticed a sign advertising a clearance on TVs. While Mom's feet were recovering, a TV in her bedroom could be handy, and no way was Caroline going to move that hefty console from the living room. Maybe it was seeing that horrible wing of the nursing home, or maybe it was just plain guilt that she'd considered institutionalizing her mother, but before Caroline left the store, she also purchased a small flat screen, a DVD player, and fun selection of Disney flicks, including the

Princess collection, which for some reason she thought her mother might enjoy.

"Looks like someone's little princess is going to have fun," the cashier said as Caroline handed him a check.

Caroline nodded. "Oh, yeah, the little princess is in for a real treat."

It was just past noon when Caroline pulled into the driveway and hurried into the house. "Sorry I'm late," she told Darlene breathlessly. "Is everything okay?"

She made a half smile. "She's a stubborn one."

"I know. Did she give you any problems?"

"She wouldn't let me touch her feet, but she did let me change her diaper. And she drank a juice box, but she refused to eat a bite of food." Darlene shook her head as she picked up her purse. "I don't know, Caroline. My mom wasn't easy, but seems to me you've got your hands full with that one."

She sighed. "Yes. But I'm not ready to give up yet. I really appreciate your help, Darlene. I hope she didn't frighten you away."

"Takes more than that to scare me off." Darlene patted her on the back. "And I hope you enjoyed some nice respite time. I'm sure you needed it."

Caroline forced a smile as she recalled her two-hour "break."

"Yes, I think it was just what I needed. Thanks so much!"

Chapter 10

JANIE

"Can I help you?" Janie turned to see a woman in her late thirties or thereabouts walking across the store toward her. The woman was dressed quite fashionably, especially for Clifden, and her brunette hair was long and wavy.

"I saw your ad in the *Clifden Weekly,*" Janie told her. "I'm renovating a house in town, and although I've found most of what I need online, I'm having a hard time deciding on tile without actually seeing it. And unfortunately, the plumber thinks it should've been installed yesterday, so I really need to resolve this quickly."

The woman's bright blue eyes sparkled. "I know just what you mean. I don't know how anyone can shop for things like tile without actually seeing and touching the product first. Interior design elements are so tactile—I think we need to experience them. Don't you? My tile section is back here." She led Janie across the crowded interior-decor shop. "If you tell me what direction you'd like to go, I can probably help you find something."

They looked for a while, considering the options, but Janie

finally decided that she wanted to go with tinted glass tiles. "I know it's probably not as interesting as some," she said almost apologetically, "but I'm fairly traditional about style, and the floor tiles will be plain white marble."

"Hey, I think glass tiles will look lovely with white marble. And those sea-glass green and blue shades are gorgeous. So spa-like in a bath. If you like I could come out to your house and measure for you before we order. There's a no-return policy on this particular line, probably because they're worried they'll get broken ones back." She smiled. "But don't worry, they guarantee that yours will be delivered in one piece."

"How long does it take?"

"That depends. You can put a rush on them if you want."

"According to the plumber, we need them soon."

"And you've picked out your fixtures already?"

Janie nodded.

"Well, you go ahead and take these samples home with you and make sure that you absolutely love them in your house, then let me know when you'd like me to come out and measure for you."

"Today probably wouldn't be too soon," Janie admitted.

"Well, my sales associate will be here at noon. How about if I come by, say, around one?"

"Perfect." Janie jotted down her address and phone number onto the notepad. "See you this afternoon." Then she gathered up the sample boards and left.

Before she got into her car, she was approached by a short Latino man in blue jeans and a work shirt.

"Excuse me, ma'am," he said politely. "Do you need someone to work?"

She bit her lip and studied him. "What kind of work?"

"I do all kind of work." He looked at the sample boards. "You need tile work?"

"Are you a tile layer?"

He nodded eagerly. "Yes."

Janie thought about the boxes of white marble floor tile stacked in her garage. They were for the bathroom floors, and the plumber wanted them installed ASAP. All the tile layers she'd called were busy until next month, and although Marley had offered to help, Janie knew that Marley needed to finish her painting.

"You no trust me?" the man asked with a sad frown.

"No, no. That's not it." Okay, this wasn't exactly true. "I was just thinking. I have a friend who might lay the tile for me."

He just nodded. "Yes. I understand." Then he started to walk away.

"No, wait," she called. "Come back."

His smile reappeared as he returned. "My name ees Mario. I have wife, Elena, she does housework," he said hopefully. "I do yard work, paint work or—"

"And you are experienced at tile work?"

He nodded. "Oh yes. I am very good."

"And you have tools?"

"Oh yes. I have tools." Now he frowned. "But no electric tile saw."

"And you need an electric tile saw?" She realized how much she didn't know.

"You can rent tile saw." Mario pointed to a light blue Chevy truck parked across the street. It was old but clean and neat. "I can pick up the saw."

Now Janie felt worried. What was she getting into?

"What kind of tile you want? I do it all. Slate, marble, granite, ceramic, terra-cotta."

"Marble."

He nodded and smiled. "Ah, marble is good. Easy to lay."

"Really?"

"Yes. Easy to cut. But you must seal it when it's done."

Okay, she was feeling more convinced, and the plumber was at her house. She could get his opinion. "Why don't you follow me home, and I can show you what needs to be done," she told him. "Maybe you can give me an estimate."

Mario shook his head.

"You don't want to work for me."

"No. I mean *no* estimate. I work by the hour."

She considered this. If she paid him by the hour she wouldn't risk giving him a check up front and never seeing him again. "That sounds perfect."

"I follow you." Mario nodded.

As she drove home, she hoped she wasn't making a big mistake. This was all still so new to her. Although Abby had been helping her initially, it seemed that she'd gotten distracted, or perhaps like Marley suggested, she was actually a little depressed. Whatever the case, Abby's suggestions for tile layers had not panned out. And now Janie was feeling a little desperate. When Mario pulled up she asked him to wait outside for her. Fortunately Ed, the plumber, was still there. She went directly to him and quickly explained about finding a "tile guy" at the home-decor shop.

"Great," Ed told her. "You get that floor and shower tile done, and we can set these things up permanently."

Janie sighed to imagine actually showering in her own house. Joining the athletic club in town had seemed like a good idea—she could work out and enjoy a real shower—but it had gotten old quickly.

"I thought maybe you could talk to the tile guy for me," she said tentatively. "Just to make sure he really knows what he's doing. I don't want to sound judgmental, but he's a Latino, and I don't know if he's—"

"Well, if he's Mexican and he knows tile, you should thank your lucky stars."

"Really?"

He nodded. "Oh yeah, they're the best."

"He's outside. Do you have time to talk to him?"

"Sure, send him in, and I'll check him out for you."

As it turned out, Ed gave Mario his stamp of approval and even offered to handle the renting of the tile saw through a construction friend. "Rod will drop the saw by this afternoon," Ed told Janie. "Mario can go to work as soon as he gets his materials."

"Materials?"

"Adhesive, mortar, grout, sealer …" Ed chuckled. "The little things that get the tiles out of the boxes and adhered to your floors."

"Oh, right."

"Just call up the hardware store and set up an account, and let Mario pick up the materials as he needs them."

"Right." She nodded. "Sounds simple enough."

It was simple. Before long, all was set, and Mario headed off to pick up some supplies while she attempted to do some rearranging in the garage. Her plan was to free up some space for Mario to use as his workshop. But then she unearthed a box she had filled with her parents' mementos—things she didn't exactly want to toss, and yet she didn't want to keep them either. What did one do with stuff like this anyway?

A good daughter would probably take it back into the house and thoughtfully go through it. But Janie had spent her entire childhood trying to be a good daughter. Not that it had gained her much favor in her father's eyes. And her mother rarely affirmed her about anything. The truth was, Janie just didn't have the energy to play that role anymore. Mostly she wanted to forget about her parents and her childhood, the pathetic little life that she'd lived within these very walls. In fact, wasn't it ironic, if not downright Freudian, that she was investing so much of herself in renovating this house? Did she think that removing ugly carpets and drapes might erase the ugly past?

"I am back," Mario hailed from the driveway. Then he rushed toward her. "No," he said as he removed the box from her arms. "I will carry for you. You show me where."

That's when she noticed the pull-down ladder that led to the attic. She remembered her dad setting mousetraps there when she was a child, and after that she'd never wanted to venture up. She reached for the cord and pulled it down. "Up there is fine," she told Mario. "Wherever you can find room. Thanks!"

Then, with that problem solved and nothing much to do until the woman from the interior shop came, Janie decided to call Marley. It should be Marley's break time now anyway.

"What's up?" Marley asked pleasantly.

So Janie explained about finding Mario the tile man. "I know I talked to you about doing tile," she said quickly, "but there's so much to do, and I know you're busy with your painting."

"I think you were smart to nab him while you could. And you're right, I do need to focus on my painting."

"How's it coming?"

"It's coming."

Janie could tell by her tone that it was still not coming easily. "Hey, I found some great glass tiles today."

"Where at?"

"That new home-decor store that just opened in town. It's a pretty cool shop."

"Bridgeport Interiors?"

"Yes. That's it. Anyway, I might go back to look at a few things again. That woman has a good eye."

"That woman?"

Janie laughed. "Yes. In the excitement of finding great tile, I forgot to get her name, but I'm pretty sure she's the owner."

"Her name is Bonnie Boxwell," Marley said in a flat voice, as if she was trying to convey something beyond identification information.

Janie's memory clicked. "Oh. Is that the *same* Bonnie—Paul's friend Bonnie?"

"That's my guess. If you were talking to the owner, that is. Abby just told me that Bonnie Boxwell opened a shop called Bridgeport Interiors."

Janie glanced at her watch now. "She should be here any minute now."

"She's coming to your house?" Marley sounded shocked. "What is she, your new best friend?"

"No, of course not. But she seems like a nice person. And I didn't get her name. Maybe she's a partner."

"Maybe." Marley sounded skeptical.

"Even if she *is* Bonnie Boxwell," Janie continued, "does that mean we all have to hate her? This is a small town, and she seems nice—and I'm not sure I want to start making enemies. And her shop is really great. I want to go back there."

"So why is she coming to your house?"

"To measure for tile." Janie looked out the front window to see a silver Jaguar pulling up in front of her house. "And I think she's here."

"Hide your men," Marley teased.

"Yeah, right." Janie glanced out to see Mario unloading a bag from the back of his pickup. "Talk to you later."

"Let me know if it's her."

Janie said good-bye and went outside to greet her visitor. "I'm sorry," Janie said as she stuck out her hand, "I never really introduced myself. I'm Janie Sorenson."

"Bonnie Boxwell."

Janie nodded to distract herself from this disappointment, then pointed toward the house. "This was actually my parents' house," she explained, "where I grew up. But they both passed on, and it was time to do something with it. When I first started renovations, I wasn't planning on moving back here."

"Moving back here?" Bonnie questioned. "Where from?"

"New York." Janie sighed. "Specifically Manhattan. I had a lovely apartment." Now, for the most part, Janie wasn't sorry for uprooting her life. But she occasionally experienced flashes of longing—unrealistic flashes, she reminded herself.

"What made you move back?"

"Lots of things. My husband passed on. It was time for a change."

"That's a pretty big change."

"How about you?" Janie asked as they stood outside on the scruffy lawn. "I'm guessing you moved to Clifden from somewhere?"

Bonnie laughed. "Yes. I needed a change too. But I only moved here from Portland. I'm wondering if that was a big mistake, though."

"A mistake?"

"It's hard to break into a new town, you know, making friends. Especially when you're single. Don't you find it to be a challenge?"

"Well, I was lucky in that I already had some friends here." Janie knew it was time to change the subject again. "Anyway, as far as this house goes, I originally thought I would fix it up and sell it. So I've had a split plan, because at first I was trying to be economical and expedient. But now, well, I like things nice." She peered up at the old ranch house, which was sorely in need of some exterior work too. "But I'm getting worried that I might be attempting to make a silk purse out of a sow's ear, as my grandmother used to say."

Bonnie laughed. "I've never heard that saying. But here's what I think: Our homes should be a reflection of who we are." She studied Janie. "And you seem like a very classic and stylish woman. Why shouldn't your home reflect that?"

Janie nodded. "Thanks. I did bring a fair amount of furnishings and things from my Manhattan apartment. Most is in storage, although I did start setting up my living room, just because I needed a place to relax in. Right now I'm working on my bedroom."

"I'd love to see it."

So Janie started showing Bonnie her house. "My parents really hadn't done anything with it over the years," she admitted. "But the wood floors were in pretty good shape, so I had them refinished." Even as she said this, she felt guilty, since it was Abby who had helped in that part of the renovation. "But now I wonder if that was a mistake," she said quickly, probably in effort to hide her real feelings.

"A mistake?"

"Well, the oak seems a little … I don't know … expected."

Bonnie nodded.

"If I'd known it was going to be my house, I might've splurged for something a bit more exotic."

"It's not too late." Bonnie's blue eyes lit up. "Something like rosewood or mahogany could really make a statement."

Janie looked at her arrangement of oriental carpets and furnishings in the living room and shook her head. "You're probably right, but the truth is I'm getting so sick of dust and waiting, I should probably just leave well enough alone."

"You could always switch it out later," Bonnie suggested.

"Yes." Janie nodded. "Later."

"Your furnishings are lovely," Bonnie said as she ran her hand over the leather sectional.

"Thank you. I worried they were a bit uptown for Clifden." Janie chuckled.

"From what I hear, Clifden is changing."

"I think you're right. Anyway, these were my things—what I was used to—and some of them had been in my husband's family."

"Like this lamp?" Bonnie pointed to the Tiffany.

"Yes. And some of the carpets."

"Your husband's family had excellent taste."

Janie nodded. "Yes, and I'm sure his mother would turn over in her grave if she knew her Tiffany was in this little ranch house."

"Do you want any suggestions?" Bonnie was standing over by the window.

"Sure." Janie nodded with a bit of uncertainty. "What did you have in mind?"

"Some rearranging of this room."

Janie frowned. "Well, good luck with that. I had a tough time figuring out how to place that sectional." Her friends had helped her to move the bulky pieces around and around the living room space. None of the options had come out quite right.

"Did you consider breaking it up?"

"Breaking it up?"

"The sectional pieces."

Janie shook her head. "Wouldn't that look weird?"

"Not if you do it right." Bonnie grinned. "Do you trust me?"

Janie felt a rush of panic. What if Abby unexpectedly stopped by, like she often did? How would she react to seeing "the other woman" rearranging Janie's furnishings? Furnishings that Abby herself had helped to put into place?

"I have an idea," Bonnie said. "Why don't you go do something else? Unpack something or go shopping or whatever it is you need to do to make your house a home, and leave me to my own devices in here."

"But I—"

"I'll do it for free. And if you don't like it better, I'll put it all back."

"I—uh—I don't know what to say."

"Just say yes."

"But it's so much work. These pieces are heavy and—"

"I have furniture slides in my trunk, and I noticed a nice piece of manpower in your driveway. Maybe he could give me a hand."

"Mario?" Janie said weakly.

Bonnie nodded. "Yes. Mario will do just fine."

Janie remembered Marley's warning—*lock up your men*—and gulped.

"Now, run along, Janie. I have work to do." Bonnie was literally pushing Janie out her own front door. "I noticed you eyeing some things in my shop earlier. Why don't you go have another look around—and keep in mind that if you're a design client, you'll get an additional ten percent off."

Well, that did it for Janie. Worried that Abby might drop in, she decided her best escape might be to do just that—escape!

==Chapter 11==

ABBY

As Abby walked away from the bank, she wasn't sure whether to feel confident or desperate. On one hand, Leslie, the loan officer, had been encouraging, talking about low interest rates, business loans, and government grants. But when she asked Abby about collateral and down payment, she seemed a bit concerned when Abby came up empty-handed. "So what do you actually have to bring to the table?" Leslie peered curiously at her. "I mean besides your dream, which I'll admit sounds like fun. But we're a bank. We need something more concrete. I assume Paul will partner with you? We've done a number of building loans with him so—"

"I want to do this separate from Paul."

"Oh?" Leslie's thinly plucked eyebrows lifted.

"I do have a nice chunk of savings," Abby admitted. "But I thought I would need most of it for supplying the house and doing some updates."

"And that's good. We always appreciate adding value to property.

But you do understand you'll need a substantial down payment, don't you?"

Abby nodded. "I've done the math. I might be able to come up with ten percent—"

"You might need more than ten percent. I'll have to run the numbers, and you'll need to provide me with some information." She slid some papers across the desk. "You'll need to fill out this paperwork."

"Yes."

"And we'll see what we can do." Leslie stood then, which Abby took as her hint that this meeting was over.

"Thank you for your time."

Leslie smiled and shook Abby's hand again. "We'll both do our homework and see where it takes us."

As Abby had smiled back, she sensed that Leslie thought Abby was never going to be able to pull something like this off. Abby drove away doubting herself. But then she reminded herself about Jackie's encouragement.

"I'm single," Jackie had reminded Abby as they ate lunch together at The Lighthouse. "And I manage all right."

"But you got in when prices were lower," Abby pointed out. "If I could purchase our house at the price we originally bought it for, I'd have it made in the shade." She sighed.

"Don't forget that everything was less back then," Jackie said. "You would've charged less for rooms, and it would all be a wash."

"I guess you're right."

"The main thing to keep in mind is that if you really want to do this—if you know that you're willing to roll up your sleeves and do the hard work, you will succeed."

"So is it really hard work?" Abby didn't like to judge people, but Jackie was even more overweight than Abby. Although Abby always managed to get her housework done, she often felt lethargic at the end of the day.

"Oh, I have a girl help with the beds and the laundry," Jackie admitted, "but it's pretty much an endless job." She smiled. "But I love it. My guests and my cat are like family. I can't imagine my life without them." Then she had launched into a story about a couple staying at her inn that very week. "They're both retired archeologists and have been on digs all over the world. The stories they tell are fascinating."

Abby nodded. "Yes, that's the part of this that interests me. Meeting new people. And I love to cook and decorate. Really, running a B and B seems like just my sort of thing."

"I have a good feeling this is really going to happen," Jackie told her as they were parting ways. "You and I will partner and help each other out, and it'll be such fun."

Abby felt bone tired as she drove through town. And yet she felt strangely driven, too. Leslie had confirmed that her old house was indeed about to go into a short sale. "I can't tell you what that price will be. But I can tell you a short sale is a lender's attempt to get back what was financed."

Abby didn't tell Leslie that she had been a previous owner of the house of interest, or a co-owner. And Leslie, new in town, wouldn't know this unless she did some research. Abby doubted she would. The good news was that, as Abby recalled, the buyers had put down more than ten percent, and they had purchased the house in a market on its way down.

Abby continued driving through town and out on the old beach road until she pulled up in front of her mom's little bungalow.

"Hi, Mom," she called as she went inside. Like her mom, Abby seldom knocked before entering.

"In the kitchen," her mom called over the whir of what sounded like a blender.

"Margaritas?" Abby said hopefully.

"Even better." Mom held up a tomato. "Salsa. My friend Elsie just dropped off a bunch of lovely tomatoes, peppers, onions, and garlic, and I thought nothing sounded better than some fresh salsa." She opened the processor, dipped in a tortilla chip, and handed it to Abby. "What do you think?"

"Needs a little more zing."

Her mom nodded and reached for a chili pepper. "Elsie warned me these are extra hot."

"Maybe you should use rubber gloves," Abby warned. "I got a bad skin burn once."

Her mother used a paper towel to protect her hand, sliced open the pepper, removed the seeds, then chopped up a small portion and dropped it into the processor. She set it to whirring again. "Try that," she said as she handed Abby another chip.

"Needs more lime juice," Abby told her.

"You're right." Her mom cut open another lime, juiced it, and poured it into the mixture, giving it another quick whirl. "How's that?"

Abby dipped another chip, tasted it, then nodded and smiled. "Perfect. A little bit sweet, a little bit sour, and hot."

"Too spicy for Paul, though."

"Probably."

"Why don't you run over and invite Marley to join us outside?" her mom said as she dumped the orange-red mixture into a large handmade ceramic bowl.

"I want to ask you about something first." Abby reached for the blender carafe and took it over to the sink to rinse.

"What?" her mom asked as she scooped some vegetable scraps into her compost bucket.

"I want to buy our old house back," Abby said.

Her mom looked curiously at her. "Is it even for sale?"

Abby explained what she'd heard about the short sale and repeated her conversations with Jackie as well as the loan officer.

"I know you've had that bed-and-breakfast dream for years," her mom said as she dried her hands. "But is it something that would be better off remaining a dream?"

"I don't think so." Abby washed off a knife. "I need something to do, Mom. Something that makes me want to get up in the morning. You have your arts and crafts. Marley has her painting. Janie has her house remodel. And Caroline ..." She sighed. "Caroline has her hands full with her mom."

"I heard about her escapade on the fishing boat." Abby's mom chuckled. "Can't wait to see that story in the paper next week."

"Yeah, I'm sure Caroline is waiting with bated breath."

"So do you have enough in your savings to swing it?" her mom asked.

"I might have enough for the down payment, but it would take all my savings, and then I wouldn't have enough to outfit the inn and do some painting and fix-ups."

"Where does Paul stand in all this?"

Abby avoided her mom's eyes, looking down at the linoleum floor, which was in need of a good mopping.

"I figured as much. He never really did like that house, Abby. When you kids wanted to buy it from us, we actually discouraged him."

"You did?"

"Yes. I told him you kids needed a fresh start, a place completely your own. And your father told him that the house needed a lot of repairs and—"

"That's for sure. That house was a money pit."

"But I think Dad's warning worked like reverse psychology. The more we talked down the house, the more Paul seemed bound and determined to buy it."

"Well, I wanted it too," Abby admitted. "And back then I actually had some influence on my husband."

Her mom didn't respond to this. Instead she found another hand-thrown ceramic bowl and dumped the bag of tortilla chips into it. Then she picked up the phone. "I'm calling Marley."

Abby sighed. Really, why had she thought her mom would have any interest in this project? Sometimes her mom was just as pessimistic about Abby's abilities as Paul was. She felt a wave of jealousy as she listened to her mom cheerfully chatting with Marley, asking about the painting and acting like they were new best friends. "Okay, honey, see you in about ten minutes." She hung up and turned to Abby. "That Marley, she insists on making margaritas."

"Well, that's nice of her," Abby said in a grumpy tone.

"What's wrong with you?"

"Just that no one, including you, seems to believe in me. No one in my family, anyway. Jackie seems to think I can do this. And the bank gal was willing to look into it. Even Marley encouraged me to check it out."

"So what do you want from me?"

Abby sat down on the kitchen stool and shook her head. "I don't know. Just a tiny bit of encouragement might be nice."

"Look, Abby, I think you can do whatever you set your mind to. I'm just not sure that you've set your mind to this. For all I know, this could be just a passing fancy. It might seem exciting or glamorous to run a bed-and-breakfast."

Abby laughed. "Exciting? Glamorous?"

Her mom held up her hands. "I don't know. I just remember that Bob Newhart show that used to be popular, and I thought running a bed-and-breakfast looked like fun."

Abby rolled her eyes. "For your information, I spent more than an hour this morning getting a tour of Jackie's B and B. She told me the chores involved, including endlessly cleaning bathrooms, changing linens, cooking, keeping the books, arranging fresh flowers, answering the phone, shopping, going—"

"All right. It seems you've done your research."

"I have." Abby nodded in a wounded way. "And I'm not ready to give up yet."

"I'm not suggesting you give up. I just think if you do something like this, you should do it with your eyes wide open."

"You mean like how you sold your house after Daddy died and bought this funky little bungalow out here on the beach by yourself?"

"I have neighbors."

"Depending on the time of year. And then you took up art—where did that come from? Did you do that with your eyes wide open?"

Her mom laughed. "Good point. No, you're right. I did that impulsively. I needed a change."

"And have you regretted your impulsiveness?"

She shook her head. "No. Not at all."

"I realize that opening a B and B is a bigger risk. But it's something I've wanted to do for years. You know me, Mom. I love cooking and cleaning and playing hostess. I always have."

Her mom nodded. "Yes. I think you enjoy it more than I ever did."

"You always acted like you liked it."

She sighed. "Maybe I did back then. I suppose I still like it, in a smaller way." She looked around her. "Not that I could do anything bigger than small in here anyway."

"*If* you ever did want to do something bigger," Abby began slowly, "like a dinner party for all your friends ... and *if* I did buy the old house ... you could use it."

Her mom laughed. "Well, I must admit, it would be fun to have a tea party there. Do you remember the tea parties we used to have?"

Abby nodded eagerly. "I was even thinking about serving high tea there, to make extra money. Can you imagine?"

"There isn't really a tea room in town."

"No, there's not."

"And you still have my Haviland china, don't you?"

"In storage. It seemed too formal for our beach house."

"But it was perfect in the Victorian."

Abby nodded. "I think it misses the Victorian."

Her mom sighed.

"Remember the roses in the backyard?" Abby asked.

"Of course. Do you think they're still there?"

"They better be."

"That house really would make a perfect inn. And six bedrooms might not be overwhelming. But could it really support the house payments, Abby?"

"I've done the math, Mom." Abby reached into her purse to pull out her notes, spreading them on the counter. "Look, even if the rooms were rented only half the time, this is how much revenue it would bring."

Her mom looked at the figures and blinked. "Really? That much?"

"That much. I based my room rates on Jackie's. She and I would have a kind of partnership. Nothing legal, just an agreement to help each other out, kind of like a co-op. We'd send overflow guests to each other and cover for each other if we needed a break."

"It does sound like you've given this some real thought."

Abby nodded eagerly. "The problem is, I don't have a whole lot of time to think about it. The bank won't say when the house is going to go to short sale, but Leslie said I better have my financing preapproved as well as my down payment in hand if I plan to nab it."

"But you said you have enough for a down payment, right?"

Abby frowned. "Yes. But then I have nothing left to get the inn ready to operate. I can't very well invite guests to visit with no furniture, no linens. I have a lot of things in storage that I can use, but there's a whole lot more I don't have."

"Okay." Her mom was pacing now. "How about this, Abby? How about if you get everything in order, you get preapproved and you use your savings for the down payment. If—and that's a big if—you're able to purchase the house, I will agree to be your partner."

Abby blinked. "You'd do that?"

"If you do the rest of it and are actually able to buy the house, I will back you with the finances to open the bed-and-breakfast."

Abby jumped off the stool and threw her arms around her mother. "Oh, Mom! Thank you! Thank you! Thank you!"

"Hey," called Marley as she came in the back door with a pitcher of margaritas and some colorful glasses on a tray. "What's going on here? Did someone just win the lottery?"

"Even better." Abby beamed at her. "My mom's going to partner with me in my bed-and-breakfast."

"Only if you are able to purchase the house," her mom reminded her. "It's up to you to pull that off. If you do, then I'm in."

"You heard her," Abby told Marley happily. "You can be a witness. Mom and I are going to partner in this business venture!"

Her mom laughed. "You think you need a witness against your own mother?"

"No, I just want Marley to remind you—when my bed-and-breakfast is a screaming success—that I had to talk you into it."

"This calls for a celebration," Marley said as she filled the glasses. "Margaritas all around!"

===Chapter 12===

MARLEY

"I'm no expert," Abby said, "but I think that's looking really good." Abby had helped bring the margarita things from next door, then paused to study Marley's seascape.

Marley laughed. "That's probably the margarita talking."

"No, it's not," Abby insisted. "This is really good, Marley. Admit it."

Marley set the margarita pitcher on the kitchen table then joined Abby, tilting her head to the side. "I guess it's coming along. It's just so different from my usual work."

"But you said you hadn't done any work for quite some time," Abby reminded her. "Maybe your style has changed."

Marley considered this. "You could be right. Now that I think about it, I did those other pieces, the ones in Jack's gallery, when I was in my crazy period." She shook her head at the memory. "At least that's what Ashton called it. He came up to Seattle to visit me shortly after I'd split with his dad. I was like a maniac—I'd barely finish one painting before starting the next, just whipping these pieces out like a madwoman. Ashton was actually worried about my sanity." She chuckled. "I remember he asked me if I planned to cut off my ear."

Abby laughed. "Well, your ears still seem to be intact."

"After a couple of months, I was so exhausted that I quit painting altogether. I couldn't stand to look at a paintbrush or tube of paint. That's when I stored all my crazy canvases and went to work at the gallery." Marley stared at the peaceful seascape and frowned. "What worries me is that Jack loves my crazy work, and now I can't seem to do it anymore. I've tried."

"Maybe this is your peaceful period," Abby suggested. "I like your other paintings, but this is more like something I would hang in my house."

"Don't forget, Janie already has first dibs on it."

"Yes, and I need to save all my money for purchasing my bed-and-breakfast anyway. Janie should definitely have it. It would look great in her house."

"Speaking of Janie, did you—" Marley stopped herself. Why had she opened her mouth?

"What about Janie?" Abby pressed.

"Oh, nothing." Marley went into the kitchen, taking the pitcher to the sink to rinse it out.

"Come on, Marley," Abby urged her. "We're the Four Lindas, one for all and all for one. You can't keep secrets."

Marley scowled as she set the glasses in the sink. "We aren't still going by all the old rules, are we? Good grief, we're grown women, Abby."

"It's an *unspoken* rule." Abby leaned forward and looked her in the eyes. "Now give! What's going on with Janie?"

Marley slowly rinsed and dried her hands then, leaning against the counter, sighed. "Well, it's really nothing ... and you'll find out eventually anyway."

"Find out?" Abby looked curious now. "What is going on? Is something wrong with Janie?"

"Not exactly. But she unwittingly went into Bridgeport Interiors. She didn't know that Bonnie was the owner."

Abby's expression was hard to read. She just shrugged. "Well, that's no big deal. Just a simple mistake on Janie's part."

Marley nodded. "Yeah, I guess."

"But?"

Marley picked up the sponge and gave the colorful tiled countertop a quick swipe.

"There's more to this story, isn't there?" Abby said.

Marley looked at her. "Well, just a little. You see, Janie needed tiles."

Abby nodded. "Yes. I know. For her kitchen backsplash and for accents in her bathrooms. I gave her a couple of good Web sites to order from."

"Well, she found some tiles at Bridgeport Interiors, and Bonnie went out to her house to help her with it."

Abby's eyebrows shot up. "What?"

Marley just nodded. "But like you said, it's no big deal."

"Bonnie went to Janie's house?" Abby looked angry now.

"That's what Janie told me. She didn't even know if it was Bonnie. In fact, she was hoping that maybe the woman she met was a partner. And maybe it was a partner. Anyway, I tipped her off. And I'm sure she has it all figured out by now."

"I cannot believe that Janie would let Bonnie into her house. Especially after I've been helping her to renovate that house. If she lets Bonnie in … well, it's like a slap in the face."

"Don't forget that Janie didn't know who she was dealing with, Abby. She simply stopped at the shop to look for tiles. It's not her fault that Bonnie insisted on coming to her house."

"She insisted?"

Marley held up her hands. "I don't know. All I know is that Janie had no idea that Bonnie Boxwell owned that shop. Think about it: It's not like we have a whole lot of interior-design stores in Clifden, and Janie is, after all, trying to finish up her house. It seems only natural that she might shop there."

"So now you're saying it's okay to shop in Bonnie's store?" Abby was really angry.

"I don't know what I'm saying, Abby. Are you saying that we should not step foot in Bonnie's store?"

Abby nodded firmly. "Yes. Out of loyalty to me, you should boycott Bonnie and her store."

Marley laughed. "Actually, I'll have no problem avoiding her store. Judging by the ad in the paper, her store is out of my price range anyway. And you know I prefer shabby chic with pizzazz. I doubt that Bonnie caters to my type."

"But she would cater to Janie." Abby shook a fist. "I wish I could drive that woman out of town."

"Okay," Marley said in a soothing tone. "You need to calm down, Abby. It won't do anyone any good for you to come unglued about this. If you lose your cool about Bonnie, it's like she wins."

"What do you mean?"

"I mean you end up looking like the jealous, crazed wife." Marley slowly shook her head. "And that's not a good look on anyone."

"So I'm supposed to take this lying down? First Bonnie comes in and tries to steal my husband, and now she's working on my friends?"

"She's not working on your friends, Abby. Don't make this into something it's not. Janie simply needed tiles. Bonnie had them. It's not like they're best friends."

Abby sat down in one of the old-fashioned dinette chairs and let out a big sigh. "It's just that I was helping Janie. If Bonnie gets involved, I will *not* step foot in Janie's house."

"That's a bit harsh."

"I don't care." Abby's expression reminded Marley of when they were girls. Sometimes Abby would pout until she got her way. It was funny then but not terribly attractive now.

"I know this is upsetting," Marley told her. "But it'll all blow over. Don't obsess over it. Besides, don't you need to focus your energy on buying your old house?"

Abby brightened. "That's right."

"And if you get the house, you'll have more than enough to keep you busy."

Abby nodded, standing. "Yes. And I should go home and start doing the paperwork." She smiled. "Sorry to act like a baby. But this thing with Bonnie, well, it just gets me a little riled up."

"It's okay." Marley hugged her. "Of all the Lindas, I should understand this better than any. If you need a shoulder to cry on, I'm here for you."

Abby thanked her, then headed on her way. Although Marley's offer of a shoulder was genuine, she hoped there wouldn't be too many moments like that. Really, what good did it do to get so angry? She hoped Abby would get the house and start her business. She needed something like that to keep her from obsessing. Marley turned back to her painting now. What if she couldn't finish it? Even worse, what if she finished it but it turned out badly? Then what?

She took in a deep breath, then squirted some dabs of acrylic paint onto her disposable paper palette and slowly started to mix them with her palette knife. She liked mixing colors, watching the pigments mingle and change, transforming into shades that resembled nature. She had just filled her brush with paint when the phone rang. Thankful for the distraction, she set down the brush and went for the phone.

"Marley?"

"Hey, Jack," she said, recognizing his voice. "What's up?"

"Not much. I was just in the neighborhood and wondered if you were home."

"You're in my neighborhood?"

"Just a ways down the road. Care if I stop by?"

"Not at all." Marley hurried to her small bathroom, flipped on the light and peered at herself in the mirror. Her glasses were smudged and her short hair was sticking out all over, but that was fairly normal.

"Okay. See you in a couple of minutes."

"See you." She hung up, quickly cleaned her glasses, then reached for some lip color, but as she was applying it, she asked herself, *Why?* Why was she so concerned about how she looked for Jack? She'd been comfortable going over to Doris's earlier without changing a thing. Why should she improve her appearance for Jack's sake? She told herself it was simply professionalism. Jack was kind of like her boss, and she wanted him to have confidence in her as an artist. She wanted to be a personality that he could proudly associate with. That was all.

She reached for a chunky choker that she'd made from rustic pieces of coral, turquoise, and silver, fastening it around her neck. Okay, the paint-spotted pale-denim shirt looked a little ratty, but she was, after all, a painter.

"Hello?" She heard his voice calling through an open front window.

"Come in," she yelled back, giving her hair a fluff with her fingers.

"Sorry to barge in on you like this," he said with a self-conscious smile.

"Hey, you were in the neighborhood," she said. "And I've invited you to come see my place if you were ever out here."

He glanced around. "Wow, this is very cool, Marley."

"I'll give you the one-minute tour," she offered. "That's as long as it takes to see everything."

But it took more than a minute, and by the time they were in the kitchen, Jack seemed somewhat impressed. "I like your style." He ran his hand over the shiny tiles. "But then why should that surprise me? However, I do have a surprise for you."

She nodded, bracing herself. Hopefully he hadn't come out here to tell her that he'd changed his mind about showing her art. She knew that nothing had sold yet, and space in his gallery was limited. It was possible he'd discovered someone with more potential.

He reached into his shirt pocket and pulled out an envelope. "Two of your paintings sold yesterday."

She blinked and wondered if she'd heard him correctly. "Two paintings sold?"

He nodded with a big grin, handing her the envelope. "Congratulations!"

She fingered the envelope. "Thank you!"

"Naturally, I deducted my commission. But I didn't want to wait until the end of the month to pay you. I assume that's okay."

Marley couldn't contain herself. She threw her arms around him. "Yes, that's more than okay. It's fantastic." Then, feeling self-conscious, she stepped away. "I can't believe it. Two paintings in one day!"

"I asked the buyer to bring them back for the art walk. I told her that would only increase their value, and she agreed."

"Oh, that's great. Where was the buyer from?"

"Here in town. She's new, just opened up a shop. Maybe you know her. She owns Bridgeport Interiors. Her name is Bonnie Boxwell."

Marley felt her heart sinking. Bonnie Boxwell had purchased her paintings?

"Is something wrong?" Jack's brow creased with concern.

Marley shook her head. "No, not really. Well, sort of. But it's nothing."

"What is it?"

"Oh, it's just that Abby … well, she's not exactly on friendly terms with Bonnie."

"Oh." He still looked confused.

So she quickly filled him in, playing it down as much as possible, then she laughed lightly. "Although Abby might want me tear up the check."

Jack looked slightly shocked. "That's a little extreme."

"I know. But Abby's a little extreme when it comes to Bonnie."

"Well, you don't have to tell Abby who bought the paintings, do you?"

"No." She stuck the envelope in her shirt pocket. "I don't."

He was looking at her seascape now. "This is … different."

She winced at his tone. "Different bad?"

"No, not at all. Just different from your other work."

She wished she'd thought to hide the painting. Instead of fretting over her personal image, she should've been concerned with her professional one. "It's not really for your gallery," she said. "My friend Janie kind of commissioned it." Okay, that was quite an overstatement, but Marley's pride and insecurity had taken over.

He nodded, then turned back to her with a hard-to-read expression. "Well, I shouldn't take up any more of your time. I just wanted to share the good news—and the check." He smiled.

"Thanks so much, Jack. You really made my day."

"And your house looks great, Marley."

"It'll look better when I get it all done," she said apologetically. "But I realized I needed to spend more time painting and less time decorating."

"Good thinking!" Then he left, and she wondered if she'd said something to offend him. Or maybe she should've invited him to stay awhile. Or offered him a drink. Or asked him to sit outside with her and enjoy the ocean view.

"Dumb, dumb, dumb," she told herself as she opened the thin envelope. Then she stopped. That was exactly how she used to scold herself when she was married to John. No, she was *not* dumb, just somewhat challenged when it came to entertaining guys in her home. This was totally new territory for her. But she could learn. She *would* learn.

=Chapter 13=

CAROLINE

"Have you been caring for your mom long?" Brent asked Caroline after the Alzheimer's support group ended.

"No, less than a month. Still, I feel like I'm barely keeping my nose above water. How about you?" She knew from the sharing time that Brent's father had Alzheimer's, and that Brent's mother (at sixty-two) had run off, saying she was too young to be trapped caring for her incapacitated husband.

"I just came up here a couple of weeks ago," Brent told her as he picked up a donut from the refreshment table. "I only expected to stay a few days, but when I saw how things were for my dad, well, I decided to take time off work and do what I can."

"That's good you could take time off. Not all bosses would be so understanding."

"My boss and I have kind of a love-hate relationship." His blue eyes twinkled. "I'm my own boss."

"Lucky you. So are you able to work and care for your dad?"

His mouth twisted to one side. "I keep telling myself that I should be able to do it, but all the distractions and demands … well, it's been a challenge. Also, I'm at a disadvantage not being down in Hollywood."

"Hollywood?" Caroline's interest level in this attractive young man just upped several notches. "That's where I'm from too."

"Really?" He grinned. "I thought you looked like a California girl."

She laughed. "California girl. Now there's something I haven't heard for a while."

"So is this a temporary thing for you, too? Will you go back home eventually?"

Caroline sighed. "This is home now. I put my condo on the market."

"Wow, that's a big commitment. You must really love your mom."

She considered this. Of course, she loved her mom, and yet in so many ways her mom seemed like a complete stranger. "I guess I thought this might be my last chance … to get to know her." She forced a laugh. "Unfortunately, I think I'm a little too late. Most of the time it's like she's not even there. Like the lights are on, but nobody's home."

"So you and your mom weren't close when you were growing up?"

She just shook her head, then took a slow sip of the metallic-tasting coffee.

"My dad and I were really close," Brent said. "He was kind of old, you know, compared to my friends' dads. He's like fifteen years older than my mom. But he always took time for me when I was growing up. Whether I was attempting to do sports, which I was totally lame at, or theater or music, there my dad would be sitting in the front row, cheering for me."

"And your mom?"

He shrugged. "She's always kind of done her own thing. In fact, I actually thought their marriage would end after I left for college. But I think Mom liked her little comfort zone. She never had to work, and Dad pretty much let her do as she pleased, buy what she wanted. It wasn't until he started putting his golf shoes in the freezer that Mom got nervous."

Caroline glanced at her watch. As much as she enjoyed chatting with this pleasant young man, she knew her respite time was limited, and she still had some errands to do.

"Looks like you need to go," he said with what seemed to be disappointment.

She smiled. "Yeah. I only get two hours, and I still need to grab some groceries."

"I hear ya." He nodded. "Maybe that's something we caregivers could help each other out with. If you ever want to email me a list, I'd be happy to get your groceries too."

Caroline blinked. "Seriously?"

"You bet." He reached for his wallet, then pulled out a business card for her.

"And I could trade the favor." She grinned as she tucked the card into her bag. "If it's any comfort, I've figured out how to get my mom's diapers and that kind of thing online."

"Hey, that's a great idea."

As they walked out to the parking lot, she told him about the local pharmacy that delivered. "And I can email you about the online drugstore if you want."

"Great. This is helpful stuff," he said as she stopped by her car. "I wasn't too keen about trying out this support group, but meeting you makes me glad I came."

"Well, thank you." She gave him a big smile. "It's been nice talking to you."

He waved and told her to email him, then walked over to a BMW convertible. She tried not to stare, but it made a nice scene. Nice-looking young guy, extremely cool car, and he even put the top down. As she drove away, she realized that she still didn't know what he did for a living. The fact that he was self-employed, lived in Hollywood, and was obviously successful suggested that he was involved in the entertainment industry. She knew that Brent's mom was less than ten years older than Caroline, so she estimated Brent would be in his late thirties at the oldest—if his mom was young when he was born. He could be as young as early thirties. In other words, young enough to be Caroline's son.

She laughed as she pulled into the grocery store parking lot. It's not like she was interested in Brent—not for anything besides a friend anyway—but if Mitch were completely out of the picture, and if Brent were ten years older, she might have been. It wouldn't have been the first time she'd dated a younger guy. But she had a seven-year rule: Any guy more than seven years younger was out of the question. Brent was definitely out of the question. Caroline had no intention of turning into the local cougar.

However, she suspected that Brent had assumed she was younger. And that felt kind of nice. Especially considering the direction her life seemed headed these days. Constantly caring for and cleaning up after her mom sometimes made Caroline feel like she was about the same age as her mother.

As she pushed her cart through Safeway, picking up packaged items like applesauce cartons, juice boxes, and pudding cups—things she'd never purchased until she'd started caring for her mother—everything felt strangely surreal.

"Caroline McCann?"

Caroline looked up from the banana section to see a middle-aged man looking at her. He looked vaguely familiar in an older sort of way.

"It *is* you," he said with a bright smile. "You don't remember me?"

Those gray eyes looked hauntingly familiar. "Adam Fowler?"

He nodded and came over to where she was standing, holding out his arms as if he expected her to hug him. Against her will and better judgment, she complied.

"How long has it been?" he asked, shaking his head.

"Well, I just went to my thirty-fifth class reunion," she told him, "and you graduated two years before me. So that would be thirty-seven years."

"No way." He shook his head in disbelief. "How did we get so old?"

She shrugged as she picked up a small bunch of bananas. Potassium was supposed to be good for her mom.

"Not that you look much older than you did thirty-seven years ago," he said warmly.

She smiled uncomfortably. "Thanks. I'd say the same about you, but it wouldn't be true."

He just laughed. "Good ol' Caroline, still speaking your mind."

She nodded, holding her head higher. "Nice seeing you again, Adam," she said in a formal tone. "If you'll excuse me, my time is limited today." Then she turned her cart around and hurried toward the dairy section. She felt warmth on her cheeks, almost as if she were fifteen again. He acted so normal, so natural, that he'd probably completely forgotten how he humiliated her in high school. Adam had been a senior jock, the kind of guy that girls dreamed of having for a boyfriend. When he asked Caroline out early in her sophomore year, she was over the moon. She dressed carefully, did her hair and makeup perfectly, and with high expectations, happily went to the movies with him.

After the movies, he took her for a soda, then drove his '66 Mustang to the cliffs to look at the moon over the ocean. Of course, the moon was nowhere to be seen, and no sooner had he turned off his ignition than his lips and hands were all over her. At first she tried to humor him, joking about how she wasn't that kind of a girl. Then, when he refused to take no for an answer, she actually slapped him, got out of the car, and started to walk home. Fortunately he picked her up. But he didn't say a word as he sped her home. Naturally, he didn't walk her to the door. That would've been fine—end of story—except that the following week at school a rumor began circulating about her. That's when Caroline got her "reputation." Fast and easy … call Caroline for a good time. It had probably been written on the guys' bathroom walls.

"We meet again," Adam said as he pulled his cart behind hers in the express lane.

She gave him another forced smile, then picked up a *People* magazine and pretended to be absorbed by a headline about Jennifer Aniston.

"So are you just visiting?" he asked.

"No," she said without looking up. "I moved back recently to care for my mother." She looked up at him now. "She has Alzheimer's. You know, that whole memory-loss thing." *Hint-hint.*

He nodded. "That's gotta be tough."

His unexpected sympathy softened her ever so slightly. Really, why was she acting like this? It wasn't even in her nature or beliefs to be unforgiving. But something about seeing him like this, such a blast from the past … well, it was unnerving. "Yeah, it hasn't been real easy." She set the magazine in her cart. "How about you? Are you just visiting or—"

"I'm actually looking at vacation property this weekend. I live over in Eugene, but it's like I hear the ocean calling."

"So you're looking at beachfront property?" she asked.

His eyes lit up. "You got any good tips?"

"Well, do you remember Paul Franklin? He married my best friend, Abby, right out of high school. Anyway, he has a development over on North Shore you might be interested in checking out. Not cheap properties, but nice."

"North Shore." He nodded. "I've heard of that."

Now it was her turn to unload her cart. Thankful for the distraction, she focused on putting her juvenile-looking groceries on the moving belt.

"I thought maybe you had kids," Adam said as she put the rubber divider behind her items. "But I'm guessing that's the kind of food your mother eats."

"That's right." She moved up to the cashier now. "Bland and boring."

"Does your mom still live in the same house?"

She studied his expression as she pulled out some cash. "Do you honestly remember where I lived?"

"Sure." He nodded with an innocent expression. "Didn't we go out for a while?"

Okay, she just had to laugh. "Yeah. We went out *once.*"

His brows shot up now like some kind of light had just gone on.

"Need I say more?" she asked as she waited for her change.

"It's coming back to me now," he said with what seemed honest embarrassment. "You slapped me."

Caroline just nodded, but the cashier looked on with interest as she carefully counted out the change.

He slowly shook his head. "I'm guessing I owe you an apology."

Now her smile was genuine. "Thank you. I'll accept it."

"I took a few blows to the head during high school," he said with a crooked smile. "I think it might've messed with my memory or something."

She laughed. "Kind of like my mom."

Caroline thanked the clerk as she took the reusable grocery bag, then she turned to Adam. "Happy house hunting."

He nodded with a slightly bewildered expression. It wasn't exactly the sort of social encounter that Caroline would've expected at the grocery store, but it was actually rather satisfying.

═══Chapter 14═══

JANIE

"I've decided that I'm an angry artist," Marley told Janie Saturday afternoon. She had popped in unexpectedly, and they were standing in the driveway so that Marley could look on as Mario cut tiles.

"What?" Janie studied Marley's face to see if she was joking.

"Anger motivates me to paint."

"Really?" Janie paused as the tile saw growled loudly.

Marley nodded. "I know it's pathetic ... but true."

"What about the seascape?" Janie moved a bit farther away from Mario's workstation, and Marley followed. "It didn't seem like it wanted to be an angry painting."

Marley let out a cynical laugh. "Well, you might not want it now." She jerked her thumb toward her car. "I brought it over."

"It's finished?"

"Yes. I got so angry that I just worked nonstop until it was done."

"Do I get to see it?"

"Of course, that's why I stopped by." Marley glanced toward the house. "You go wait in your living room, and I'll bring it in for the great unveiling."

"How exciting!"

"I'm warning you, you might not like it. So don't feel like you're beholden. I just figured I should give you the first chance to reject it."

"Oh, Marley." Janie shook her head. "Go get it. I'm dying of curiosity." Then Janie went into the house, left the front door open, and went to sit and wait. She felt a little bit concerned though. What if she really didn't like the painting? Would she have the nerve to tell Marley that? And considering the way Marley was acting today, talking about being angry ... what if Janie's rejection really cut deep? And yet, how could she purchase a painting she didn't like? Where would she hang it?

"Okay, now close your eyes," Marley called.

"All right." Janie leaned back in the chair and shut her eyes.

"Okay," Marley said after a minute or so. "Open your eyes."

Janie looked up to see the painting perched on the back of part of the sectional, leaning against the bare wall. "Oh, Marley." Janie stood and went closer. "It's fabulous."

"Really?" Marley looked shocked.

"Absolutely." Janie stared at the surf pounding onto the rocks and nodded. "I love it. I want it. It's perfect."

Marley let out a huge sigh and sank down onto a club chair. "You don't know how happy you just made me."

"It's so much better than I hoped for." Janie kept staring at it.

"You're not just saying that to make me feel better?"

"No. But I'll admit I'm relieved. You had me worried when you started talking about being an angry painter." Janie turned to look at her. "What did you mean by that, anyway?"

Marley ran her hand through her short hair and smiled sheepishly. "Oh, Jack came by and looked at the painting while it was still unfinished, and I got the impression he didn't like it."

"He didn't like it?" Janie found this hard to believe. "I thought the man had pretty good taste."

"Well, he said it was 'different.' But he said it in a way that sounded like criticism, like it wasn't as good as my other works."

"Well, it is different. The colors alone are different. But it's a seascape. You couldn't very well have used magenta and turquoise, and if you had, I wouldn't have wanted it."

"I started to doubt myself after Jack left. And then I got mad. And then I went to work. I realized that I'd done the other paintings in a state of anger too." She gave Janie a hopeless look. "What if that's the only way I can paint? Out of anger?"

"It might not be good for your blood pressure."

"Not to mention my stomach. I think I went through half a bottle of Tums."

"That's not good."

Marley shook her head, then stood and walked around the room. "Hey, you changed things around in here. Didn't the sectional used to be over there?"

"Yes. What do you think?"

"I like it." Marley nod approvingly. "Much better. It feels roomier and more balanced. Very nice."

"Bonnie Boxwell did it."

Marley's mouth twisted into a questioning look.

"I couldn't stop her," Janie explained. "She came in and told me to leave and to just trust her. So I left and came back to this."

"Are you going to tell Abby?"

Janie sat back down. "I don't know. Really, I don't see why I should. She doesn't know all the deep dark details of my life." She chuckled. "Not that I really have any."

"She does know that Bonnie came to your house."

"You told her?"

"Sorry, it kind of slipped out. Besides, this is a small town. Abby might've found out anyway."

"How did she react?"

"Probably just like you would imagine."

"I honestly didn't know that it was Bonnie's shop when I went in. I don't want to hurt Abby for anything, but Bonnie is really nice. And she's smart. And she has a great eye for design." Janie wondered how much to say now.

"All things Abby will not want to hear about."

"Then let's not tell her."

"Hopefully she'll qualify to buy her old house."

"Her old house? You mean the one she grew up in, the one she and Paul raised their girls in?"

Marley filled her in about the bed-and-breakfast and how Paul was less than enthused. "Abby wants to leave Paul out of it."

"Oh?"

"It might be a good thing. Abby seems pretty jazzed. She's getting her ducks in a row."

"Good for her." Janie got up to get her purse. "I'll write you a check."

"You don't have to pay me today if you don't want to," Marley said. "I just sprang it on you, and I know you're trying to cover a lot of ground here on your renovations."

"Well, I just had a bit of good news." Janie returned with her purse. "My Realtor got a cash offer on my Manhattan apartment yesterday."

"Wow, that's great. And fast, too."

"We didn't really expect it to be on the market for long," Janie admitted. "It's a pretty great neighborhood, and word travels fast when a place goes up for sale."

"Well, congratulations." Marley grinned at her. "I had some good news too—a couple of my paintings sold at the gallery."

"Then congratulations to you, too!"

Marley told her who bought the paintings.

"Did you tell Abby about *that?*"

"It hasn't come up."

"Oh dear." Janie shook her head. "This Bonnie biz is getting more and more complicated, isn't it?"

"We all grew up here. We all know what a small town is like."

"So now that your art is starting to sell, I should ask whether you've raised the price." Janie waited.

"No, of course not. If I were a better friend I'd just give it to you."

"No, you would not," Janie said sharply as she took out her checkbook. "You need to start acting like a businesswoman, Marley."

"So you really do like it?"

Janie laughed as she wrote out the check. "Do you think I'm faking it?"

Marley was over by the painting again. "No. I believe you."

As Janie subtracted the amount from her balance, Marley walked around admiring the room. "Abby is going to be pea green," she said finally.

"Pea green?" Janie tore off the check and handed it to Marley.

"Pea green jealous of how Bonnie made this room look so great."

"Well, I have to give it to Abby. She's pretty good at design and picking out materials. But Bonnie has a real gift. Also, she understands my style. Just don't tell Abby I said that, okay?"

"Don't worry. And the same back at you about my paintings."

"I might as well get this off my chest: I'm consulting with Bonnie for Victor's boat, too."

"His new sailboat?"

Janie nodded.

"So will your friends ever get to see this sweet little boat?" Marley smiled hopefully.

"I'm sure Victor will be happy to show it off. Maybe we should plan an open house. Or would that be an open boat?"

"We could whack it with a bottle of champagne."

Janie laughed. "I'm not sure Victor will agree to anyone whacking the *Heavenly* with anything."

"The *Heavenly?*"

"He renamed the boat."

"Nice."

"I can see how this whole Bonnie thing could get awkward." Now Janie wished she hadn't invited Bonnie to walk through the boat with her. Really, what if Abby happened to see them together?

"Tell me about it."

"I guess we'll just have to keep our fingers crossed that Abby is able to buy her house again. That would probably keep her so busy that she might forgive us for associating with her nemesis."

"Yes, let's hope."

"Thanks for the check." Marley chuckled as she tucked it into her bag. "Now I'm going to go home and attempt to start a new work. I've decided I have to prove to Jack—no, prove to myself—that I can still paint. Hopefully I won't have to get angry to do it."

After Marley left, Janie started to worry about Abby. Really, how would it feel to have not just one but two of her closest friends consorting with the very woman who had tried to steal her husband? And what if Abby did see Janie with Bonnie as they were going out to look at the boat? Or even coming out of Bonnie's store? Or what if Abby popped in while Bonnie was here dropping off an order? Or vice versa? No, this was not good. In Janie's line of work, she always felt it most prudent to prevent catastrophe whenever possible. So she called Abby and invited her to meet her in town for lunch. They would face this thing head-on—and in a public place.

As Janie walked into town, she came up with an idea. The more she thought about it, the more the idea morphed into a plan. And as she walked up the boardwalk to the Chowder House, she realized it might actually be a rather ingenious plan. Oh, some might assume that guilt was motivating her. But no. If anything was motivating her, it was simply genuine interest.

"Hey," Abby called out as Janie entered the restaurant. "You made it."

"Sorry." Janie looked at her watch. "It was such a nice day, I decided to walk. I guess it took a little longer than I anticipated."

Abby hugged her. "That's okay. I was so glad to get out of the house, I can't complain."

"Why were you stuck in the house on a day like this?"

Abby launched into a description of all the paperwork that was needed to get her financing for the house.

"Marley told me about that," Janie admitted after they were seated. "It sounds like a fantastic opportunity for you."

Abby frowned. "Kind of a long-shot opportunity. But I'm going to give it my best effort."

"Do you know when the house will go into short sale?"

"Not exactly, but the gal at the bank said it could be by the end of the month." Abby shook her head. "I just hope I can get it together in time."

Janie was tempted to spring her idea on Abby then, but years of practicing law reminded her that timing was everything. So she looked over the menu, then ordered Manhattan clam chowder and waited as Abby decided between fisherman's stew and Boston clam chowder.

"It figures you'd go for Manhattan," Abby teased. "You can take the girl out of the city, but you can't take the city out of the girl."

"That reminds me of something," Janie began cautiously.

"What?"

"I know that you know that I went into Bonnie Boxwell's design store," Janie said, "but I didn't know it was her store when I went in."

Abby smiled. "Yeah. Marley told me all about it. No hard feelings."

Janie sighed. "But Marley might not have told you that Bonnie came out to my house and measured for tile, and then she rearranged my living room and—"

"You let her rearrange your living room?" Abby looked so shocked that an eavesdropper might have assumed Janie let an ax murderer rearrange her furniture.

"She actually did a good job. You know what a time I had with that sectional, how I wished I'd left it behind in the apartment."

Abby nodded. "It was an awkward layout."

"Well, Bonnie insisted I give her a chance. So I did, and she worked her magic."

"Her magic." Abby made a disgusting face. "More like witch-craft."

"Bonnie isn't a witch."

"Not to you, maybe."

"Clifden is a small town, Abby. It's unavoidable that your friends are going to run into Bonnie. We can't treat her like a pariah."

"Why not?"

"Because that will only make things worse."

Abby frowned. "What are you suggesting? That I welcome my husband's lover with open arms?"

"She's not Paul's lover, Abby. You know that."

"She'd like to be."

"Don't be too sure."

"What do you mean by that?"

"I mean she's an attractive and talented woman, and I've noticed that men seem drawn to her. She has that way about her. You know, kind of like Caroline."

"You mean she's a flirt."

"I'm not saying Caroline is a flirt," Janie said. "I'm just saying Caroline has a certain demeanor ... a way that men like. It's a skill I've never mastered." Janie laughed. "I've actually never wanted to master it. But Bonnie has it too."

Abby looked angry. Or maybe she was hurt.

"Look." Janie reached over and placed a hand on Abby's. "I didn't invite you here to make you feel badly about Bonnie. I just wanted to be honest with you. I happen to think honest friendships last longer."

Abby slowly nodded. "Yes, I'm sure you're right. It's just that ... well, Bonnie is a bit of a sore subject with me."

"I know, but I'm hoping you can move on, Abby. For your own sake. And I really think your idea to do a bed-and-breakfast is brilliant."

Abby's blue eyes brightened. "You do?"

"Absolutely."

"That's what I told Paul. I need something to pour myself into, to take my mind off of feeling sorry for myself or being jealous. Well, I didn't actually say that, but I told him I need my own business. I've always regretted letting that house go, but now, hearing that it could be available, and at a pretty good price, well, it almost feels like fate." Her brightness faded. "If I can just make the numbers work."

The waitress set their soup and bread down. Janie took in a deep breath, then began. "Abby, I have a proposition for you. My Manhattan apartment looks like it's sold, and I've been thinking I need to invest some of it. Also, I've been thinking I need an office space, because I'm considering practicing law again. Not corporate law. But more like family law. And maybe even some legal aid if there's a need for it in Clifden, which I suspect there is."

"You're going to buy office space?"

"I'm not sure. I was actually wondering about being a silent partner in your bed-and-breakfast."

Abby's eyes opened wide. "You'd do that with me?"

"I'd like to consider it. If you're comfortable with the idea."

"Are you kidding? I love the idea."

"I'd have to go over all the paperwork."

"I'd love you to go over the paperwork. The truth is I'm feeling a little overwhelmed."

"And part of the deal would be for you to let me have the basement for my law office."

"But it's so dingy down there, would you really want—"

"I'd probably want to do some renovations, but the truth is I have such great memories of being in that basement. Remember how we hung out there when we were girls, back before you and Caroline got so popular that you left Marley and me in the dust?"

"We didn't leave you in—"

"Never mind, that's water under the bridge."

"Oh, Janie, I'm so excited. This could be so perfect. Would you really want a law office located at an inn?"

"Why not? It's a great location. I think the basement could be remodeled into a very cool office. You'd be around to keep me company. Maybe I could even lend you a hand at times."

"I can't believe it." Abby was so happy that her eyes filled with tears. "This could be so wonderful, Janie. I just can't believe you want to do this."

"Well, like I said, I need to carefully look over all the details. You know me, I won't agree to anything that I haven't thoroughly studied first."

"I'm just so relieved." Abby leaned back and exhaled. "I really, really wanted to do this, but I was worried I was getting in over my head, and that if I went under, no one would be around to throw me a line."

"It's a lot to take on all by yourself."

"Even though my mom is willing to get involved, I get the feeling that she halfway expects me to fail before I even get started."

Janie's legal mind was kicking into gear now. "So how about you make copies of all your paperwork so I can look over it?"

"I'll go home and gather it all up, then drop it by your house later today." Abby reached for the bill. "And when Paul hears that you're involved—I mean that you *might* be involved—well, I'll bet he'll probably start singing a different song."

Janie extended her hand. "So, it's a deal." She shook Abby's. "If everything looks good and all goes well, we might be partners."

=Chapter 15=

ABBY

Abby was still feeling slightly stunned as she drove through town. That Janie would even consider partnering with her in this new venture was truly amazing. Of course, it was possible that Janie would review the numbers and decide the whole thing was foolish. But if that happened—and as disappointed as Abby knew she would be—it might be for the best. It wasn't as if Abby wanted to risk everything and end up losing her savings.

She couldn't resist driving down her old street, parking across from the stately old house and just looking at it. She knew this was a big dream, perhaps even an impossible dream. But it was her dream. And yet it was a dream she was willing to share, if that was what it took. Still, she was relieved not to have to share it with Paul. She knew that was probably selfish and perhaps even stupid. But she was glad he had no interest in participating in her dream.

She took in a deep breath and closed her eyes and attempted to focus her hopes and her energy on God. Faith wasn't exactly her strong suit, and prayer seldom felt comfortable, but more than ever, she wanted God's blessing on this endeavor. She knew that God was the one who could open and close doors, and she really wanted him to open this one. If it was for the best.

"And if it's not for the best," she whispered quietly, "then just close this door, lock it tight, and help me to find something else to pour my energies into." Then Abby said amen and started her car. As she drove toward home, she remembered that winter was coming, and that her usual volunteer efforts at the soup kitchen and food bank would be needed. Also, she could get involved in the quilters guild again. It wasn't as if she had nothing to do. It was simply that what she had didn't seem to be enough. She felt like a river that had become stagnant over the past couple of years. For some reason, her energy and enthusiasm had been blocked. As much as she loved having her old friends around her, she couldn't help but compare their lives to her own. It was as if they were reinventing themselves, starting over, and enjoying a freshness that she longed for.

To be fair, she knew that Caroline didn't see her life like this at all. But even the prospect of caring for a needy parent felt more appealing than just sitting around her lovely new home and doing nothing.

As Abby turned down her street, she remembered Caroline's challenge for Abby to get a checkup. Caroline had been concerned that Abby's struggle was as much physical as emotional. And while Abby knew Caroline might be right, she also knew that being busy always made her feel better.

She pulled into the driveway, surprised to see that Paul was home already. To be honest, she was a little disappointed. She had hoped to gather up her paperwork, slip into his office, and make the copies at home. In all likelihood he would be in his office, and if she started making copies, he would want to know why. She wasn't ready to divulge everything to him quite yet.

To her relief, he wasn't in his office. So she turned on the copier and quickly began reproducing her paperwork, sorting, stacking, stapling. She was almost done when she heard his voice.

"What are you doing in here?"

She jumped. "Just using the copy machine." She turned and forced a smile. "You don't mind, do you?"

"No, of course not. What are you copying?" He was looking over her shoulder as she pulled out a file folder and slid Janie's packet of papers into it.

"Just some stuff for the B and B."

"You're still thinking about that?" The tone of his voice seemed to say it all, but she was determined not to go there.

She simply nodded. "But I'm being very careful about it. Janie is going to look over everything for me. You know, being an attorney and all, she can help to decide if it makes sense or not." She didn't want to divulge Janie's investment interests yet. Not until Janie gave it her seal of approval anyway.

"I'm impressed."

She turned off the copier and stared at him. Was he just jerking her chain, or was he serious? "Really?"

Paul nodded. "Seeking legal advice. That's a good move, Abby."

She gave him a genuine smile. "Thanks."

He sat down in his desk chair and let out a long sigh.

She studied him more closely now. "Are you feeling okay?"

He nodded, but there seemed to be a shadow over him.

"Paul?" She sat in the chair across from his desk. "Is something wrong?"

"No … no." He slowly shook his head. "Not really."

"Not really?"

"Nothing out of the ordinary anyway."

"What do you mean?"

"It's just business. You know, too much real estate sitting around … winter coming. You know the drill, Abby. We've been down this road a few times."

"Oh." She did know this road. It could be bumpy when the economy was down, but she had hoped they were beyond that. She also knew that the market hadn't picked up as much as they had expected it would by now.

"Nothing to worry about," he assured her.

"You're right," she said in a confident tone. "We've weathered far worse than this, haven't we? Remember the eighties?"

He nodded. "Yeah, three little kids, not much work. We were barely scraping by then."

"But we made it." She waved her hand toward the big window that looked out over the ocean. "And who would've guessed we'd ever live in a place like this?"

His lips curved into a weary smile. "Yeah. Go figure."

"Really, is that *all* that's troubling you?" She studied him closely, worried that perhaps this was something more, something related to a certain businesswoman in town.

"Isn't that enough?"

"Yes, of course. But I just want you to be honest with me, Paul. If something else is going on, you would tell me, wouldn't you?"

"Are you obsessing over Bonnie again?"

She shrugged, then looked out over the ocean. A low fog bank was rolling in.

"Well, don't waste your time on it, Abby. I promise you there's nothing there."

For some reason she believed him.

"I think I'm just tired." He chuckled. "Plus I had a lousy golf game this morning. Gary whupped me big time."

She laughed now. "Well, that's probably bothering you more than anything else."

He nodded with a sheepish grin.

"How about if I fix you some lunch before I go run some errands?"

He smiled hopefully. "That'd be nice."

Abby felt unexpectedly happy as she made him a turkey sandwich. She took her time putting it together just the way he liked it and even made a quick potato salad out of last night's red potatoes, then took it in to him with a linen napkin and a tall glass of lemonade.

"Thanks, Abby. You're the best."

Not used to this kind of praise, she tried not to look too surprised. "Well, thank you." She set his lunch on his desk, then leaned over to peer more closely into his eyes. "You really are feeling okay, aren't you?"

"Just tired."

She frowned. "Caroline has been nagging me to go in for a complete physical, and I'm thinking maybe I should schedule appointments for both of us."

He let out a reluctant groan as he reached for the sandwich. "You know how I hate going to the doc, Abby. I'm way more fit than most guys my age. You go ahead and schedule something for yourself if you want."

"But you haven't been in for ages."

"I'll make an appointment later this fall," he said with his mouth full. "When things aren't too busy."

She wanted to challenge him, remind him that maybe things weren't too busy right now, but that might sound like she was coming down on him. He was being so sweet today ... well, she decided to just let it go. She could always schedule him an appointment anyway.

She leaned over and pecked him on the cheek. "I'm running over to Janie's with this paperwork. Then I might check on Caroline. She's pretty much in a lockdown these days."

"Lockdown?" He forked into the potato salad.

Abby explained about how Caroline's mom needed round-the-clock care and supervision.

He shook his head. "That's gotta be hard."

"Anyway, I'll be back in a couple of hours. I've got some steaks for dinner, but since you're having a late lunch, maybe we can eat a late dinner, too."

"No complaints from me."

Abby still felt caught off guard as she got her bag and headed back out to her car. Though Paul was being strangely congenial, she believed him when he'd promised his mood had nothing to do with Bonnie. As she drove toward town, she realized his attitude might've had as much to do with Abby as with him. Maybe it was because she was being nicer to him. In fact, that's exactly what their counselor had recommended.

"Remember how you treated each other when you were courting?" she'd said last week.

Paul had laughed. "Courting?"

Abby had tried to conceal her aggravation. "You see, we dated
in high school and got married right after graduation. *Courtship* isn't
exactly how I'd describe it."

"Well, maybe that's part of your problem. You both still rely
on some old habits—I'm guessing they're habits you picked up in
adolescence. I'm just suggesting that you take a more grown-up
approach. Practice a bit more respect and civility toward each other.
Mind your manners as if you were courting. Does that make sense?"

At the time it hadn't made sense, but Abby thought maybe she
was getting it now. She and Paul did have some immature habits.
They were too quick to speak their minds to each other, which sometimes resulted in blowout fights where they both lost. So maybe their
counselor was right. Maybe they did need to act like they were courting. Abby thought maybe she'd open a bottle of wine and light some
candles for dinner, show Paul that she still thought he was special.

When Abby got to Janie's she thought the silvery sports car in
front of the house was her friend's, but as she was walking toward the
house, she realized that Janie's silver Mercedes was parked over to the
far side of the garage. On closer inspection, she saw that the car in
front was a late-model Jaguar.

Abby considered turning around and getting back into her car,
but then she heard the front door opening. As irrational as it seemed,
Abby had the distinct and uncomfortable suspicion that the Jaguar
belonged to Bonnie Boxwell and that she was about to meet this
woman face-to-face. She hoped she was simply being dramatic and

imagining things. Abby had seen Bonnie a couple of times from a distance, but they'd never officially met.

"Abby," Janie said in a voice that sounded a little tight around the edges.

"I brought the paperwork by," Abby said in a voice even more tightly wound.

"Abby, I'd like you to meet Bonnie Boxwell," Janie said in a way that Abby suspected she hoped sounded totally innocent, although Abby knew better. "Bonnie, this is my dear friend Abby Franklin."

Bonnie stuck out her hand, but Abby pretended not to see it. "I didn't mean to interrupt," she said directly to Janie. "But here's the paperwork I promised you." She shoved it toward Janie.

"Abby Franklin?" Bonnie sounded curious. "I think I may know your husband."

Abby's mouth dried up.

"Abby's husband is Paul Franklin," Janie offered. "He's the developer of North Shore and—"

"Of course," Bonnie said. "I have a lot there, and I spoke to Paul about building a house." She smiled at Abby as if she thought Abby was totally in the dark in regard to Bonnie's relationship with Paul. "Small world."

Abby nodded stiffly. "And Clifden is an even smaller town."

"Bonnie opened up that design shop," Janie continued, "Bridgeport Interiors. I think I mentioned it to you."

Abby just nodded, trying not to obsess over how irritatingly pretty and young Bonnie was, even better-looking up close than from a distance.

"Abby's the one who helped me start the renovations here," Janie prattled on, having a conversation of one. "She knows where to get almost everything and who to call and all that."

"I'm sure you've learned a lot from your husband." Bonnie smiled.

"Yes. I used to help him with decor choices on all the new spec houses," Abby told her in a voice that sounded much too cheerful. "We had such fun. Then he began building custom homes, and most homeowners hired professional decorators."

"I've been trying to talk him into working out a deal with me," Bonnie said. "I could handle the interior designs and—"

"I think Paul has everything under control," Abby said in a frosty voice.

Bonnie laughed. "Yes, so it seems."

"Abby," Janie said suddenly, grabbing her arm as if worried that Abby was about to go for the jugular, which was strangely tempting. "You have to come inside and see the glass tile. Bonnie just brought it over, and Mario is going to start installing it. It's just beautiful and—"

"And I must be going," Bonnie said. "Nice to meet you, Abby. Give my regards to Paul."

"Oh, I will," Abby snapped as Janie tugged her into the house, closing the door before Abby had a chance to say something really mean and nasty. Not that she wanted to be mean and nasty, especially when she'd already been having such a great day. But hearing that woman saying to give Paul her regards was just too much.

"I'm sorry, Abby," Janie said. "She just popped in with the tile, and I was trying to hurry her out in fear that your paths would cross, but she just kept sticking around."

"Like she wants to be your new best friend?" Abby said sarcastically.

"I don't think she has many friends."

"Well, she better not start taking mine," Abby snarled. When she saw Janie's expression, she regretted her reaction. "I'm sorry, Janie. But that woman really gets my dander up."

"Gets your dander up?" Janie laughed. "That's an old one."

Abby looked at Janie's rearranged living room. "So this is the work of Ms. Boxwell?"

Janie nodded. "You have to admit she improved it."

"I guess." Abby looked at the seascape now. "Is that Marley's?"

"Yes, isn't it beautiful?"

Abby went closer. "It really is. I can't believe how quickly she finished it. I saw it just a few days ago and it wasn't even close."

"She said she painted it in anger."

Abby kind of laughed. "Maybe I should take up painting too—especially if I plan to run into that woman again."

Janie linked arms with Abby, leading her into the kitchen. "No, you just need to let that all go. Really, I think it's for the best that you actually met her today. Now if you happen to run into her—"

"Run over her is more like it."

Janie released Abby's arm and shook her finger. "If you happen to run into her, you can act more natural and cordial."

"If that's even possible."

"You know, Abby, if you seriously want to become a businesswoman—a successful businesswoman—you will have to learn to control that tongue of yours."

Abby frowned. "Yes, you're probably right."

"Of course, I'm right. And you'll have to develop thicker skin, too."

Abby sighed. "Maybe I'm not cut out for this after all."

"Maybe you're not."

"Or maybe I am," Abby countered. "Maybe Bonnie is just my boot camp."

"Bonnie boot camp." Janie laughed. "Now that's a good attitude to have."

"What doesn't kill you makes you stronger, right?"

"Precisely." Janie picked up a piece of aquamarine tile and held it up to the light. "What do you think?"

"Very nice." Abby nodded. "It looks great with those dark cabinets. Very classy."

"Come see the bathroom," Janie urged.

Soon they were lost in talking about tile and various types of design and the kinds of renovations that would improve the B and B if all went well and they became business partners. By the time Abby left Janie's house, she had almost successfully blocked the image of Bonnie Boxwell from her mind—until she remembered Bonnie's arrogant suggestion that she might become Paul's new interior designer for his spec houses. Over Abby's dead body she would!

Chapter 16

MARLEY

Marley's XM Radio was tuned to a classic rock station and playing loudly—her attempt to manufacture anger to paint by—and right now it was working. As the Stones grinded out "Get Off of My Cloud," Marley's brush and palette knife were flying. She grabbed up color with abandon, swiping it across the canvas in large movements, slashes of gold and coral over a background of intense blue. But something was distracting her. Realizing that the phone was ringing, she dropped her brush, grabbed the remote and muted the radio, then reached for the phone.

"I was about to give up on you," Janie said. "Did I interrupt anything important?"

"Just the mad painter at work." Marley looked at the clock to see that it was getting close to quitting time anyway.

"How's it going?"

Marley studied the colorful image on her canvas. Inspired by a postcard sent from Ashton while on vacation in the Bahamas last year, it was an impressionistic scene of an island fruit stand and a woman wearing a flowered dress and big yellow hat. "Not bad," Marley said. "I think."

"Well, Victor stopped by my house," Janie explained. "He's been admiring your work, and we're wondering about commissioning you for a couple of small pieces for his boat."

"Really?" Marley set down her brush, feeling her anger melting away.

"Yes. Something nautical and fun. Does that seem doable?"

"Sure. Although, I've never really done commissioned work. I guess there's always the concern that the customer might not like it."

"I think Victor's confident you can pull it off."

"And I might be able to put it in the One-Legged Seagull if Victor changed his mind."

"I doubt that'll be the case."

"Then, sure, I'm interested."

"We're heading over to the boat now," Janie said. "I want to measure some things, and then Victor wants to take it out. Any chance you'd like to join us? I told Victor that you'd been hinting."

Marley laughed. "You told him that?"

"Well, it's true."

Marley dropped her dirty brushes into a jar of water. "I would love to see the boat. How soon are you going out?"

"In about an hour. We'll probably only stay out an hour, just long enough for sunset. Let's meet at the dock a little before six. I plan to grab us something to munch on while we're out."

"Cool. I'll clean up and head over."

As Marley drove to town, she wondered how many more delicious Indian summer days they would enjoy before winter came.

Having grown up on the coast, she knew that summerlike days could pop up in January, too. Maybe coastal weather was a good metaphor for life: Snatch the sunny days when you can, because tomorrow might be wet and windy.

She parked near the wharf, getting out her hat and windbreaker as well as a bag that she'd filled with some crackers and cheese, and a bottle of good zinfandel for Victor's boat. She would've brought champagne if she'd had any handy, but hopefully Victor wouldn't want to smash this one onto the stern of his boat.

As she approached the dock, she spotted Janie walking just ahead with a grocery bag in hand. Marley called out, then jogged up and joined her. "This is so great," she told Janie. "What a perfect evening for a nice little sailing trip. Thanks for inviting me."

"Victor said she's all set to go too. He's been out already today."

"Where is he?"

"Picking up Jack."

Marley stopped walking. "Picking up Jack? You mean my Jack? I mean, not *my* Jack. But you mean Jack-from-the-One-Legged-Seagull Jack?"

Janie laughed. "Yes, that would be the correct Jack. Is that a problem?"

Marley felt puzzled. "Why?"

"Why what?"

"Why is Victor picking up Jack?"

"Oh, didn't I mention that we were in the gallery earlier today? Victor was admiring your work, although the pieces there were too large for his boat. Anyway we got to talking with Jack, and Victor invited him to come out and sail with us this evening."

"Oh."

"Seriously, Marley, is this a problem?" Janie peered curiously at her. "I actually thought I mentioned this when I spoke to you."

"No. You didn't."

"Is something wrong between you and Jack?"

"That's just it," Marley explained as they continued walking out onto the dock. "There isn't anything between me and Jack. We're business acquaintances. That's all. No one should go around assuming we're anything more than that."

Janie chuckled. "Who's assuming anything? Victor just happens to like Jack, and Jack just happens to like sailboats. Jack probably doesn't even know you're coming sailing either. You guys will be in the same boat." Janie grinned at her pun.

Marley rolled her eyes. "Great. But now Jack will probably think that I set this whole thing up."

"Why would he—"

"Never mind." Marley shook her head. "I'm sure I must sound like I'm in junior high again. You know the truth, Janie. I've just never been good at any of this."

"Any of what?"

"You know. The guy thing."

Janie laughed loudly now. "What does that mean?"

"It's outside of my comfort zone. I haven't dated since my divorce."

"Not at all?"

Marley shook her head. "Not at all."

"But what about Jack? You guys seemed to hit it off. I suppose maybe I did assume that maybe something would come of it … someday."

Marley pointed at her. "See, I knew you were assuming."

"Here's the boat." Janie stopped in front of a pretty sailboat. Holding her grocery bag in one hand, she gracefully hopped aboard, then reached for Marley's hand and helped her to board as well.

"This is nice." Marley nodded in appreciation. "Very nice."

"I'll give you the tour," Janie offered. While using official boating terms, which Marley was sure she wouldn't remember, Janie walked her around the deck and around the outside of the cabin. Then she led Marley below.

"See, this is one of the spots where I think a painting would look nice." Janie pointed out a small bit of mahogany wall next to the galley. "Maybe a vertical piece. Like a sailboat with its sails up tall, maybe with a sunset. We want it to be in your more colorful palette. More like the pieces in the gallery. In fact, those colors have inspired my plans to outfit this place. I'm thinking bright tropical colors. Kind of like your house."

Marley nodded. "Now you're talking my language."

"Your art will really punch it up."

"I'm already getting an image in mind."

"The other piece—maybe even two pieces—will be in here." Janie opened the door to reveal very compact sleeping quarters. "See there, alongside that bookshelf. I think a couple of paintings on either side would look nice. Just to brighten it up."

"Ahoy," called what sounded like Victor from above.

"Ahoy," Janie called back. "I'm giving Marley the tour. We'll be up in a second."

Marley felt a wave of nerves and wondered why. What difference did it make to her if Victor invited a friend to join them? It's not like this was a double date or a prom. Good grief, they were middle-aged adults. *Just grow up.* Forcing what she hoped looked like a natural smile, she followed Janie on up to the deck, where Victor was showing Jack around.

"Marley?" Jack said in surprise. "I didn't know you were joining us."

She smiled bigger. "Same back at you. But it's nice to see you."

"I'm going down to the galley to throw some things together for us to snack on," Janie told Victor.

"I'll help," Marley offered.

"And I'll play first mate." Jack grinned at Victor and rubbed his hands together. "I haven't done anything like this in years."

It didn't take long to get the cheeses and olives and fruits and crackers organized onto a couple of plastic platters, ready for whenever they all decided to stop for a little break. As the boat was starting to pick up speed, Marley and Janie went back on deck, settling themselves in the cockpit where Victor was at the helm, navigating the boat through the bay. Meanwhile, Jack was busily doing something with a rope.

"Ah …" Marley pulled her hat down more tightly onto her head and sighed. "This is the life."

"Victor thought a little sailing trip might inspire you," Janie explained as she leaned back into the cushions. "Not that you have to paint anything you see out here. But you never know."

Marley reached for her bag. "That reminds me, I brought my camera along for just that purpose. I better keep it handy."

"Guess who Abby met coming out of my house yesterday?" Janie's eyebrows arched mysteriously.

"No!" Marley shook her head. "Not Bonnie Boxwell."

Janie nodded solemnly.

"Oh, dear."

"I did everything I could to avoid it. Bonnie just popped in unexpectedly, and I knew Abby might stop by. And then—well, it was just too late. The two planets collided."

"Was there any bloodshed?"

"No, but it was close."

As Janie colorfully relayed the story, Marley watched Jack. He gracefully ducked to get beneath the sail, then maneuvered his way to the other side of the deck. He seemed fairly comfortable in his role as first mate and, to Marley's surprise, he looked much younger in his faded denim Levi's and white T-shirt than what she'd been telling herself he was. Just as Janie finished up her tale of Bonnie and Abby, Jack turned and looked directly at Marley. She couldn't believe he'd caught her staring at him. But he simply nodded and grinned like it was no big deal. Feeling embarrassed and self-conscious, she turned back to Janie, trying to think of something to say and at the same time wondering why she was being so juvenile. Was it possible that she really did have feelings for Jack? Was she more attracted to him than she was willing to admit?

"There's a seal." Janie nudged Marley, then pointed.

"Oh, yeah." Marley grabbed up her camera. Aiming and focusing and pretending to be quite interested, she took a couple of shots, knowing full well that the seal's head would appear as a small dark spot in the water—nothing particularly subject-worthy for a photo or a painting. The distraction was worthwhile. The more she looked around through the lens of her camera, the more she began to spot scenes that might actually lend themselves to a canvas, including another sailboat with a rose-colored light on its sails, heading in the opposite direction.

After about half an hour, Victor turned the boat toward a small cove and Jack, as ordered, did something to the sail; the boat slowed down, and they dropped the anchor. Marley followed Janie back down to the galley to put the finishing touches on their mobile feast. Janie uncorked the wine, and soon they were all topside again, sitting in the cockpit with the guys, enjoying the scenery, food, and friendship.

"This is perfectly lovely," Marley said to Victor. "You really know how to live. I'm torn between envy and admiration."

He grinned. "I'm not sure I deserve either one. It took almost my whole life to figure things out."

"You mean the first *half* of your life," Jack told him. "Because you're only embarking on the second half now."

"I'd have to live to be well over a hundred to make your math work."

"Some scientists are predicting our generation will live past a hundred," Janie said. "I actually used that theory in a lawsuit once."

"Did it work?"

Janie grinned. "It didn't hurt my case."

"I think everyone should reinvent themselves at least once in their lifetime," Jack said.

"Did you reinvent yourself?" Janie asked.

"As a matter of fact, I did." Jack told them how he used to teach art in a community college in California. "I was one of those guys— you know, the losers. You can't make a living at your craft so you teach it instead." He shook his head. "I felt like such a hypocrite telling kids to embrace the artist's life and express their creativity and all that while I was an adept failure at it."

"But you're an excellent artist," Marley said.

His brown eyes twinkled as he smiled at her. "You really think so?"

She nodded. "I absolutely do. Your watercolors are delightful. And I know watercolor is the hardest medium to work with." She looked at Janie. "Did you see his paintings?"

Janie looked slightly embarrassed. "I'm not sure." She pointed a finger at Marley. "But that's your fault. I was so busy showing Victor your art that I don't think we looked at much else."

"We'll come back and look around more thoroughly," Victor promised Jack.

"You should've heard Janie," Jack directed to Marley. "She was going on and on about this wonderful seascape that had just been delivered to her house. Like she was trying to rub it in." He feigned a hurt expression. "Here I thought Janie was such a nice person, and she was practically stealing business right out from under my nose."

Janie grimaced. "I probably added insult to injury when I stood there in your gallery telling Victor how we might commission some pieces directly from Marley."

"Ruthlessly cutting out the middle man completely." Victor chuckled. "I'm surprised you even agreed to come out here with us today, Jack."

Jack reached for a cracker. "Well, I did worry that you had some diabolical plan to tie an anchor around my neck and throw me overboard."

"With friends like us ..." Victor held up his hands.

"Poor Jack." Janie refilled his wine glass. "Please, accept my sincere apologies for my heartless attempt to drive you out of business."

"Yes, and when I'm starving and the wolf is at my door, I'll remember who took me down, Janie Sorenson."

They all laughed.

"Seriously," Jack said, "I consider myself a staunch supporter of the arts. And I'm thrilled to see Marley's work being so well received, whether in my gallery or your living room."

"You didn't really like that seascape anyway," Marley said in an offhand way.

Jack blinked. "Are you serious?"

"I got the impression you didn't care for it."

He shook his head with a perplexed expression. "I guess I better be more careful of the impressions I leave. Obviously, the painting wasn't done when I saw it, but make no mistake, Marley, I could tell it was going to be good. I liked it just fine."

"You did?"

"I came back to my gallery and started looking for a place to hang it."

Marley felt slightly guilty. "I had no idea. I honestly thought you hated it." Now she started to giggle.

"What's so funny?" Jack reached for a gray hooded sweatshirt and pulled it over his head.

Marley's giggling turned into full-blown laughter.

"What is it?" Victor asked.

"Share with the class," Janie urged.

Marley took a deep breath, recovering. "I was so certain you hated my painting that I kind of went into this mad rage." She chortled. "And I was squirting out paint and whipping around my brushes and working late into the night. Really crazy."

"Oh, yeah," Janie said. "I remember you said you were an angry painter."

"All because of me?" Jack smiled at her. "I don't know whether to be flattered or worried."

"Probably both," she admitted.

"Now I suppose I'll need to provoke you to get those paintings for Victor," Janie teased.

Marley made a face. "Yeah, come on over and insult me and make fun of my art and tell me that I should hang up my paintbrush. That should do the trick." Now she looked around, noticing that the light was getting really gorgeous. "Hey, if I could get onto shore right now, and if you pulled the boat over there, I could probably get some photos that might lend themselves to a good painting." She hadn't even finished her sentence when both Jack and Victor sprang into action. The next thing she knew, Jack was helping her to shore.

She perched on a rock and started snapping shots of the boat against the rosy sky and water. "Hey, Janie," she yelled across the water, "can you turn on some lights?"

Before long, Janie had lights turned on, which made the shots even more interesting. "This is looking really good," she told Jack as she continued to shoot.

"Come back around," Jack yelled toward Victor.

"Yes," Marley agreed. "That's going to be perfect."

Before long, the light faded, and to Marley's surprise the boat kept going. "Are they abandoning us here?" she asked with concern.

Jack laughed. "I had a feeling I was being shanghaied."

Marley shivered. "I wish I'd thought to grab my jacket."

Just like that, Jack peeled off his sweatshirt and wrapped it around her shoulders like a cape. She didn't know how to react, but she welcomed the warmth. "Thanks, Jack. You didn't have to do that."

He just nodded. "Oh yes, I did."

The sailboat was slowly turning back around now. "Looks like they might be coming back after all."

"Too bad." He chuckled.

Although she wasn't totally sure what he meant by that, she suspected he intended something flirtatious. And that bothered her some.

Chapter 17

CAROLINE

"Thanks for meeting me," Caroline told Janie as they took their coffee to a table by the window. "I can't believe how much I look forward to something as ordinary as getting coffee." She sighed as she sat down. "Kind of pathetic, huh?"

"No, not pathetic, Caroline." Janie made a sad smile. "I remember feeling very much like that toward the end of Phil's life. He wanted his last days to be at home."

"Did you care for him yourself?"

"We had a nurse to help. She came daily and was worth her weight in gold. There's no way I could've done it on my own. But I did feel the need to remain with Phil twenty-four/seven." She took a sip of coffee. "I was never sure which day was going to be his last. And I wanted to be there for him."

"That must've been so hard."

"There were times when I felt like I wasn't going to survive it. I actually thought when Phil died, I would be next. If not for my kids, maybe I would've."

"Wow. I had no idea."

"It's not something I like to talk about. Even now it's hard to remember those days."

Caroline set her spoon on the napkin. "So you understand how it feels to be stuck at home. I mean maybe you didn't feel as stuck as I do. I realize you loved your husband dearly—and it's not that I don't love my mom." Suddenly Caroline was crying. "I'm sorry, Janie." She reached for a napkin to wipe her eyes. "I think I'm just a little more bummed than usual today."

"It's okay," Janie assured her.

"For some reason it felt like a really long weekend. It didn't help that the weather was absolutely gorgeous. Everyone else was out having a great time, and I was trapped in an old-folks' home." She shook her head. "I felt like a caged tiger, like I wanted to just kick down the doors and run free."

"Can you go outside?" Janie asked. "Just in the backyard for some fresh air?"

Caroline rolled her eyes. "You obviously didn't see Mom's backyard."

Janie nodded. "I can guess. It probably looks a lot like my parents'. Overgrown with weeds and neglected."

"Worse. It's overgrown and neglected and a garbage dump." She made a face. "I keep the curtains closed because I can't stand to look at it. My mom's pack-rat syndrome wasn't just limited to the confines of her house. I'm afraid to walk in the backyard. A person could trip over something and not be found for days—not to mention I have a feeling there are rats back there. Sometimes when a window is open I hear stuff scurrying around."

"Oh dear." Janie shuddered. "That's terrible. But maybe you're hearing cats. There are a lot of feral cats in our neighborhood."

"I hope it's cats."

"Hey, I've got a handyman, Caroline. Maybe he could come over and give you a hand too."

Caroline frowned. "I seriously don't know how I could ask anyone to go back there, Janie. Not in good conscience. And I doubt I could afford to pay anyone what it would really cost to clean that place out. Plus, my mom would have a fit if she knew what was going on."

"You could keep the curtains closed."

Caroline nodded, trying to appear interested in what she knew was a hopeless cause. "Well, I'll think about it."

"How are your mom's feet?"

"Better. We've been soaking them in Epsom salts every day. The nurse's aide suggested some aloe vera, which seems to be working. Mom's actually been enjoying getting around in the wheelchair. Kind of like a kid with a new toy."

"And the respite care … that's working out okay?"

"Mom is never too happy to see Darlene, but that's not surprising. Naturally, Mom doesn't remember her from last week. Hopefully she won't pull any stunts while I'm gone. But at least Darlene's got my number." Caroline chuckled now. "She's not the only one, either."

"What do you mean?"

"Do you remember Adam Fowler from high school?"

"Popular sports guy a few years older than us?"

"That would be the one."

Janie nodded grimly. "I remember him. Kind of a jerk as I recall. But a lot of kids were jerks in high school. I try not to hold that against them."

So Caroline told her about the grocery store incident and how Adam actually apologized in the checkout line.

"You're kidding!" Janie laughed. "He said that right in front of everyone?"

"It was crazy." Caroline chuckled to remember it. "But it gets even crazier."

"How so?"

"He's called me several times."

"Why?"

"He's interested in getting to know me again." Caroline made a face. "And how's this for pathetic: I was so bummed this weekend, I kind of encouraged him."

"You encouraged him?"

"I was lonely." Caroline gave her a weak smile. "Mitch is still in Thailand, and Adam was being so sweet on the phone. It's like he told me his whole history. I pretty much told him mine, too."

"Interesting. Do you see it going anywhere with him? I mean, in a serious relationship?"

Caroline thought about this. "Probably not. He's not my type. Not really. Although I'm not so sure about how he feels."

"I'm guessing he's interested," Janie said. "Why else would he call so many times? I assume he was the one doing the calling."

Caroline nodded. "He wanted to come over and visit, but I just couldn't bear the idea of having him in my mom's house. It's embarrassing enough to have my friends drop by, which I totally appreciate, but I can't even imagine what someone like him might think or say about that place. You know what it's like."

"So what is he like now? What's he been doing since high school?"

"He's a high school football coach."

Janie laughed. "Well, that's not surprising. Let me guess— Clifden High?"

"No, he lives in Eugene. He's divorced and has a couple of grown kids who live in other states. He seems kind of lonely. It sounds like he's a little disenchanted with his job, too."

"So what was he doing here?"

"Checking out real estate. After his divorce, he scaled down. He lives in what sounds like a pretty modest condo, but he wants a beach house over here."

Janie broke off a piece of the pumpkin muffin they were sharing. "That sounds like a good plan."

"I just hope I wasn't leading him on," Caroline said with guilt.

"Maybe he just wanted someone to talk to."

"That's what I told myself." Caroline decided it was time to change the subject. The point of meeting with Janie was to get her mind off of her own troubles. "Hey, I heard about the Bonnie-Abby showdown at your house."

Janie filled her in on the details as well as the other latest bits of news that Caroline had been hungry for. On one hand, it was reassuring to hear how her friends' world continued to turn without her; on the other hand, she felt left out.

As they finished their coffee, Caroline asked how Janie's renovations were coming, and Janie invited her to stop by on her way home. "You can see the tile and Marley's latest work."

Caroline eagerly agreed. "I have about thirty minutes left. I'll meet you there." Feeling like a kid who knew recess would soon be over, she drove over to Janie's. The next thing she knew, Janie was introducing her to a guy named Mario and discussing the possibility of him cleaning up Caroline's backyard.

"Oh, I don't think so." Caroline held up her hands. "It's a pretty big mess. I can't even imagine how—"

"I have a friend—Lorenzo. He's looking for landscape work."

Caroline scowled. "Landscape work would be lovely, but this yard is more in need of a dump truck than a rake. It's full of junk. It's probably not even safe."

Mario nodded with concerned eyes. "Yes … I see."

"But thanks anyway." Caroline smiled, relieved to have averted what could've turned into a very embarrassing situation. She didn't want anyone going into that backyard—ever.

"Come see Mario's lovely tile work," Janie said as she led Caroline through the garage, which though slightly cluttered with boxes and tools and things, was nothing like that horrible, foul-smelling mess Caroline's mom had created in her garage.

"Wow, that's beautiful," Caroline said when Janie showed her the hall bathroom. She ran her hand over the marble countertop, admiring the pale green and blue tiles on the backsplash. "Very, very nice." Again, Caroline compared this showplace to her mother's sorry house. Who would believe that the two homes had been built at the same time and by the same builder?

"I got lucky with Mario. He's a real craftsman. And he's fast."

"I feel bad acting uninterested in his friend," Caroline admitted. "But I just can't let anyone in that yard, Janie. It's too horrible." She looked at the tile in the shower stall, which looked almost done. "Your house is going to be drop-dead gorgeous, Janie." Caroline fought to hold down her envy as she saw the other nearly finished rooms, reminding herself that life wasn't meant to be fair ... and that Janie's life wasn't as perfect as it appeared.

"Oh, Janie," Caroline gushed, "this place could be featured in *House Beautiful*."

Janie laughed. "Thanks, but I don't think so. Especially if anyone saw the exterior. Plain-old ranch houses don't usually make *House Beautiful*."

"Well, this one would." Caroline walked around admiring everything. "Look at your kitchen," she said. "It's nearly done too."

"Maybe I can have an open house in a couple of weeks."

"It's all coming together for you." Caroline forced what she hoped was a convincingly happy smile. "And how about Victor's boat? How's that project coming?"

As Janie described what sounded more and more like a fairy tale, Caroline's cheeks began to ache from the fake smile she had plastered there. She couldn't believe that she'd just spent her last precious minutes of freedom being tortured like this. As much as she loved Janie, she could've done without this little peek at the lifestyles of the rich and deliriously happy.

"Well, it all sounds like fun." Caroline glanced at her watch. "But I promised Mom a McDonald's lunch, so I better get going."

"Call me if you need anything." Janie hugged her. "I mean it, Caroline. I'm here for you and just a few blocks away."

"Thanks." Caroline nodded, swallowing against the lump that was growing in her throat. "I really appreciate that."

Caroline waved to Mario, then got in her car and drove slowly down the street. Her unshed tears were making it hard to see, so she continued cautiously. While waiting in line for the drive-up window, Caroline put on her sunglasses and just cut loose, letting the tears flow freely. She hated feeling jealous of Janie, but she would do almost anything to be in her shoes. Oh, not literally … but compared to Caroline's pathetic excuse of a life, Janie's looked absolutely perfect. Even though she knew Janie had been through hard times, it wasn't easy standing on the outside looking in. Even the news that Janie's apartment had already sold hurt. So far Caroline hadn't even had a bite, and she could actually use the money!

As Caroline slowly inched her SUV forward in the line of cars, her tears eased up a bit. She reached for a tissue and blew her nose and told herself to get it together.

As the girl was giving her change for her mom's lunch, Caroline's cell phone rang.

"Hey, Caroline," the now-familiar voice of Adam said pleasantly. "How's it going?"

"Okay." Caroline quickly explained that she needed to keep it short because she would be on the road in a minute or two.

"I'm on my lunch break too," he admitted. "But I was thinking of you. I just wanted to tell you to have a good day. I know it's not easy doing what you do—in my opinion there should be a special place in heaven for people like you. Your mom's lucky to have you, Caroline."

The kindness in his voice made her start crying all over again. "Thanks," she told him in a choked voice.

"Are you okay?"

"Yes—yes—I'm just fine," she blubbered as the girl handed her a bag. "Perfectly fine." She tossed the bag to the passenger seat, put the car in gear, and pulled forward.

"You don't sound fine."

"Okay, I'm *not* fine. The truth is I'm having a meltdown. I'm in the middle of a pathetic little pity party. Pity party of one. But my respite time is about up so I really need to get home, Adam. But thanks for calling."

"Can I call you back later this evening?"

"Sure … if you want." She knew she should tell him that it was futile to pursue a serious relationship with her. She was simply using him, selfishly filling in the empty spaces of her life with his voice.

"Okay, talk to you later. Now you drive carefully, you hear?"

"Thanks."

"Hang in there, kiddo."

She sniffed loudly as she hung up. Really, this was getting ridiculous. She had to pull herself together. Other people, including her young friend Brent, who'd been emailing her almost daily, survived these things. Surely, Caroline could too. Still, the old image of that white knight coming to rescue her, even if it was only Adam Fowler, was more appealing than ever right now.

=Chapter 18=

JANIE

"Does your friend Lorenzo speak English as well as you?" Janie asked Mario as he was setting tiles onto the kitchen backsplash.

Mario's brow creased as he pressed the glass into place. "No. Lorenzo's English is not so good."

"And my Spanish is not so good," Janie admitted.

Mario stood up straight. "But Lorenzo's brother, Roberto, he speaks English pretty good. He works at El Capitan."

Janie nodded, wondering how that helped.

"Roberto works nights in the kitchen," Mario continued.

Janie brightened. "So he might be available to work during the day?"

"Oh, yes. He is happy to work days."

"Can you call them for me, Roberto and Lorenzo?"

So she quickly explained her plan, waiting as Mario called his friends, speaking to them in Spanish. She could only make out a word or two. Then he paused, holding the phone down. "When you want them?"

She shrugged. "When can they come?"

He grinned. "Now."

"Oh." She nodded, trying to decide if she was really up to this. "Okay. Sure. Tell them to come over. Do they have pickups?"

"Lorenzo can use my pickup," Mario offered. "We trade sometimes."

"Great. And they have tools?"

"Oh, yes. They have tools."

It was a little past one when Lorenzo and Roberto showed up. They talked to Mario in Spanish, then Mario introduced them to Janie. "Senora Sorenson is your boss," he said in a formal way. "Her Spanish is not so good."

Janie laughed. "So you'll have to be patient. And you can call me Janie."

Mario translated this to them in Spanish, and they smiled and nodded. Then Mario proceeded to tell them Janie's plan. At least she assumed that's what he was telling them. It was hard to say for sure, but the two guys kept nodding and agreeing, as if they really got it. She could only hope.

"You guys follow me," she said after Mario finished. "I will help get you started." As she drove the few blocks to Caroline's, she hoped this was not a big mistake. What if Caroline felt invaded? Or what if it upset Caroline's mom? Caroline *so* didn't need that right now. At Caroline's house, Janie asked the guys to wait in the pickup, promising to be back shortly. Then she quietly knocked on Caroline's door. She didn't want to ring the bell because she knew how it upset Ruby.

Caroline looked surprised. "What are you doing here?"

"I'm on a mission." Janie nodded to the blue pickup parked out front. "My friends and I are here to work on your backyard and—"

"Oh, no." Caroline shook her head. "I can't let you do that, Janie."

"Look, I'm not taking no for an answer, and I've already put together a plan. I've got several boxes of black yard bags as well as a roll of tape. The guys are going to tape the bags over the back windows so your mom can't peek out there. And they know they're supposed to be extremely quiet. I had Mario tell them a very sick woman lives here and cannot be disturbed. They also know they're to only go alongside of the garage to and from the backyard. So, really, there's not much chance your mom will see or hear them. Please, say you don't mind."

Caroline pressed her lips tightly together. She looked as if she wanted to slam the door in Janie's face. Instead she just shrugged and made what seemed a forced smile, but her eyes looked worried. "Whatever."

"You have to promise not to look out there or go back there," Janie continued. "Until I tell you it's okay. *Okay?*"

Caroline grimaced at the sound of her mom's voice calling out. "Oh, Janie, this really isn't a good idea. You don't know how bad it—"

"*Please,*" Janie said firmly. "Just trust me, okay?"

"Well, I know no one can do anything to make it any worse back there. I just don't want anyone getting hurt then suing me."

Janie smiled. "I'm an attorney, remember? Between you and me, I've got a pretty strong hunch these guys are here illegally, so they're not going to want to get involved in any judicial issues."

Caroline nodded. "Still, I don't want them to get hurt."

"I agree. But I'm pretty sure they can take care of themselves. And Mario recommended them."

"But what about you?" Caroline glanced over her shoulder as her mom called again, louder this time.

"I won't work back there until it's safer," she promised. "I'm only here to get them started, okay?"

"Okay." Caroline was backing up now. "I have to go."

"Yes. Don't even think about it. Just trust me. And make sure you pull the drapes and blinds on windows that face the backyard until the guys get them blacked out, okay?"

Caroline nodded and waved, then closed the door. Janie returned to the pickup, directing her instructions to Roberto. "It must be very quiet," she said, holding a forefinger in front of her lips like sign language. She showed them where to park the truck, off to the far side of the driveway and out of sight of the front window. Then she showed them which route to take, but when they attempted to open the gate, it seemed stuck. Roberto gave it a good shake and it came off the hinges.

"That's okay," she told him. "We will replace it."

He nodded. "*Sí.*"

Janie took a plastic bag and held it up over a garage window, holding up the roll of tape. "Cover the windows first," she said quietly.

They both nodded and she handed them the materials, then slowly picked her way past trash cans and rotten boxes and all kinds of broken things. It really did resemble a small junkyard, and Janie suspected that if the city had any idea what was back here, they would've intervened long ago. Really, this was a mission of mercy.

She just stood there staring, trying to take it all in, trying to imagine how this was even possible, and she soon became completely overwhelmed. No wonder Caroline didn't want anyone back here. Not only was this a mercy mission, it was mission impossible. The two guys were quietly moving junk away from the house so they could reach the kitchen window. They had found a stump that they were using as a step stool, and before long they had the kitchen window completely covered.

Janie picked her way over to the fence to see that it, like the gate, was rotted. The only thing holding it up seemed to be blackberry brambles. She wondered how many trips to the dump this project would take, then realized these guys would need some money to cover that expense. She slowly made her way over to Roberto. Whispering, she asked him if he knew where the garbage dump was located.

"Sí," he said quietly. "I know it."

Janie reached into her purse now, pulling out two twenties. "To pay for dumping the garbage," she explained. "For today."

"Sí. *Gracias.*" He pointed to a decaying cardboard box of glass jars. "And for glass … it is free."

"Oh." She smiled. "Recycling?"

"Sí." He nodded eagerly. "Recycling."

"If you have questions or need more money for the garbage dump, you come by my house, okay?" she whispered.

He nodded. "Sí."

"Or call Mario." She held up her cell phone.

"Sí … sí … No problem."

"Sí," she echoed him. "*Bueno.* And gracias."

"Gracias," he said.

She held her forefinger to her lips again. "Shhh."

He mimicked her now.

Feeling that Caroline's backyard was in good hands, Janie left. When she got home, she called the county refuse-disposal number and asked some questions. As it turned out, Roberto was right. Not only were glass, metal, and several other recyclable items free, they would discount the dumping fees in exchange. Also, if the guys waited until Saturday, the dump was holding their annual free disposal of hazardous waste materials. Janie wasn't sure if there were hazardous waste materials there, but she would be surprised if there weren't.

Finding Mario now grouting the tile in her kitchen, Janie explained everything to him, asking him to convey the information to his friends for her. He promised that when they exchanged vehicles at the end of the day, he would do this.

"Also, please, tell them I will pay them at the end of the day," she said. "And that the dump closes at six."

With this settled, Janie decided to pay a visit to the local home-improvement store. Not only would she shop for things for Caroline's place, but for her own as well. She'd wanted to get things started in her own backyard, and there seemed to be no time like the present.

It was getting close to five by the time Janie made her selections and purchases. She arranged to have most of it delivered to her house, where Roberto and Lorenzo could sort things out and transport them to Caroline's as needed. Encouraged by the fact that her check for the Manhattan apartment was supposed to clear by the end of the week, and enticed by some big clearance reductions, she'd probably gone overboard. She picked out ceramic planters and shrubs and pavers and a small fountain and birdbath and some outdoor furniture. All in all, it was just plain fun, and, despite the fact that she had no specific plan or blueprint to work from, she hoped that her selections would come together in some pleasing design once in Caroline's yard. And yet, she reminded herself, anything would be an improvement over what was there now.

Even so, she decided to call Abby for some reinforcement. She explained having coffee with Caroline and how depressed she seemed. "The poor thing, she can't even go into her backyard because it's literally a dump site." Then she told Abby about her Mexican helpers and what they were doing, as well as her little spending spree just now.

"Wow," Abby sounded impressed. "You've had a busy day."

"The reason I'm calling is that I'm a little worried about putting it all together. And you have such a good eye for design that—"

"So you didn't call your friend Bonnie?" Abby teased.

"Did you want me to?"

"Of course not. Although Caroline might've enjoyed meeting her."

"That's true. But I was hoping you could help. And maybe Marley, too. I just don't want the yard to look like it came from the clearance section of the—"

"I'm getting an idea," Abby said. "You said there's a lot of junk back there, right?"

"That's about all there is back there. Junk."

"Well, why don't you save some of the more interesting pieces?"

"Save them?"

"Yes. I saw a cute idea on HGTV where they spray painted some funky old things in bright colors, then positioned them in a garden like found art. It was really fun and lively—and unique."

"Oh, yeah. I get it."

"So maybe you could ask your guys to set a few things aside to be reused."

"I'm on my way." Janie started her car. "I'm so glad I called you."

"I'll let Marley know what's up," Abby said. "How soon do you think the guys will get the place cleared out so I can come and look around?"

"I have no idea. It could be next week or next year. It's a huge mess, Abby. I'm surprised the city hasn't gotten involved."

"Well, just make sure you go over and save some things. I'll go through my landscaping files for more ideas."

"You have landscaping files?"

Abby laughed. "Oh, I've been clipping magazines for years. You just never know when they might come in handy."

"Well, I can see I called the right person. But I better go if I'm going to salvage some junk."

Of course, as Janie drove through town, she questioned this idea. Did she really want to salvage anything from that yard? To her surprise, the guys already had the pickup loaded and were about to leave. So she quickly explained to Roberto this new plan. To her relief, he seemed to get it.

"So I'll go back and mark some things," she said quietly, taking the roll of duct tape from him. "I'll stick some of this tape on the items I want saved. And you will set them aside—and not take them to the dump. Okay?"

"Sí." He nodded, pointing to the silver tape. "Tape—no dump."

As she walked alongside the garage, she still wondered about the sensibility of this whole plan. Really, what had made her think she could accomplish something like this? What had motivated her? Caroline, of course. She was doing this to lift her friend's spirits. Hopefully neither of them would be disappointed.

But Janie did feel disappointed when she saw the backyard. Not only did it not look improved since earlier, it almost seemed worse. Suppressing the urge to turn and run the other way, Janie forced herself to walk around the yard. And then she spied something near the fence—Caroline's old bicycle! Nearly covered in blackberry vines, a rusty blue fender stuck out. Janie leaned down and grabbed hold of the tire and gave it a pull. She tugged and yanked and finally dislodged the bike. She pulled off a piece of duct tape, stuck it to the blue fender in what she hoped was an obvious way, then went off in search of some other items.

By the time Janie gave up her search, she'd marked the bike, a wheelbarrow, a watering can, an old Tonka dump truck, a couple of old metal chairs from the fifties that (although falling apart) could probably hold up a potted plant, and a number of other items that might or might not be useful. She'd let Abby decide.

Now all she wanted to do was go home and take a nice long shower and get all this grime off. Unfortunately, the final plumbing fixtures and faucets wouldn't be installed until the end of the week, after Mario finished the last of the tile work. Deciding to forgo her regular workout, since she was already sweaty not to mention filthy, Janie drove over to the fitness club and headed straight for the showers with her gym bag in hand. She walked through the club's posh lobby feeling like she was the object of some questionable attention. She wondered what her Manhattan friends would have thought if they'd seen her picking through the junkyard just a little bit ago.

===Chapter 19===

ABBY

"How are you holding up?" Abby asked Janie as they met at the bank parking lot on Friday morning. "You look a little worn out."

"Short of needing a good manicure, I'm fine." Janie held up a hand to show off her raggedy-looking fingernails. "Really, the guys have made amazing progress. In fact, if you have time later today, I wish you'd come over and share your expertise. Gardening isn't exactly my strong suit."

"I'd love to come."

Abby pushed open the door to the bank. "I'm so excited," she confessed. "I can't believe how this is coming together."

"That's because you did your homework, Abby. If you hadn't been on top of things, this would've been a missed opportunity."

"Leslie sounded surprised that the short sale came up as quickly as it did," Abby explained as they went over to the loan officers' area. Noticing that Leslie's desk was unoccupied, Abby felt concerned. "Leslie said she'd be here."

"Maybe she's just running late." Janie pointed to the chairs by Leslie's desk. "Why don't we just wait for her?"

Abby sat down, placing her purse in her lap and nervously twisting the strap. What if the deal had fallen apart at the last minute? Maybe they felt Abby was a loan risk or wondered why Paul's name wasn't on the loan too. Maybe this whole thing was a mistake.

"Are you nervous?"

Abby nodded, glancing over her shoulder to look for Leslie. "I hope nothing went wrong. Leslie said it wouldn't be easy, but she promised to have the loan approved by now."

"It's convenient that the short sale is being handled by your own bank," Janie said lightly, as if she wasn't the least bit concerned. Janie was probably used to making big deals like this. Abby wished she had that kind of calm confidence. Instead, she was drumming her fingers on the smooth surface of Leslie's desk.

"Remember to just breathe," Janie reminded her.

Abby took another deep breath and stopped drumming. "Thanks. I needed that."

"Trying to purchase real estate is a bit like having a baby."

Abby nodded. "It is, isn't it? All this apprehension, waiting … wondering how it's all going to turn out, hoping it'll be healthy."

"And remember," Janie said, "getting the loan approval and making our offer is simply the first step. We have no guarantee that it will even be accepted."

"But it's a full offer," Abby pointed out.

Janie just nodded.

"Paul thought we should've offered less," Abby admitted. "So we'd have some bargaining room. But I reminded him this was my business, not his."

"Do you want to reduce the offer?" Janie said quietly. "It's not too late. We haven't signed anything yet."

"Here comes Leslie now." Abby waved with relief. "No, I think the offer is fine as is."

"Sorry to be so late," Leslie shook both their hands with a warm smile. "I was just getting the final sign-off on this." She held up a folder of paperwork. "Now was that quick or what?"

Abby nodded. "Yes. I appreciate that."

"Well, you and Paul have been good customers for ages." Leslie smiled at Janie now. "And we're happy to have your new business partner transferring her account to our bank as well." She handed them both a pen. "Are we ready to sign?"

"I am," Abby said, and Janie nodded. Then Leslie began to explain the various pages, and, to Abby's relief, Janie actually took the time to read through each one before signing. Doing this transaction without Paul's blessing was hard enough, but he really was the one with the business experience.

"It's so nice to be partners with an attorney," Abby murmured after Janie gave her the okay to sign the first section. On and on it went, taking nearly an hour to finish.

"Now you both already know that a short sale is different in a number of ways," Leslie said finally. "In this case there will be no inspections. Everything is as is. The decision will be made quickly, and the sale closes upon acceptance."

"Do you know how many other offers there are?" Abby asked.

Leslie just smiled. "All I can say is that you're not alone."

"So we're done?" Janie asked.

"We are for now." Leslie shook both their hands. "Good luck," she told them.

"How soon will we know?" Abby asked nervously.

"I'll let you know as soon as I hear back from corporate. That could be as soon as the end of today or not until early next week."

"Is there much chance our offer will be rejected?" Abby asked.

"I can't say, but I'll let you know as soon as I know. I have your phone numbers." Leslie shook their hands again. "Have a good day."

Abby let out a little groan as they exited the bank.

"You've done all you can for the time being, Abby. Now you just get to wait."

"Like having a baby." Abby had a sinking feeling—what if this baby was stillborn? All her doubts assaulted her. "Hopefully we'll hear something today," she said nervously. "I don't know how I can wait until next week."

"I have just the solution to distract you," Janie said in a teasing tone. "Bring your own gloves." She waved her chipped fingernails under Abby's nose.

"Yes." Abby nodded. "I'll go home and change into my gardening clothes and meet you at Caroline's."

"Thanks. Remember, be sneaky."

"Sneaky." Abby nodded. "Now I get to be both pregnant and sneaky."

Janie laughed. "Who would've thought?"

Abby tried not to obsess as she drove home. Really, there was no point in worrying. So far, she'd done well to keep praying about everything, and this was no time to give in to despair. So, once again, she gave the whole thing to God, asking for his will to be done. By the time she got home, she was surprised at how relaxed she felt. She was also surprised to see that Paul hadn't left for work yet. She found him in the bathroom popping a couple of Tums.

"Is that a bad reflection on my breakfast?" she asked.

He smiled. "No, your blueberry waffles were great as usual. My problem is just that, as usual, I ate too many."

"See, this is exactly why I should be running a bed-and-breakfast. I always cook too much."

He nodded, but she knew he wasn't fully on board with this idea, and she suspected that he'd be hugely relieved if their offer was rejected and someone else bought the old house.

"Aren't those your gardening overalls?" he asked as she pulled them out of the closet.

She told him about the Caroline project. "If you don't have anything better to do, you're welcome to come over and join us."

"No, thanks. I'm already running late. I've got an appointment with a building inspector at eleven."

Abby told him good-bye, then braced herself as she pulled up her overalls. She hadn't worn them for a couple of years, and she knew she'd put on a few pounds since then. But the soft worn fabric of the overalls was forgiving. Then she dug out her old green Crocs and her floppy straw hat, and before long she was happily on her way to Caroline's.

"Wow," she said quietly to Janie as she came into the backyard. "Talk about a blank slate."

Janie just shook her head. "You have no idea how much hard work went into erasing this particular chalkboard."

Abby looked over to where a couple of Latino men were busily laying sod. "That grass will be a nice touch," she told Janie.

"And the covered patio survived," Janie said, pointing to a small square of pavement that looked freshly washed. "The plan is to make it larger with those." She nodded to stacks of cement pavers.

"Aha." Now Abby spotted what looked like a small junkyard over in the corner of the lot. "Is that our stash of found art pieces?"

Janie nodded and they both walked over to investigate. "The guys thought I was crazy for wanting to save this stuff, and I must admit I'm still a bit skeptical."

"Caroline's old bike." Abby smiled at the rusty old Schwinn. "It's perfect."

"I'll trust you on that."

"I've got spray paint in my car."

"Feel free to go at it." Janie held up a can of landscaping paint. "I just stopped by to mark where the pavers should go so the guys can start on that after they finish with the lawn, but I'm not really sure how to arrange them. Do you have any ideas?"

Abby followed Janie back to the small patio, talking even more quietly close to the house. "The obvious plan would be to outline the patio, but you could also change its shape."

"Change its shape?" Janie frowned. "How?"

Abby moved the toe of her shoe through the dirt, drawing a rounded section along one side. "You could fan the pavers out like this," she said, "make kind of a half circle. Then do the same over there. Then fill in around the corners with some pea gravel and add some potted plants or whatever—something to add interest."

"Like a small water feature or birdbath?"

"Sure," Abby said. "Either would be great."

Janie handed her the landscaping paint. "Why don't you handle *all* the spray painting today?"

"You trust me?"

"Totally." Janie stepped back and held her hands up. "I knew I was in over my head, but I was hoping you or Marley would bring in some creativity. I sure didn't want to have to call in Bonnie."

Abby made a face. "Thanks a lot."

"Anyway, you have fun. I'm heading back to my house to fill pots. I decided to plant them over there, and then the guys can transport them back here all at once so they don't get in the way."

"Smart idea." Abby walked back out to her car with Janie. "Has Caroline seen any of this yet?"

"Not that I know. I made her swear to not look until I give her the go-ahead. My biggest challenge now is how to replace that fence without making noise. The guys tried to prop it up as best they could, but come next big wind, it'll be flattened."

"Why not get some of those prefab sections of fence delivered?" Abby suggested. "The guys can plant the posts in the old holes with some cement, then bolt the eight-foot sections onto the posts in relative silence."

Janie blinked. "You are brilliant."

Abby beamed back at her. "Why, thank you. That's not something I hear a lot."

Janie patted her back. "Well, maybe that's about to start changing."

Abby thought about that as she got the box of brightly colored paints from the trunk of her car. It would be nice to do something that utilized her various talents, because despite Paul's sometimes-dismissive attitude, Abby knew she had something to offer. Running a bed-and-breakfast seemed the perfect answer. A rush of excitement ran through her as she imagined working in her old garden, redecorating the bedrooms, outfitting her old kitchen, and all the other tasks associated with a successful inn. She just knew she could do it.

She propped Caroline's old bike up against a tree and began cleaning off the dust and spiderwebs with a dry rag, then paused. What if their offer was rejected? What would she do then? Not that she wanted to think negatively, but she knew acquiring her old house was not a done deal. It could go either way. Maybe she should make some kind of backup plan, something to keep her from feeling crushed if the short sale fell apart. She smiled to herself as she spread out a disposable drop cloth over the dirt. Laying the bike on its side, she picked up a can of spray paint. Who knew? Perhaps she could start her own landscaping company, featuring recycled yard art.

"What's going on back here?"

Abby peered up from under her straw hat and saw a strange woman approaching. "Who are you?"

"Darlene Kinsey." The woman smiled, nodding toward the house. "The respite caregiver for Mrs. McCann."

"I'm Abby Franklin, a friend of Caroline's." She lowered her voice. "We're supposed to keep it quiet out here. Did we disturb her mom?"

"No. She's napping." Darlene held up what looked like a baby monitor.

"How's she doing?"

Darlene sighed. "She seems to be going downhill, but that's not unusual at this stage of the disease."

"I wonder how long Caroline will be able to continue caring for her."

Darlene shook her head. "I don't know. But I do know it's wearing on her. She seemed really depressed this morning. She had a hard time with her mom last night. It's taking a toll on poor Caroline."

Abby explained a bit about what they were doing in the backyard and how they hoped it would cheer up Caroline.

"Well, you're good friends. And I look forward to seeing the results." Darlene waved and went back into the house.

Abby picked up the can of hot-pink spray paint again, shaking it vigorously. She aimed it at the old bicycle and started to spray, thoroughly coating the surface, then leaving it to dry in the sun. Then she continued cleaning the other junk pieces and painting them various bright colors. It was actually really fun—almost enough to take her mind off the house-buying business.

Seeing Roberto and Lorenzo finishing up the lawn, she realized she needed to get the design for the patio pavers laid out. So while the guys trimmed the edges of the lawn and set up the sprinkler, Abby marked out the plan for the pavers.

The harder Abby worked, the more she thought about Caroline and the challenges she faced, and the more she hoped that Caroline would be encouraged by their efforts. The yard seemed to be coming together quickly now. With the lawn in place and the pavers going down, it was taking a nice shape. As Abby finished painting the various "art pieces" around the yard, she began to get some more ideas. She remembered seeing some brightly colored outdoor dishes and patio things on the clearance rack of a discount store. Wouldn't it be fun to really set this place up? Abby walked over to a corner of the yard and called Janie, quietly explaining her plan. "I know the whole yard won't be completely finished," she said, "but it seems Caroline was feeling pretty bummed this morning, and I thought a little unveiling party might cheer her up." Abby looked around the yard. "The guys have the sod laid, and the pavers are going down fast. It's really looking good, Janie."

"Mario is helping me with the potted plants, so that's going well. He'll deliver them this afternoon. And he might as well bring over the outdoor furniture and other things." Janie sounded excited.

So it was agreed: They would finish it up and have a surprise party for Caroline. Abby knew it wouldn't make up for all the hardships in Caroline's life, but it might lighten her load a bit. Wasn't that what friends were for, to lend a hand and lift someone's spirits? Abby wondered how she'd gotten along all these years without her friends. Of course, she'd had her girls, but more often than not it seemed that Abby was the one who did all the lifting and lending. Then her girls had grown up and left her behind. Oh, she still had Paul. But in some ways her relationship with him wasn't much different than it had been with the girls. Abby did most of the maintenance. If Paul was down, Abby did her best to lift him. If he needed help, she was the one who was right there, rolling up her sleeves. But when the tables were turned, did Paul come running? Abby sighed as she tossed an empty spray can into the trash. No, if Abby needed help, she could probably count on her friends more than she could count on her own husband.

Chapter 20

MARLEY

"That's okay." Marley dropped her paintbrush into the water jar and switched the phone to her other ear. "I think I'm due for a break anyway."

"I know you need to stay on task for next week's art walk," Janie said in an apologetic tone, "and I really want to respect your time, but Caroline's been so down, and Abby and I thought it would boost her spirits to see the backyard all finished and—"

"And I think it sounds like a hoot. Really, Janie, I'm practically out the door."

"I appreciate this so much."

"Hey, I appreciate that you're doing this for Caroline. It's really sweet of you. I'm glad you're letting me help out."

"You can park your car at my house and help me finish up some of the stuff here. Then we'll head back over there after Caroline gets home from her support group."

"So you really think Caroline doesn't know what you're up to?"

"She promised not to peek. And she thinks the guys are just removing the junk—she was pretty skeptical about that happening."

"Is there anything I can bring?"

"You might want to bring some paints. We're trying to do some yard art. Abby spray-painted some old pieces of junk, but you might have some ideas for how we could liven it up even more."

"I'm on it." Marley started tossing some tubes of acrylics into a basket.

"The color palette is bright and bold."

"This is sounding like way too much fun."

"Abby's going to fix us a little something for the unveiling party."

"Great. I haven't had lunch yet."

"See you soon. Just come around to the backyard. That's where I'm working."

Marley gathered up some old brushes and a few more tubes of brightly colored paint. Then, as she tossed her camera into her bag, she remembered the cheerful Mexican blankets she'd purchased from a street vendor a while back, far more than she could use in her little bungalow. She grabbed up the extra ones and threw them into her car as well.

On her way to Janie's, she thought about Caroline's life. Despite her surprisingly sunny disposition, Caroline had experienced more heartache and hardships than any of the other Lindas. She had her heart broken early on, then was unable to have children as the result of that abortion. She never really succeeded at her career choice of acting. She'd been diagnosed with breast cancer and underwent a double mastectomy and chemo. Now she was caring for her ailing and slightly wacko mother, living in that horrible pack-rat house, financially strapped until her condo sold. No wonder Caroline was feeling bummed. It made perfect sense that her friends should roll up their sleeves and help brighten her world. Marley was more than happy to help.

She parked in front of Janie's house, then gathered up her paints and blankets and went around back to find Janie bent over a wheelbarrow and up to her elbows in mud. A dark brown smudge crossed one cheek, and her white T-shirt was probably never going to be white again. Marley grinned. It was the first time she'd seen Janie looking less than elegant since their school days. Realizing the photo op in front of her, she reached for her camera and snapped a couple of shots.

"What's that for?" Janie made a face as Marley stuck her camera back in her bag.

"Just for fun."

"Because blackmail is illegal, you know."

Marley laughed. "Are you making mud pies or getting ready for a facial?"

"I think I lost my ring in here."

Marley blinked. "Your wedding ring?"

Janie nodded sadly. "I should've taken it off, but I hadn't planned to get my hands dirty."

Marley grimaced. "Looks like you were wrong."

"You see, I dumped this potting soil in here for Mario. Then I'd dampened it with some water, and that's when I noticed my ring was missing." Janie looked up with worried eyes. "I feel like such a fool for leaving it on. What was I thinking?"

"You weren't. But you really can't find it?"

Janie looked close to tears. "If the soil had been dry, I might've been able to sift through it. But it was already wet." Janie wrinkled up her nose. "For some dumb reason I thought if I added more water, the ring might sink to the bottom and I could feel my way to it."

Marley couldn't help but laugh. "Which explains the mud bath."

"What should I do?" Janie, the one who always seemed so together and in control, looked completely helpless.

Marley thought about this. "Actually, the water idea does make sense."

"Except that it hasn't worked."

Marley went over and picked up a five-gallon bucket as well as a smaller pail. "Maybe you should add more water and then dip out one pailful at a time, going through it to be sure the ring's not there."

Janie nodded as she reached for the hose. "Good idea."

"You go through the pail and then I'll slowly pour it out over here, just to make sure you didn't miss it."

"I hate wasting this time," Janie said as she stirred the brown soupy mess with her hands. "But I hate even more to lose my ring."

Marley wanted to ask Janie why she continued wearing the wedding ring, especially when it seemed that Victor and Janie were getting more serious, but she couldn't think of a way to put the question without sounding pushy. Marley had to admit that the big solitaire was a beautiful piece of jewelry. Why shouldn't Janie keep wearing it? After about ten minutes of dipping pail after pail of mucky mud, Janie let out a happy shriek.

"Eureka!" she yelled. "I found it." She victoriously held up what looked like a small brown mud ball and actually started to cry as she pushed it onto her finger. Then, with the hose on low, she washed her arms and her hands and finally the muddy ring until the diamond shone brightly in the sun.

"You found it?" Mario came over to see.

She held up her hand. "Yes."

"That is good." Mario looked at the wheelbarrow full of muddy water. "Now I will take care of this for you." Then he carefully wheeled the sloshing mess away.

"What's that?" Janie pointed over to the Mexican blankets that Marley had set on a lawn chair.

Marley explained. "I thought they might be fun to use in the backyard. You know, for an accent of color, like a tablecloth or on a bench or even as a wall hanging." She shrugged. "Unless you would rather go a different direction."

Janie nodded eagerly. "No. I like that direction. Those are all great ideas."

Marley held up her basket of painting supplies. "I thought maybe I could decorate some of the pots, too. You know, make them look festive and fun."

"More good ideas." Janie smiled. "See, that's why I needed you and Abby to help. You're the ones with all the imagination." Janie waved to the pots sitting around her yard. Some were already planted with small shrubs and flowers, and some were still empty. "I leave you to it, Marley. Work your magic. Meanwhile, I'll focus on the less creative tasks like planting flowers and mixing dirt."

"Uh, Janie." Marley pointed to her ring. "Don't you think you should take that off and put it in a safe place?"

Janie stared at the ring with a sad expression. "You know, I never really took it off before."

"Never?"

"Not really. Oh, to be cleaned and have the setting checked periodically." She held it up to the light again. "I had the wedding band and engagement ring soldered together about ten years ago. But other than that, I've always worn it. Even to bed."

"Oh."

"But I think you're right."

"Well, you don't want to lose it."

"No. Besides, maybe it's just time for it ... you know?"

"Time for what?" Marley studied her.

"To ... to put the ring away." Janie looked close to tears. "I should probably save it for Matthew, in case he ever gets married."

Marley went over and placed a hand on Janie's shoulder. "I'm sure Matthew would be honored to have it."

Janie nodded. "Phil would understand."

"Of course he would, Janie." Marley was fairly certain that Janie was referring to Victor. "It's obvious that Phil loved you very much, and that makes me think he would want you to be happy."

Janie looked at Marley with tear-filled eyes. "It's hard, you know? Phil truly was the love of my life. I never expected to care for anyone again."

"I doubt that Phil would've wanted you to spend the rest of your life being lonely. You have to know that, don't you?"

"Yes, but still ... it's hard." Janie slipped off the ring and made an uneasy smile. "Maybe losing it today was like a sign ... like it's time."

Marley nodded. "I think so."

Janie went into the house, and Marley focused her attention onto a big black pot, making a plan for stripes, dots, and zigzags to brighten it up. By the time Janie returned with a clean face and fresh T-shirt, minus one very large diamond ring, Marley was halfway finished painting the pot.

"That looks fantastic," Janie said.

For the next couple of hours Marley decorated pots, planted flowers, and even helped Janie and Mario to assemble the patio furniture. She and Janie helped Mario load his pickup, then followed him over to Caroline's house, where the other workers quietly unloaded the goods and began placing them throughout the backyard. Before long, it looked like the heavy work was done.

Janie paid her workers, thanking them for all their help and telling them she'd be in touch in regard to building the fence next week.

"This is turning out to be a lovely little oasis," Marley told Janie as they plugged in the water feature and waited for it to start gurgling.

Abby had gone for food, but she returned in time to help them decide where to place the furniture to its best advantage. Then the three of them went around and tweaked the decor, placing the junk art here and there, the planted pots in just the right places. Then they hung the colorful patio lights and set out brightly colored plates and glasses and draped the Mexican blankets various places. The finished effect was absolutely delightful.

"I love this," Marley quietly told Janie as she admired the cheerful colors. "I could totally live here."

"At least if you lived outside." Janie tipped her head toward the house. "If you had to live in there, you'd be singing a different tune."

Marley nodded. "Yes. I'm sure you're right."

"The food is in the cooler," Abby told them. "And I made an arrangement to have Darlene come back here at five. She can only stay an hour, but that should be long enough to have a little party. And I asked Darlene to swing by McDonald's for Mrs. McCann." She chuckled. "Trying to cover all the bases."

"That's perfect," Janie said. "Good thinking."

"I want to get some photos." Marley grabbed her camera and started shooting. "Abby, these junk-art pieces are so fun," she said as she snapped the hot-pink bicycle with petunias growing in the basket. "Caroline's old bike is my favorite."

"I love the Tonka truck," Abby said as Marley snapped a shot of the tangerine-colored dump truck with a load of happy purple violas planted in back.

"And I like the lime green wheelbarrow." Janie pointed to the planter full of daisies.

With about ten minutes until five, the three of them sat down at the table. "I'm so excited about this, I feel like I'm about seven years old," Janie said with sparkling eyes.

"I know," Marley agreed. "This was so much more fun than painting at home."

"How's it coming?" Abby asked her.

"I think I'll have three new pieces for Jack's show." Marley winked at Janie. "Two of them will hopefully end up on Victor's boat."

"Really?" Janie looked surprised.

"If you and Victor approve."

"You'll mark them sold?"

"Of course."

"Are you nervous?" Abby asked Marley. "You know, since this is your first real art show?"

Marley nodded. "But I try not to think about it."

"People are going to love your work," Janie assured her.

"Not everyone," Marley said. "I worked in a gallery long enough to know that's not possible."

"Well, you know what they say about pleasing all the people all of the time," Abby pointed out. "Why even try?"

"Don't worry, I'm not. But I am bracing myself for rejection and critiques."

Abby looked at her watch. "Speaking of bracing yourself, I guess we won't be hearing from the bank today, Janie."

"The bank?" Marley looked curiously at them.

"We made an offer this morning," Janie explained.

"Congratulations," Marley told Abby. "You must be excited."

"Excited and worried and trying not to obsess," Abby admitted. "Working on Caroline's backyard was a great distraction, but now I'm going to have the whole weekend to turn into a nervous wreck."

"Maybe you should do another yard project," Janie teased. "I know mine could use some work."

Abby laughed quietly. "Well, it's occurred to me that if our offer is rejected, a good backup plan might be for me to go into landscaping." She pointed at the nearby pair of spray-painted turquoise chairs with flowerpots sitting in them. "Recycled junk art could be my signature."

"If my art flops or I run out of inspiration, maybe I'll go into business with you," Marley said, only half joking. "Because this was fun."

"It's nearly five o'clock," Abby whispered. "I wonder if Darlene is here yet."

"Should we jump up and say 'Surprise!' when Caroline comes out?" asked Marley.

"We don't want to freak out Caroline's mom," Janie reminded her. "We better just keep it quiet."

"What about the blackout stuff over the windows?" Marley realized that the plastic trash bags covering the windows took away from the overall pleasing effect. "Should we take them down now?"

"Yes." Janie stood. "Hurry and be quiet about it."

So they quickly scrambled from window to window, quietly peeling off the ugly black coverings and stuffing them into the trash can. Though it was an improvement, Marley realized that the house, badly in need of paint, was still a bit of an eyesore. On second thought, who would be looking at the house when the yard looked so fantastic?

=====*Chapter 21*=====

CAROLINE

All Caroline wanted this afternoon was a nap—a nice long nap. She would've settled for a short one, not that she was going to get *any* rest. Her mother had snoozed during Caroline's respite time, and she was wide-awake now. Wide-awake and cranky. As Caroline attempted to fix a second food tray—this one with applesauce and Vienna sausages, per her mother's request—she replayed her two hour "break" from earlier today.

She had actually been looking forward to the support group. In all honesty, it was probably because she wanted to chat with Brent again. They'd been emailing, and she was interested to hear more about his work as a screenwriter. To her disappointment, Brent was not there, and a woman named Moira seemed to have the need to express herself—or else she just liked the sound of her own voice. Whatever the case, she had monopolized the group's time with her hard-luck, poor-little-me stories. Caroline left feeling even more depressed than when she'd arrived.

When she got down to the parking lot, she discovered that in her rush to be on time for that second-rate meeting, she'd locked her keys in the car. This resulted in a long wait in the parking lot and a bill for fifty bucks. By the time she was back behind the wheel, she had only about twenty minutes to make a run to the store. Then she got home to learn that her mom had slept nearly the whole time Caroline had been gone, which meant she'd missed out on a blessed two hours of peace and quiet.

Caroline noticed a small slip of paper still sitting on the window ledge by the sink. She'd torn this off a flyer at the grocery store. She'd seen a young woman sticking it on the bulletin board, but it was the photo that got her attention—a happy-looking golden Labrador retriever with amber eyes and a red bandana. The heading above the photo read: Free Dog for Good Home. Of course, Caroline knew it was nuts to even consider a pet, not to mention a dog of that size. But those eyes in the photo melted her heart, and Caroline had torn off a phone number tab and slipped it into her pocket. Back at home, her mother's foul mood had provided a much-needed reality check. Caroline knew it would be pure insanity to call that number.

"Here you go," she said pleasantly as she set the tray in front of her mom. "Applesauce and Vienna sausages just like you wanted. Enjoy."

Her mom scowled, poked a sausage with her finger, then looked away as if disgusted. Caroline braced herself, hoping her mom wasn't going to throw her food again. Even if she did, Caroline told herself she was not going to clean it up. Not this time. Oh, she knew it was ridiculous and childish to react this way. She also knew she would clean it up. She always cleaned it up.

"Do you want to watch Animal Planet while you eat?" Caroline asked cheerfully, picking up the remote and turning on the TV. This distraction might entice her mom to nibble on her food. Sometimes it worked. Sometimes it didn't. Knowing this could go either way, Caroline returned to the kitchen, stood in front of the sink, and blinked back the tears. She looked at the window, which, thanks to whatever Janie had put back there, looked black and bleak behind the faded yellow curtains. Kind of like Caroline's life.

The slip of paper with the handwritten phone number caught her eye again, and before she could think or reason, Caroline reached for her cell phone and started to dial. As the phone on the other end rang, she told herself to hang up. In the same instant she told herself it would be too late anyway, because a great dog like that would've been snatched up already, which was just not fair. If anyone needed that lovely golden dog, it was Caroline. She hurried to the bathroom now, closing the door behind her with her heart pounding.

"Hello?" a female voice answered.

"Yes, I'm calling about the free dog," Caroline said nervously. "Is he still available?" She waited.

"He is."

"Oh?" Caroline felt a mixture of surprise and apprehension. Perhaps she should say thank you and hang up like a sensible person. "So ... may I ask why you're giving the dog away?"

"He was my husband's dog."

"Was?"

"I mean he was my *ex*-husband's dog. My husband left me, you know, for another woman. He left his dog too."

"He doesn't want his dog back?"

"No. He can't have a dog where he lives."

"Oh. I understand."

"I was going to keep the dog, but I went and enlisted in the army."

"The army?"

"Yeah. It was kind of an impulsive thing to do. But I did it anyway."

"Wow."

"I leave for boot camp on Monday, and I thought my friend was going to take Chuck, but then he changed his mind, and my parents sure don't want him, and I just really need to find him a good home and fast. That's why I put that flyer up."

"Oh … his name is Chuck?"

"Yeah. He's a good dog. I just want to see him get a good home where he'll be treated special, you know what I mean?"

"Special?" Caroline looked around at the tight little bathroom filled to overflowing with too much of her mom's old clutter and junk. "How do you mean, exactly?"

"Like I hope he's the only dog in the home. He's used to being the only dog, and sometimes other dogs intimidate him. He doesn't really like small yippy dogs either. I guess he's a little bit spoiled. But he does like kids."

"I don't have kids."

"Any other dogs?"

"No. Just me." She almost added *and my mom* but couldn't force those words out of her lips. Maybe it was just denial.

"Chuck's used to being inside. I mean he's a big dog and likes to go outside sometimes, but it's like he thinks he's a person, you know?"

"Sure. I think so." Caroline wondered what kind of questions a potential pet owner should ask. "Uh, does Chuck have any bad habits? Like does he chew things or bark all the time ... anything like that?"

"Not really. But he does like to run."

"I like to run," Caroline said wistfully.

"He's about three years old. My ex got him a year before we married."

"You were only married two years?"

"Yeah, not even."

"I'm sorry."

"Thanks. Me too."

"The truth is, I've never had a dog," Caroline confessed. "But I always wanted a golden retriever. I just never lived in a place where a dog made sense. When I moved back here, I decided I had to get a dog. I want a dog to run on the beach with me."

"Chuck loves the beach."

"So do I." Caroline felt seriously depressed to think how long it had been since she'd actually been on the beach. Especially when she'd imagined herself going there every day.

"Would you like to come over here and meet him?"

Caroline considered this. "I would. But, you see, I'm kind of caring for my mom, and I can't leave her alone right now."

"If you live in town, I could bring him by for you to see, but I'd have to do it right now because I'm going out with my girlfriends tonight."

Caroline imagined this young woman taking one look at her mom's house and running the other direction. "Let me see if I can get a friend to come sit with my mom for me," she said. "Not tonight. But maybe tomorrow. Is that soon enough? Would that work?"

"Yeah. I guess so. I mean if you're really serious. I did have another guy interested in Chuck, but he already has a dog, and I'm not sure it's a good fit."

"I'm very serious," Caroline said. "I think I really need Chuck. I've been through a lot of stuff the past few years, and getting a dog feels important to me."

She gave the woman her name and phone number and almost offered her a credit card as security but remembered the dog was free.

"My name's Morgan, and you've already got my number. I plan to be here all morning tomorrow. After that, I can't promise you anything. I mean I've got a lot to get done by Monday. But it's my parents' house, and I suppose someone will be here to show you Chuck if you make it." She gave her address, which Caroline jotted down then tucked into her jeans pocket.

"I'll do everything I can to be there tomorrow by ten. Please, don't give him to anyone else before that," Caroline urged her.

"Well, since I'm going out tonight, there's probably not much chance of that. Unless my mom gives him away." She laughed like that was a real possibility.

"Please, don't let her do that."

"If you promise to come by tomorrow, I'll tell my mom that I think I've found Chuck a good home. I'm sure she'll be relieved."

"Thank you so much." Caroline heard a noise in the living room and slipped out to see that her mother had, once again, thrown her plate of food onto the floor. Well, at least the dish was plastic this time. "Now you have a nice evening," she told Morgan. She wanted to add, *Be sure to enjoy this freedom while you have it, because someday you may end up caring for your mom too.* Of course, Morgan was going into the army. Maybe that experience wouldn't be much different. Although a short stint in the army almost sounded like a vacation compared to this.

As she cleaned up the mess her mom had just created, Caroline thought a dog might come in handy at times like this. Chuck would probably make those sausages disappear like magic. He might even like applesauce. Not that she wanted him to be her garbage disposal or cleanup crew. Really, was it even fair to bring a dog into this house? Was Caroline being selfish? She dumped the remains of the uneaten dinner in the trash and took out a can of protein drink. She tried to use these as the last resort, because her mom needed to continue eating solid foods for as long as possible. And yet Caroline couldn't let her go to bed on an empty stomach. Caroline popped open the can and stuck a pink straw in. While her mom was staring at the television, Caroline set the can on the TV tray and slipped away, knowing that her mom would eventually notice it and take a sip.

Caroline thought about Morgan and Chuck again. She should call Morgan and apologize. It was a crazy idea, and Morgan should just find another home for Chuck. A large furry thing wandering the house would probably be upsetting for Caroline's mom. It might just push her right over the edge.

On the other hand, her mom had always liked dogs, and she loved watching the dog shows on Animal Planet. What if her mom really liked Chuck? What if it perked her up? Didn't some of the more progressive nursing homes use dogs and cats to help in their patients' recovery? And what if having Chuck made Caroline feel happier? Wouldn't that be an improvement in this living situation? *And* maybe Chuck needed Caroline as much as she needed him. After all, she had a lot of love to give, and she could lavish it all on the right dog. She remembered those soulful amber eyes. Chuck seemed like the right dog.

Was she being a fool?

She was washing down the countertop when she heard someone knocking at the door. Hopefully it wasn't a solicitor again. Thanks to some unwanted interruptions, she'd actually posted a No Solicitations of Any Kind sign on the front door just yesterday. To her surprise, it was Darlene.

"What are you doing here at this time of day?"

Darlene smiled. "Just giving you a little break."

Caroline was stunned. "You're kidding."

Now Darlene held up a familiar paper bag. "Has your mom eaten yet?"

Caroline gaped at the bag, thinking she was about to fall over. "You went to McDonald's?"

She nodded. "May I come in?"

"Of course." Caroline stepped out of the way. "You're like an angel, Darlene. How did you know I needed you just now?"

"A little bird told me," she said mysteriously.

"Huh?"

They were in the kitchen, and Darlene was pointing to the back door. "You're supposed to go out there."

Suddenly Caroline realized that something was different. The windows that had been blacked out were now letting in the afternoon light. "What do you mean?"

Darlene took Caroline by the arm and led her to the back door, unlocking the deadbolt then opening it wide, letting the sunlight in. Caroline gave Darlene a curious look then glanced out the door, expecting to see the usual piles of rubbish and junk, or perhaps a path cleared through it all. Instead she stared out to what looked like someone else's backyard. She actually steadied herself on Darlene's arm as her jaw dropped. "No way."

Darlene grinned. "Why don't you go check it out while I check on your mom? I can only stay an hour."

Caroline burst out the back door. There, standing on a perfectly lovely patio, complete with furnishings and plants and everything, were her three best friends. "What? How?" Caroline couldn't even form a complete sentence as she looked around, attempting to take it all in. The whole yard was transformed. Everywhere she looked was something pretty or fun or interesting. There was even grass—*real grass!*

"Here." Janie took Caroline by the arm and led her to a lounge chair. "Sit down and let the shock wear off."

"And here." Abby placed a full lime-green margarita glass in her hand.

Caroline leaned back in the chair and just kept looking. "Am I dreaming?" she finally said. "Is this for real?"

They laughed. "It's for real," Abby told her. "Janie organized the whole thing. She and her worker dudes did most of the work. Marley and I only came along to do the finishing touches."

"This is incredible." Caroline took a sip of the icy drink. "I feel like Alice in her wonderland. Or maybe Alice in *Through the Looking-Glass.* It's like I've gone to somewhere I've never seen before, and yet it's in my own backyard." She stared across the green lawn. "Is that my old bike?"

"Yes," Marley told her. "That was Abby's idea. Recycled art."

"I love it." Caroline got to her feet and started walking around the yard, pausing to examine every square foot and listening as her three friends described everything with nearly as much enthusiasm as Caroline felt. "It's incredible."

"We had so much fun," Marley told her.

"I just don't know what to say." Now Caroline was crying. But unlike before, these were tears of joy—and gratitude. "I have the best friends on the planet. The best friends in the universe." Then she hugged each of them, long and hard. "I don't even know how to thank you all."

"We just wanted to brighten your world," Janie told her. "You've been through a lot."

"Now if you need a break, you just bring the baby monitor out here and sit back and breathe a while," Abby said. "Call it a mental-health break."

"A change of scenery."

"It's like a vacation." Caroline wiped her eyes with a bright napkin.

"Or a staycation," suggested Marley.

"You guys have no idea how much I needed this right now." Caroline sat back down and sighed. "You just threw a life preserver out to a drowning woman. No, I take that back. You just rescued a drowning woman and set her on the deck of a beautiful cruise ship!"

Chapter 22

JANIE

"Is she asleep?" Janie asked as Caroline returned from the house.

"Yes." Caroline nodded with wide eyes. "I can hardly believe that Darlene got her to bed this early. It's not even six."

"Think she slipped her a mickey?" Janie teased.

"I don't think so." Caroline chuckled as she set the baby monitor on the table and sat down across from Janie.

"Marley and Abby said to tell you good-bye." Janie stretched her arms and let out a yawn. "I should probably go too, but it's so nice here."

"Oh, please, don't go," Caroline urged. "Unless you need to. This is the most fun I've had in weeks. And with Mom sleeping, well, I might just stay out here all night. I could almost make myself believe that this afternoon, the temper tantrums, the food throwing … that none of that even happened. Mom was really in a snit today."

"Guess you can't blame her," Janie said sadly. "Can you imagine what it would feel like to be in that kind of condition?"

Caroline nodded. "Actually, I can imagine. In fact it's like I'm living it. Sure, it's from the outside looking in, but it feels very real. If I end up with Alzheimer's, I hope that someone will simply put me out of my misery."

"Really?" Janie studied Caroline. "You believe in euthanasia?"

Caroline frowned. "Not exactly. I certainly wouldn't try to shorten my mom's life." She laughed in a slightly cynical way. "Oh, I might feel like killing her sometimes, but it seems I spend more time obsessing over ways to entice her to eat something or to improve the quality of her life. Not that it's working any."

"It's got to be frustrating."

"It is." Caroline smiled now. "But having this sweet little oasis is going to help a lot. I still can't believe you accomplished this."

Janie surveyed the yard again. In the dusky evening, tiki torches burning and colorful strings of patio lights glowing, the whole place looked more magical than ever. It was rewarding to stick around and enjoy the fruits of her labor. "I can hardly believe it myself," Janie admitted.

"Seriously, when you said you were going to clean up my back-yard, I was like—yeah, sure, good luck, Janie." Caroline rolled her eyes. "I honestly didn't think it was humanly possible."

"It wouldn't have been possible without my three amigos." Janie was glad that she'd given them each an extra tip. "Roberto, Lorenzo, and Mario were the real workhorses here. And of course, I had Abby and Marley to help with the finishing touches. I can't take all the credit."

"Anyway, it's just perfect." Caroline held the monitor to her ear, then smiled. "I hope someday I'll come up with a way to repay you."

Janie waved her hand. "It's like karma—what comes around goes around. It all equals out, right?"

"I hope so." Caroline's expression turned teasing. "I'll bet you can't guess what I'm going to do tomorrow."

Janie chuckled. "Have a luau?"

"I wish. No, not a luau. But maybe someday."

"What then?"

"Well, I'm not totally sure, but I called a woman about a dog."

"You're getting a dog?"

Caroline looked uneasy. "Does it seem crazy?"

Janie thought for a moment. "No. Not really. Not if you really want a dog."

"I do. I saw a photo of the sweetest-looking golden retriever, and it just feels like it might be right."

"Aren't those fairly large dogs?"

Caroline nodded. "Do you think it's a mistake?"

"I don't know." Janie looked around the small yard and tried to imagine a big, rambunctious dog running around. Hopefully he wouldn't mess the place up.

"Morgan, that's the owner, she said he's used to being in the house and that he's really good and doesn't have any bad habits. He's about three years old, so it's not like he'll need to be trained."

"Why's she getting rid of him?"

Caroline explained about Morgan's failed marriage and the army, and the more Caroline talked, the more Janie thought maybe it actually did make sense. Caroline seemed to be genuinely excited about it.

"You seem to really want this," she told Caroline.

"I really do. I told Morgan that I'd come check him out tomorrow." Caroline looked hopefully at Janie. "You don't happen to be free around ten in the morning, do you?"

"I told Victor that I'd drive up with him to visit Ben at college. It's parents' weekend."

"Victor invited you to go with him to parents' weekend?" Caroline's brows arched.

Janie just nodded. She hadn't meant to mention this to any of her friends.

"Does that mean you guys are more serious than I realized?"

"I think Victor just wants some company. It's a long drive."

Caroline pointed to Janie's left hand. "I noticed that something is missing."

Janie stared down at her ring finger. It did look bare. "I actually lost my ring working on your yard," she explained.

"You lost your ring?" Caroline looked shocked. "I feel so terrible, can't we—"

"I lost it, and then I found it again," Janie clarified.

"Thank goodness." Caroline sighed. "Because, seriously, that's quite some ring. I have to admit I've admired it a time or two. So where is it?"

"Marley suggested I put it in a safe place." Janie rubbed her ring finger.

"Absolutely." Caroline peered curiously at Janie now. "So do you plan to leave it in a safe place … indefinitely?"

Janie forced a smile. "Maybe it's time."

Caroline nodded. "Yes. It seems like it might be. Do you think Victor will notice?"

Janie considered this. "You mean, like will he think it's a hint?" She frowned. "I don't want him to think I'm—"

"No, he probably won't think that. I bet he'll just be relieved. Some widows take forever to get over a loss. Not that I'm saying you're over it." Caroline looked embarrassed. "Wow, I really have a way with words, don't I?"

"I know what you mean."

"Anyway, I think Victor will appreciate it."

"This doesn't mean we're really serious," Janie said. "I'm not ready for anything really serious. I think it simply means I'm open … you know … to the possibilities." Janie really wanted to change the subject now. "How about you, Caroline? Any word from Mitch?"

"I get an occasional email, but it's always just a brief hello. He sounds pretty busy over there."

"What about your other admirer? Adam Fowler? Have you heard from him lately?"

Caroline chuckled. "Oh, yeah, Adam calls fairly regularly. I wouldn't be surprised if he called tonight, but I turned my cell phone off."

"So do you see that going anywhere?" Janie was still just trying to keep the conversation away from her relationship with Victor.

"No, I don't think so, but I do enjoy chatting with him." She grinned. "I have a younger man too."

"You have another guy?" Janie blinked. *That Caroline, still stringing them along.*

"I met him at the Alzheimer's support group. Although he stood me up today. I hope his dad isn't having a problem. Anyway, his name is Brent and he's a screenwriter."

"A successful screenwriter?"

"Yes. If only he were about twenty years older." Caroline made a dreamy sigh.

"How old is he?"

"Thirty-four."

"Yikes. He could be your son."

"Thanks for that reminder. Anyway, we're just friends, although I suspect he thinks I'm younger than I am." She smiled in a catty sort of way. "At least I hope he does."

"I'm sure he does," Janie assured her. "You can easily pass for forty, maybe even late thirties on a good day."

"In that case, Brent would be fair game."

"Fair game?" Janie imagined Caroline hunting the young man down with a spear.

"I used to have a seven-year rule. I would date younger guys, but not anyone more than seven years my junior. See, if I were forty—or passing for forty—that would make Brent just six years younger."

"You mean *if* you were forty. It's not like you can turn back the clock, Caroline, even if you do look younger. Our age will eventually catch up with us."

"I guess."

"Sorry. I didn't mean to burst your bubble."

"I know." Caroline looked slightly crushed. "I suppose I still suffer from delusions of youth."

Janie laughed. "We should all stay young at heart, Caroline."

"Hey, speaking of staying young, don't you have a birthday coming up?"

Janie was surprised that Caroline remembered this. "I was trying not to think about that," she admitted.

"When is it?" Caroline pressed. "I remember it was the first week of October, because I always used to be jealous when you turned a year older than us so early in the school year."

"Now no one wants to get older."

"So, really, Janie, when is it?"

Janie wasn't sure she wanted to say.

"Come on," Caroline urged.

"Okay, it's Sunday."

"*Sunday?*" Caroline's eyes lit up. "You'll be fifty-four on Sunday?"

Janie nodded. "Thanks for reminding me."

"Does Victor know?"

Janie firmly shook her head. "And that's how I plan to keep it."

Caroline seemed disappointed. "That's no fun."

"It's just the way I am," Janie said gently. "I've always disliked attention on my birthday."

"Why?"

Janie thought about that. "Well, probably because it was the same day as my parents' anniversary, and that always seemed to create conflict when I was growing up. My dad usually forgot to get my mom anything, and she'd be sad, and then I'd feel guilty if anyone remembered me on my birthday."

"That's so sad."

"And weird. It's like I thought it was my fault my parents weren't celebrating their anniversary. Like I was personally responsible for all their marital dysfunction."

"Trust me, I totally understand. I used to feel guilty about all kinds of things related to my parents. Kids are like that. They blame themselves for things they can't control."

"Anyway, birthdays don't mean a lot to me, and I'd appreciate it if you kept mine to yourself." Janie leaned forward and looked intently into Caroline's eyes. "Okay?"

Caroline seemed reluctant, but she nodded. "Okay."

"Thanks. Now, as lovely as this evening has been, I suppose I should head for home."

First, Janie helped her take the dishes and things into the kitchen. They were both very quiet so as not to disturb Caroline's mom. As Janie said good-bye, she couldn't help but observe the striking contrast between the dismal interior and the renovated backyard. But doing an inside makeover was probably not even a remote possibility. Janie hugged Caroline and wished her good luck with her dog decision.

A few minutes later, Janie pulled into her own driveway and noticed, not for the first time, how similar her house and Caroline's looked from the outside. Same era, basic ranch style, one story, small front yard.... Once Janie got inside the house, though, everything was different. Thanks to Mario's tile work, Janie's renovations were nearly complete. Next week, she planned to move the rest of her belongings in. She walked from room to room, turning on the lights and wondering how she would arrange the furniture and if she would require Bonnie's help again. She hoped not.

Finally, Janie stopped in the room she planned to use as her home office—the same room her dad had used for his office when she was a kid, which was why she'd left his old rolltop desk pushed up against one wall. Looking at the piece now, she wasn't too sure she wanted to keep it. It was an attractive antique, but it just wasn't her style—plus it was a bit bulky and awkward. She sat in the old leather chair, listening to the familiar squeak as she rolled it into place. Then, for no particular reason, she pulled open a side drawer. She hadn't taken the time to empty the desk, thinking she might need a shredder to properly dispose of the old papers. Neatly hanging in the drawer were the usual file folders of paperwork. She thumbed through the old things that her dad once thought were important: information about the house, outdated insurance policies, ancient appliance warranties, and the usual kinds of papers that rendered themselves generally worthless over the passing of time.

All of the important papers—deeds, titles, bonds—had been stored in a safe-deposit box, which was also in Janie's name. Everything in this desk was probably just trash, and yet it had once been her dad's treasure.

Janie remembered being a child and feeling like an intruder if she stepped even one foot into her dad's office. Everything in this room, and most of the rest of her father's life, was pretty much off-limits to her. It was as if her father assumed that Janie, being a silly child, would come into his space and wreak havoc. She'd always assumed that was the result of having older parents. They were just stodgy.

She opened another drawer then paused, looking over her shoulder as if she expected to see her father's stern face about to scold her for getting into his private things. But no one was there. This too was a file drawer, but unlike the other drawer, it had no hanging folders. Instead, a stack of old hunting magazines filled the bottom. She pulled the top one out and studied the image of a bull elk, then looked at the date. September 1964. She carefully pulled out the other magazines, each one older than the previous and going clear back to the late forties. They were probably collectible. She set the stack on the floor.

Next in the deep drawer was an old candy box tied securely with string. She lifted it up and could tell by the weight that it contained papers. Curious as to the contents, she searched the desk until she found a pair of rusty scissors and used them to cut the string. She removed the lid to discover the box was full of musty old letters and what looked like a bundle of yellowed telegrams, or what had commonly been called V-mail during World War II.

Janie knew that her dad had been in the war. Not that anyone had ever said as much, because it was a taboo topic in their house. But she was sure she'd heard it mentioned. In some of her friends' homes, war memorabilia was proudly displayed on shelves and mantels. In her house, however, no one ever would have guessed that her father had served. Janie had always wondered if it was because of something shameful. She even suspected he had received a dishonorable discharge, perhaps for desertion. Janie had often felt her dad was a bit cowardly. Oh, she had nothing to base these assumptions on, but as a child, she had the feeling that something bad had happened. That seemed the most plausible reason for the stoic silence.

Most of the correspondence seemed to have been between her parents during the war years. She organized the letters chronologically and began reading them in order. They started out stateside while her parents were in college, then moved on to when her dad had been stationed with the Army Air Force in Florida, and eventually switched over to V-mail while he was in Europe. To her surprise, the exchanges were actually very sweet and sounded heartfelt. It was obvious—in a somewhat shocking way—that her parents had at one time been very much in love.

She pulled out a piece of blank paper and a pencil so that she could create a timeline in regard to her parents' relationship. Feeling like a detective, she discovered that they'd met in college in the fall of 1941. Her dad, then twenty-one, had been in his third year at Portland State, and her mom had been in her second year at the teachers college in Corvallis. It seemed that mutual friends had introduced them, and it had been love at first sight.

Their love seemed to intensify in December of 1941, because following the drama of Pearl Harbor, they became engaged at Christmas. But they continued attending college in separate towns. Janie was almost embarrassed to read some of the early letters. Their love was so open and candid and youthful—so sweet and unspoiled—Janie could hardly believe that her parents had actually written those words.

There was also the serious talk of the war in the letters. Her mom's older brother, Howard, had gone off to serve in the Pacific, and it was obvious that her mom was both proud of and worried for him.

In the summer following his college graduation, her dad decided to enlist in the Army Air Force. Her mom's response was surprisingly supportive, even saying how handsome he would look in uniform and how proud she'd be to be a military wife. A small wedding was planned in October of 1942, just two weeks before her dad was scheduled to go overseas.

The tone of the letters and V-mail remained sweet, and it was clear the young couple was desperately in love. But with each new letter, Janie could tell that something in her dad was changing. Not necessarily his love for his wife, but perhaps his love of life and his worldview in general. His tone grew increasingly sad and slightly jaded. How could it not?

The V-mail letters abruptly ended in late May of 1944, and Janie knew enough of history to know this was shortly before D-day. Disappointed, Janie looked back in the drawer and was surprised to see a thick manila folder on the bottom, also tied securely with string. In this folder, she found an official telegram informing her mother that her husband was missing in action and possibly a prisoner of war. The other correspondence, some from military friends and some from state officials, eventually confirmed that her dad's plane had been shot down over Germany and the survivors captured.

Janie tried to grasp this. Her dad had been shot down, captured, and imprisoned? And no one had ever said a word about it?

Feeling something else in the legal-sized manila envelope, she extracted several small parcels wrapped in tissue paper. She unwrapped them to discover they were medals. Although she was no expert on medals, she suspected they were important ones. Why were they wrapped in tissue and stuffed into the bottom of a drawer?

Weary and confused, Janie carefully straightened up the old letters, arranging them neatly on the surface of her father's desk so that she could continue her exploration on another day. Then she reverently laid the medals on top and slid the rolltop closed with a thud. She had the startling sense that she'd been wrong about a number of things concerning her father. For the first time in her life, she wondered if she might not owe him an apology.

Chapter 23

ABBY

As Abby pulled the car up in front of Caroline's house on Saturday morning, she was still feeling a little uneasy. Not that she didn't want to help Caroline, because she absolutely did, but being alone with Mrs. McCann was a bit unsettling. What would she do if the old woman stripped off her clothes and insisted on going for a stroll through the neighborhood? Was Abby supposed to physically restrain her? And, if so, how? Abby wasn't even on the porch when Caroline stepped out the front door and quietly explained that her mom had just dozed off in her recliner.

"Mom's been up since around five thirty this morning, so I think she's due for a fairly long snooze," Caroline whispered as she slipped the strap of her bag over her shoulder.

"Okay." Abby nodded, trying to appear more confident than she felt.

"I've got my phone, and I'll be less than a mile away. If you need me, just call."

"Don't worry." Abby forced a smile. "We'll be just fine."

Caroline hugged her. "Thank you so much. I'll make it as quick as I can."

Abby waved, then quietly stepped into the house. She could hear the TV, a bit loud it seemed, but she was not going to touch it for fear of waking the old woman. Instead she tiptoed into the kitchen and just stood there and looked around. Everything about this place was so depressing. She wondered how Caroline could stand it and, once again, was very thankful that Janie had taken on the backyard project. Abby peeked out the window over the sink to see that Caroline's "wonderland" looked just as good as it had yesterday. If Abby knew where the baby monitor was, she'd go out there and sit. As it was, she figured she better stay close by.

To pass the time, and because it simply came naturally, she decided to attack some cleaning. Thanks to the clutter, which was everywhere, this was a bit of a challenge, and after scrubbing the sink and what she could reach of the worn Formica countertops, she eventually gave up. Too bad Caroline couldn't clear this place out too. Perhaps with a bulldozer. She had told Abby that her mom threw fits anytime she saw anyone touching or removing anything, including the trash. However, Abby wondered if Mrs. McCann would notice if she was asleep when it happened. Just the same, Abby wasn't ready to be the one caught in the act.

Abby was trying not to think about the offer she and Janie had made on the house, or about how badly she wanted to get to work on creating a state-of-the-art bed-and-breakfast. In her effort to "let go and let God," she had prayed about the whole thing while having a little beach walk this morning, and she was determined not to obsess over it now. Monday was only two days away. She could wait.

She sat down and flipped through a recent issue of *People* magazine, surprised to find herself actually amused by the Hollywood
drivel that Caroline seemed to thrive upon.

It was a bit past ten thirty when Abby heard a moaning sound
coming from the living room. Her first response was to ignore it and
hope the old woman was just having a dream or indigestion problems.
When the groan grew louder, Abby decided to peek out and make sure
nothing was severely wrong.

Mrs. McCann appeared to be trying to extract herself from her
chair but hadn't bothered to put the extended footrest down. Perhaps
she'd forgotten how the mechanism operated. She had pushed herself
precariously close to the edge of the chair and looked as if she was
about to tumble down.

"Let me help you," Abby said as she hurried over, bracing the
old woman with one hand as she reached for the lever to lower the
footrest. "There you go."

Mrs. McCann sat frozen in her chair, staring at Abby with wide,
frightened eyes. Her lips moved, but no sound came out.

"Remember me?" Abby said in a friendly tone. "I'm Abby.
Caroline's friend. I've known you since I was a little girl."

"Little … girl?" Mrs. McCann looked even more confused.

"Abby." Abby pointed to her chest.

"Abby."

Abby smiled. "Yes. That's right."

"Abby." Mrs. McCann pointed to her own chest now, as if she
thought her name might be Abby too. At least her fear seemed to
have resided some.

Abby sat down on the sofa, wondering what to say next.

"Caroline is looking at a dog," she finally said.

Mrs. McCann's brows drew together. "Dog?"

"Yes." Abby nodded eagerly. "A dog." Then, feeling a bit silly, Abby imitated a dog, even barking in case Mrs. McCann didn't quite get it. Fortunately, this seemed to amuse the old woman.

"Dog ..." Mrs. McCann repeated the word as if trying to recall something.

Abby was tempted to tell her that Caroline would be bringing home a dog, but she didn't know for sure, and it seemed mean to go into the details if Caroline decided not to. Instead, Abby pointed to the TV, where a small dog was jumping in the air. "There's a dog," she said. "A little dog."

"Little dog."

"Yes." Abby peered at the screen. "I think that's a Pekingese." Then Abby pretended she was talking to her granddaughter, Lucy, and continued chattering on and on about a lot of insignificant small things. To Abby's relief, Mrs. McCann didn't seem to mind this a bit. Nor did she seem to miss her daughter.

It was nearly eleven when Abby heard Caroline coming into the house. Abby glanced toward the small foyer to see Caroline poking her head around the corner with a curious grin.

"Your mom's awake," Abby informed her.

"I've brought someone with me," Caroline announced. Then she and a fairly large golden retriever burst into the living room. Mrs. McCann jumped back, pulling up her knees and holding her clenched hands to her chest as if she expected to be eaten alive.

"It's a dog," Abby explained gently. "A big dog."

"His name is Chuck," Caroline said as she came closer, holding the dog's leash securely. "He's a very sweet dog. Do you want to pet him, Mom?"

Mrs. McCann shook her head. "No! Go 'way!"

Abby reached out and petted the dog's head. "Nice doggy," she said in a gentle voice. "Good doggy."

Caroline sat on the sofa next to Abby, telling Chuck to sit as well, which he did. "Chuck *is* a good dog," she told Abby as they both petted him. "Isn't his fur soft?"

"Yes," Abby agreed. "He's very soft. Did he just have a bath?"

"I don't know. But his fur is so silky and smooth." Caroline glanced nervously at Abby. "He's such a *good* dog. Don't you just love him?"

Abby continued petting the dog, saying nice things about him, about how pretty he was, how soft his fur was, all the while sneaking peeks at Mrs. McCann, hoping that maybe she was being convinced.

"I'm going to take Chuck outside," Caroline finally announced. "Unless you want to pet him first, Mom."

Her mom still looked a bit uncertain. But Caroline walked Chuck over to her chair anyway. "See how nice he is?" She slowly took her mom's hand and set it on Chuck's back.

Still frowning, Mrs. McCann moved her fingers on his coat, then slowly ran her hand down his back as if trying to decide whether this was a positive experience or not.

"He's a good dog, Mom," Caroline said. "He's going to be our friend."

"Friend." Mrs. McCann's hand still rested on Chuck's back.

Now Chuck turned his head around and licked Mrs. McCann's fingers, but she jerked her hand back so quickly that Abby expected her to shriek as if he'd bitten her. Instead, her mom giggled like a child.

"He *likes* you, Mom," Caroline said happily. "Chuck likes you."

Mrs. McCann petted him again, smiling shyly now. "Chuck."

"Chuck *is* a good dog," Abby said with wonder. "A *really* good dog."

Abby decided to stick around for a bit, since Paul would be golfing for a couple more hours anyway. Plus she knew Caroline appreciated the moral support. When Mrs. McCann was in need of "a little freshening up" as Caroline discretely put it, Abby offered to take Chuck outside and introduce him to the backyard.

She and Chuck were walking around in back when Abby heard a man's voice calling out for Caroline. Chuck barked and ran straight for the gate by the garage, and Abby joined him to see who was on the other side.

"Oh." A young man looked at her in surprise. "I thought this was where Caroline lived."

"It is." Abby tipped her head toward the house. "She's inside."

"Are you her mom?"

Now, although he seemed a decent young man, Abby suddenly wanted to throw something at his head. "No. I'm *not* her mom. Caroline's in the house *with* her mom."

"Oh, I'm sorry." He looked embarrassed now. "Anyway, Caroline emailed me last night. She wanted me to sit with her mom while she went to look at a dog. I emailed this morning but didn't hear anything back, so I decided to just pop in."

"Yes, well, I stayed with her mom," Abby explained, still feeling disgruntled over the confused identity. "And obviously, Caroline got the dog. This is Chuck."

"Oh." He nodded. "I'm Brent. I'm in Caroline's Alzheimer's support group. Mind if I let myself in?"

She stepped away from the gate. "Sure, come on in. I'm Abby—Caroline's friend."

Brent came in, then knelt to pet the dog, gently tugging on his ears as if familiar with dogs like this. Since Chuck seemed to like it, Abby simply folded her arms and watched. "So you care for someone with Alzheimer's too?" she asked when Brent finally stood up.

"My dad. It's not too advanced, although he definitely needs help with some things. I'm trying to find someone to live with him." Brent looked hopefully at Abby. "Hey, you're not looking for a live-in situation, are you?"

For the second time, Abby wanted to hurl something directly toward this young man—maybe that shovel. "No," she said curtly. "I'm not looking for work."

"But you help care for Caroline's mom?"

"Not exactly." Abby walked over to the patio and sat down with a thud. "I just watched her mom for her this morning so that she could look at the dog. As I mentioned, Caroline and I are friends." She wanted to add that they'd been friends since their school days—hint, hint—but controlled herself. If Caroline wanted to pretend she was thirtysomething, that was her problem. Still, Abby was curious as to what kind of relationship Caroline might be having with this young friend. Brent ventured over to the grassy area, playing with Chuck like he was a kid. Actually, he was a kid. Probably about the same age as Abby's oldest daughter.

"Hello?" Caroline stuck her head out of the patio door. "Abby, do me a favor, will you, and go open the gate for—"

"I already did," Abby told her.

Caroline looked confused now. "Adam is already back there with you?"

Abby frowned. "Adam?"

"Yeah. He just knocked on the front door, and I told him to go around back so Mom doesn't get upset."

"Adam?" Abby glanced over at Brent, who was out of Caroline's view.

"Remember?" Caroline said impatiently. "Adam Fowler from high school."

Abby blinked. "He's here?"

Caroline nodded. "I have to go finish up with Mom. Thanks!"

Feeling like she was in some kind of hidden-camera show, Abby cautiously walked over to the gate where, sure enough, another guy was waiting. This was a much older guy, to be sure, but he looked vaguely familiar.

"Oh, hi," he said congenially. "Caroline said someone would let me in."

"Come on in," Abby told him. The next thing she knew, she was performing introductions and wondering if she should be offering these guys something to drink.

"You're not the *same* Abby?" Adam's brow creased as he studied her. "From high school? Abby Lund?"

Abby smiled. "Yes. But it's Abby Franklin now. I married Paul Franklin."

"Oh, yeah. I remember Paul. He's the one with the housing development on North Shore."

"That's right."

Adam nodded to Brent. "I'll bet you're Abby's son."

Abby just laughed. "No. Brent is Caroline's friend from her Alzheimer's support group. Brent's dad has Alzheimer's too."

"Oh. That's got to be hard." Adam focused in on Abby again. "Your husband is actually the reason I came back to Clifden this weekend. He's going to show me a house this afternoon."

"After his golf game," Abby supplied.

"Yes. He mentioned a nice golf course in the area."

Abby glanced at her watch now. "Speaking of Paul, I promised to have lunch ready for him by one. I suppose I should be going." She stood. "I'm sure Caroline will be out shortly." She had no idea when or if Caroline was coming out, but that wasn't really her problem. That was for Caroline to sort out. With the way these guys seemed to be sizing each other up, Abby suspected there would be some sorting out to do, which was what motivated Abby to go through the house. She wanted to give Caroline a little heads-up. She found Caroline in the living room getting her mom resettled in the recliner. Abby grinned mischievously.

When Caroline was out of her mom's earshot, Abby spilled the beans. "I let Adam into the backyard. And in case you didn't notice, your young friend Brent is back there too."

"Brent's *here?*" Caroline looked shocked.

"Yes. I introduced him and Adam. Adam thought Brent was my son." Abby shook her head with a frown. "Worse than that, Brent thought I was your mother."

"Oh dear." Caroline grimaced as she took a juice box from the fridge. "Did you straighten them all out?"

Abby just smiled. "No, dear, I'll leave that to you."

Caroline's cell phone rang, so Abby took the juice box from her, stuck in the straw, then took it over to Mrs. McCann, who seemed to appreciate it.

"Mitch?" Caroline said in a slightly high voice. "You're home?" She tossed Abby a startled look. "You're here? Here in Clifden?" Now she made a helpless look. "And on your way over? No, that's not a problem. Sure, see you when you get here." Caroline closed her phone and looked at Abby. "Mitch is on his way here right now. He got home from Thailand yesterday and flew up here this morning."

"How exciting." Abby glanced toward the patio door. "Now you have four guys to hang out with."

"Four?"

"Brent, Adam, Mitch, and Chuck."

"Oh, yeah. Chuck." Caroline's hand flew to her hair. "What am I going to do?"

Abby just laughed. "Have fun, I suppose. I have to go fix some lunch for my guy. Thank goodness there's only one."

Abby drove away feeling nothing but relief. Really, if Caroline was up to caring for her mom, acquiring a dog, and entertaining three guys simultaneously, more power to her. Just thinking about all that made Abby tired.

Chapter 24

CAROLINE

Seeing that her mom was comfortably stretched out in her recliner, Caroline picked up the baby monitor, then braced herself and went into the backyard.

"There you are." Adam hugged her, perhaps a little too long. "How are you doing, Caroline?"

"Okay." She stepped away from Adam then nodded to Brent, who was kneeling by Chuck and scratching the dog behind the ear. "Hey, Brent, I didn't see you back here earlier. How's it going?"

"Not bad." He grinned. "I see you got your dog. Chuck seems like a real good boy."

She went over and knelt on the other side of the dog. "He is a good boy. Aren't you, Chuck? My mom even likes him."

"Brent tells me he's in your support group," Adam said in the sort of way that seemed to beg for an explanation of some sort.

Caroline stood. "Yeah. Brent's going through a similar thing with his father."

"Sorry I didn't get here in time to help with your mom," Brent said. "And sorry if I insulted your friend Abby. I think I offended her when I asked if she was your mom."

Caroline chuckled. "Yeah, she wasn't too cool with that."

Adam was laughing. "You thought Abby was Caroline's mom?"

Brent nodded.

"Abby's the same age as Caroline."

Brent looked shocked. "No way."

"It's true," Caroline confessed. "We went to school together." She pointed to Adam. "He went to school with us too."

"No way!" Brent looked from Caroline to Adam and back again. "I actually thought maybe Adam was your dad."

Caroline couldn't help but hug Brent. "You are so sweet. I think I should keep you around to stroke my ego."

"You thought I was Caroline's *dad?*" Adam sounded wounded. "I look *that* old?"

"Hello back there," called what sounded like Mitch's voice.

"Come on in." Caroline went over to the gate and waved. "Join the party."

He looked puzzled as he came into the backyard. She gave him a quick hug and started introductions, but before she sorted them all out, she heard her mother calling for help. "Sorry, I need to check on Mom," she called over her shoulder as she hurried inside.

On one hand she was relieved to escape from the unlikely trio gathered in her backyard. On the other hand, she was worried about what might transpire during her absence. There wasn't much she could do about it, though. Her mother had decided she was hungry, and that was a good thing. Caroline wanted to get some food in front of her before she changed her mind.

She opened a can and poured some chicken noodle soup in a large mug, then put that into the microwave. Then she opened a package of vanilla pudding, set some Ritz crackers on a plate, put these along with a napkin and spoon onto the tray, and still had a few seconds left on the microwave.

"Here you go, Mom," she said cheerfully. "Lunch is served."

Her mom scowled as she slowly picked up a spoon and tentatively stuck it into the soup.

"Chicken noodle soup," Caroline said, "your favorite."

"Harrumph."

"And vanilla pudding."

Her mom looked up at her with a confused expression. "Dog?"

"The dog is outside."

"Outside."

Caroline nodded. "Yes. Do you want me to go check on him?"

"Yes."

"Okay. You eat, and I'll go check on Chuck."

"Chuck." Her mom looked down at her food again, then slowly lifted the spoon to her mouth.

With the baby monitor still in hand, Caroline went back outside to find Adam standing on the patio with his fists planted on his hips and feet spread apart in what seemed a confrontational stance. "Mitch here tells us that he's your boyfriend." Adam cocked his head to one side. "Is that true, Caroline?"

Caroline wasn't sure how to respond. "Well, Mitch and I have gone out—"

"I didn't know you had a boyfriend either," Brent said with a sad expression.

"I guess it never came up." Caroline held up her hands helplessly. "I'm not even sure I'd call it that ... I mean we've dated."

"It seems these guys thought they were dating you too," Mitch added with a tone of accusation.

"I wouldn't go that far," Brent explained. "But I was hoping to date her."

"I thought you and I had a serious relationship," Adam told her. "We talk all the time ... I tell you things I never even told my wife."

"You have a wife, too?" Brent asked him.

"An ex-wife."

"It appears we're all a little confused," Mitch said with aggravation. "Maybe you'd like to straighten us out."

"And I want you to tell these guys just where I stand with you," Adam insisted.

Brent stepped over and patted her on the shoulder. "I really didn't know you were that old, Caroline. Not that I wouldn't date an older woman ... but you're almost my mom's age."

She nodded. "I know. I don't really want to be a cougar."

He smiled. "I'm not too comfortable being cougar bait either."

"But I hope we can still be friends."

"Yeah. I'll see you at group next week."

With Brent gone, Adam focused his angst onto Mitch. "What kind of boyfriend are you anyway? Gone all the time. Never call, never write."

Mitch laughed. "You sound like the poor little woman."

"Poor little woman?" Caroline repeated. "Is that how you see me?"

Mitch pointed to Adam. "I was talking about him."

Adam stepped closer to Mitch now. "You calling me a woman?"

"Hey, guys." Suddenly feeling worried, Caroline stepped between them. "Let's not get carried away here."

"So what is it then?" Adam demanded of her. "Him or me?"

Mitch just scowled.

"I'm not sure I have a choice," Caroline confessed. "But, Adam, the truth is that I never wanted to get into a serious relationship with you. I thought I made that clear right from the start."

He shook his head. "Not from the way I saw it."

"I'm sorry."

"Well, I can tell when I'm not wanted." He started walking toward the gate, and Caroline's mom called out again.

"I'm sorry, Mitch," she said. "I'd like to explain, but Mom needs me."

"Looks like everyone does."

Her mom called again, and Caroline knew it was pointless to try to figure this out right now. So she went inside and saw to her mother, but when she came back out, only Chuck remained in the backyard.

"Come on into the house, old boy," she told Chuck. "Mom and I are in need of your canine company."

* * *

"So what is it then?" Mitch asked Caroline later that evening. She'd finally gotten her mom to bed, and now she and Mitch were sitting outside, wrapped in blankets and sipping cocoa she'd heated in the microwave.

"What do you mean?" Caroline studied his expression in the dim light.

"I mean are you stringing me along or not?"

Caroline suppressed the urge to laugh. "Me? Stringing *you* along?" She leaned over to take a slow sip of cocoa, trying to wrap her mind around this unexpected attitude. Was Mitch just being jealous, or was something else going on here? Maybe she didn't know Mitch as well as she'd assumed.

"Well, I fly up here, thinking you'll be so happy to see me, and then I find you here with two other guys."

Caroline shook her head. "I tried to explain all that to you already."

"Yes, and I apologize for overreacting. It was rude for me to take off like that. But I felt like I'd been tricked."

"Tricked?" She frowned.

"It's just that every email I got from you sounded so down and out, like you were so lonely. I imagined you out here pining away, caring for your ailing mother night and day, being depressed and on the brink of totally losing it, Caroline."

She nodded eagerly. "Yes. That's almost exactly how it's been."

"Sure could've fooled me."

Caroline felt a rush of irritation now. "Are you suggesting I was lying to you?"

He ran his hand through his hair. "No ... no ... I just feel confused."

Caroline knew the morning's circumstances had looked odd. "I already told you that I didn't invite any of you guys to visit," she told him. "And I really don't appreciate the attitude you're taking with this whole thing, acting like I'm running a brothel or something."

He actually laughed. "Is that what you think I'm saying?"

"Well, your tone is pretty accusatory. Excuse me for being offended."

"Okay, Caroline." His voice softened. "Let's back up the truck. What if the roles between us were reversed? What if you were the one worried about me, and you made a special trip down to California to surprise me, and you found me hanging out by my pool with a couple of gorgeous girls?"

Caroline looked around her yard and frowned. "You have a pool?"

He smiled, then nodded. "But you're missing my point. How would you feel if you were in my shoes?"

She set down her cocoa cup. "Well … I can see how things may have appeared. But are you willing to hear the whole story?"

"Yes. I'm actually rather curious."

And so Caroline started by explaining how the Lindas had surprised her on Friday with their amazing backyard transformation. "It was a fabulous pick-me-up. I was so encouraged." Then she told him about how she'd called about the dog and really wanted it but had no one to help with her mom. "So I'd emailed Brent last night. Because he's in my support group, he'd offered to help me."

"Weren't you aware that Brent was nurturing a small crush on you? Or that he assumed you were his age?"

Caroline felt her cheeks grow warm. "I honestly didn't think he had a crush on me, but, yes, I suspected he was under the wrong impression about my age."

"You obviously didn't see Brent's face when Adam announced that he'd been your high school sweetheart and that you and he were involved in a serious relationship."

"First of all, Adam was *never* my high school sweetheart. Not even close. And as for a relationship, we've never been anything more than telephone buddies. We've both been lonely and depressed, but I swear to you that I had no intention of getting involved with him beyond that. I didn't expect him to pop in here like that either." Caroline thought for a moment. "So Brent seemed really surprised that I'd gone to school with Adam?"

"Well, you have to admit Adam could pass for sixty-five."

She laughed. "I guess so. But poor Brent."

"Poor Brent?"

"Well, you know it wasn't his fault. But … I'm sorry. I should be saying *poor Mitch.*"

His brow creased. "I'm not looking for pity, Caroline. Just honesty."

"That's all I've ever been with you. I know it looked like Crazyville here this morning, but it was all just a fluke." She started to giggle now. "A great big silly fluke." She patted Chuck's head, rubbing his ear. "In fact, a couple of hours ago, I thought I might quit men altogether. It could be just me and Chuck from here on out."

"Is that how you really feel?"

Caroline thought for a long moment. "You know, I'm not even sure how I feel. Despite what you think my life is like, these past few weeks have been really, really difficult. There've been times when I've questioned my own sanity. Not to mention my mom's. It's like I don't know what I'm doing or why, and then I question whether it's right or wrong. Seriously, caring for a parent with Alzheimer's is the hardest thing I've ever done. Harder than my broken marriage, going through cancer treatments, never having children. I honestly thought I'd already experienced the worst parts of my life, but compared to this, well.... If it hadn't been for my friends—the other Lindas I mean—I just don't know if I could go on."

"Maybe it's time to stop, Caroline."

"Stop?" She peered at him. "You mean quit caring for my mom?"

He looked uncertain. "It seems like you should be asking yourself if it's really for the best. For you as well as her."

She studied him. Was he about to tell her what she should or should not do, how she should live her life? If he did, would she want to listen? "I honestly don't know the answer to that, Mitch."

"I respect that."

She blinked. "You do?"

"I know that the answers to life's questions aren't always crystal clear. It's not always black and white."

"That's right." She nodded. "There are moments when I think I can't do this for another minute ... when I think Mom doesn't care anyway ... that she's not in her right mind ... and that it's killing both of us."

He just nodded.

"And then there are times—like this morning when Mom smiled and patted Chuck and fed him a piece of her toast—and I think, okay, I can do this a while longer. I think, yeah, maybe my caring for her does make a difference." Caroline was crying. "I guess it's just, you know, a day-by-day thing."

Mitch wrapped his arms around her, holding her tight as she let the tears flow. "Thanks for telling me what's really going on. I'm sorry I doubted you, Caroline." He stroked her hair, and she let out a long sigh, just resting against his shoulder and wishing that she could feel this protected forever.

"I just wish you weren't so far away," she said quietly.

"It's just the nature of my work."

"I know." She pulled away from him and looked at his face. "And I know I need to be strong and keep figuring out my own life. I don't expect some brave knight to arrive on a big white horse to rescue me."

He chuckled. "I'll have to admit that I thought I was doing that. Oh, not rescuing you, but maybe helping you just a little. But then I get here and discover that you have all kinds of people—guys, a dog, the Lindas—and maybe you don't even need to be rescued."

She laughed. "Are you kidding? I'd love to be rescued, even if it's only briefly."

"Unfortunately, it is going to be briefly," he said sadly. "I have to fly down to LA tomorrow for a big meeting."

"It figures. And then I suppose you'll be off doing some more globe-trotting."

He made a half smile. "Just Italy."

"Italy." She groaned. "You don't have to rub it in."

He grabbed her hand. "Hey, why don't you come with me? I leave the end of October, and I've heard Italy is enchanting in the autumn."

As tempting as Italy in the autumn sounded, Caroline knew it was impossible. There was no way she could get in-home care for her mom that quickly. Even if she found a good nursing home, which was unlikely, she wasn't sure that her mom was really ready for that. "You know I can't go," she said quietly. "I can't leave my mom yet."

"I know. I admire your loyalty to her, Caroline."

"Thanks ... I guess."

"I just don't want to see your loyalty crush the life out of you."

"I don't either."

"And I wish I were around to help you. One of the reasons I keep my emails so brief is because I feel guilty. You need someone by your side ... like maybe I should encourage you to give up on me and move on." He sadly shook his head. "That's probably why I got so upset when those guys were here today. I thought maybe that's exactly what you were doing."

"No. Not at all. You understand that now."

"I do." He touched her cheek. "But I still wish I were around more so you could lean on me. I'd like to take care of you."

She put her hand on his. "Thanks. I appreciate that. If it makes you feel better, my friends—the Lindas—not the guys, are taking really good care of me." She nodded toward the yard. "Like the way they pulled this off ... well, it was just so amazing. I don't know when I'd ever felt so totally loved."

"Well, I hope you'll share my appreciation with them. Maybe I should send them all chocolates."

"Or something from Italy." She grinned. "Like shoes."

He laughed. And then they talked and talked until they both realized they were starving. "Do you think you could sneak out with me to get a bite to eat?" he asked.

"I wish I could. But it's weird. It's like my mom has radar or something. I just can't risk having her waking up and getting into trouble."

"Then I'll go out and bring back something."

While he was gone, she set the patio table and lit the tiki torches and turned on some music, and when he returned with pizza (since that was all that was open) they ate and talked until Caroline could hardly keep her eyes open. Then they kissed good night, and he promised to call her from LA.

As Caroline went to bed, she felt a strange sense of satisfaction. As great as it had been having Mitch there, and as much as she'd imagined she'd wanted him to show up and rescue her, it was almost a relief that he wasn't able to do that. Although she might think differently about this tomorrow, tonight she liked the idea of standing on her own two feet … with her trusted friends nearby, and her dog. It felt good not to be obsessed with the need for a man to fix her life. With or without Mitch, she was going to be just fine.

Chapter 25

MARLEY

Marley was glad the fog rolled in this afternoon. It was hard enough forcing herself to stay indoors to paint, but having sunshine and blue sky outside made it even worse. No, this fog suited her just fine. Her goal was to have this piece finished by the end of the weekend, which was now only hours away. She was just squirting out some more cobalt blue paint when her phone rang. To her surprise, it was Jack.

"I'm sorry to bother you," he began. "I know you're in the midst of painting, but I have a bit of an emergency."

"An emergency?" She set down the tube of paint.

"Not a life-or-death emergency, exactly. But it's Jasmine."

Marley knew Jasmine was Jack's only daughter and not entirely predictable. She worked for him at the One-Legged Seagull, and Marley had met her on occasion. "Has she been hurt?"

"No. She's just missing."

"Missing?"

"Yes. She was out with an old boyfriend last night, and she left Hunter with a babysitter. The sitter just called to say that Jasmine never came home last night or today. And now the babysitter has to go to work, and she doesn't like to leave Hunter alone. Naturally, I'm stuck at the gallery or I'd go get—"

"Do you think Jasmine's okay?"

"I hope so." He let out a low groan. "I'm sure she's fine, maybe a little hungover. It's actually Hunter I'm worried about. I don't like her being alone."

"No, of course, not. Do you want me to go and get her?"

"Or come mind the shop while I get her?" he said hopefully.

"Whichever is best for you."

"Well, you're closer to Jasmine's place than I am. Maybe, if you didn't mind, you could go pick up Hunter. I know how she's scared to be by herself. She's only seven."

"Should I bring her to the gallery?"

"If you don't mind."

"Or, if you like I can bring her back here until you close."

"Whichever is easiest for you, Marley. I really do appreciate it."

"Hey, that's what friends are for." Then he gave her the address, and she headed over to some rather rundown apartments off of Beach Road. She'd never actually met Hunter before but had heard Jack mention his granddaughter a number of times. It was obvious that Jack really loved the little girl.

A dog barked as she walked up the rickety metal stairs. Then, wondering how she would introduce herself, she knocked on the door of apartment 11, and when no one answered, she called out. "Hunter? This is your grandpa Jack's friend Marley. He's working at the gallery and asked me to come get you." Still no answer, but Marley could hear a shuffling sound inside.

"Hey," Marley called even louder now. "I'll bet you're not supposed to let anyone in when your mom's not home. And that's a good thing. So can you call your grandpa, Hunter? Do you know his number?"

She heard a muffled, "Yeah."

"Tell him that Marley is here to get you and see if he says it's okay." Marley waited, trying to listen through the door to see if the girl was calling or not. Finally, after what seemed a very long time, Hunter called out to her.

"What's your *whole* name?" she asked.

Marley thought for a moment, unsure of what the girl meant. "Linda Marlene Phelps," she said tentatively. "But my friends call me Marley."

There was a pause, then the door slowly opened, and a little girl with red curly hair stood looking at her with big brown eyes. She still had the phone to her ear. "Grandpa says you can come in."

"Thanks." Marley stepped in, closed the door behind her, and looked around. The small apartment was messy and smelled a bit rank.

"She's here," Hunter said into the phone. "Okay." Then she hung up. "Grandpa says I can go with you."

"Good." Marley smiled. "Do you have some shoes and a jacket?"

"Uh-huh." Hunter disappeared into another room.

"And anything else you'd like to bring with you," Marley called out, "like a backpack or pajamas or whatever." Marley could hear the girl rustling around in the room. Meanwhile, Marley did some quick sleuthing, or perhaps it was snooping. While it appeared that Jasmine's housekeeping skills were lacking, her artistic talent was not. There were a number of unfinished drawings on the dining room table, and some were actually quite good. But the sink and counters were heaped with dirty dishes, and the garbage, which was overflowing, seemed to be the source of the smelly aroma.

"I'm ready," Hunter announced. She had on shoes and a jacket. Her backpack hung over one shoulder in a slightly dejected fashion.

"Okay." Marley nodded. "Let's go."

Once they were outside, Marley wondered about locking the door. "Do you have a key?" she asked Hunter.

Hunter just shrugged. "I used to have one, but I don't know where it is anymore."

So Marley just locked the doorknob. She'd let Jasmine figure it out later. She considered leaving a note, but then decided that it might not hurt this MIA mom to get a little worried. Besides, Jack would handle it.

"Here's my car," Marley said as she opened the door for Hunter.

Once they were inside and Hunter was securely buckled in, Marley asked if she wanted to go to the gallery until closing time, but Hunter let out a low moan. "I *always* have to wait there," she complained. "It's sooo boring."

Marley nodded. "Yes, I suppose it is."

"Do you have a TV?" Hunter asked hopefully.

Marley made a sympathetic smile. "Sorry, but I don't."

"Oh." Hunter looked down at her lap and sighed.

"But I have a friend who has a TV," Marley said. "She doesn't live far from here, and I'll bet she has some movies you'd like too." Marley called Abby's number and quickly explained the situation.

"Sure, come on over," Abby said cheerfully. "Paul's just napping, and I'm baking cookies."

"Cookies?" Marley winked at Hunter. "We're on our way."

"What's your friend's name?" Hunter asked as Marley drove.

"Abby. She has a granddaughter who's probably a little younger than you. I think she's five."

"I'm seven," Hunter said proudly. "That's a lot older than five."

"Yes. Of course."

"Is the granddaughter there?" Hunter looked hopeful.

"I don't think so. She lives a ways away."

Now Hunter looked disappointed.

"But I'll bet Abby's got toys and things. She's a good grandma. And, as you heard, she's making cookies."

"What kind of cookies?"

"I'm not sure, but knowing Abby, they'll be good."

A few minutes later, they were walking into Abby's beautiful home, and Hunter was taking it all in with wide eyes. Before long, Hunter was seated at the breakfast bar with a warm snickerdoodle and a glass of milk, *The Little Mermaid* playing quietly on the kitchen TV.

"You are a godsend," Marley quietly told Abby as they went into the living area to sit down. "Disney movies *and* cookies. Why, you should win some kind of a grandmother award."

"I was baking to keep my mind off of the house-buying business."

"Do you think you'll hear tomorrow?"

"I hope so. One way or another, I'm tired of waiting on pins and needles. I think Paul's getting a little impatient too."

"But he's still supportive?"

"*Supportive* might be an overstatement. But for Paul, I suppose he is. Mostly I think his work is wearing him down. He just doesn't seem to have his same energy." She shrugged. "Or else we're just both getting old."

"Like it or not, age does slow us down." Marley glanced over to where Hunter was still happily munching, her eyes riveted on the small flat screen.

"It doesn't slow everyone down." Abby launched into a slightly unbelievable retelling of how Caroline had been entertaining three guys in her renovated backyard yesterday.

"Three guys?" Marley was skeptical. "Seriously?"

Abby filled her in on Caroline's surprising social life, then glanced over to Hunter. "What's the story here?"

Marley quietly explained. "After I picked her up, she didn't want to be stuck in the gallery. Said it was boring."

"It probably is, for a child."

Marley frowned. "I just don't understand a mother doing that, running off and leaving her child alone for so long."

Abby shook her head. "Some parents."

"Jasmine seems like a nice person. And I do like her. Plus she's a talented artist."

"That doesn't mean she's a good mother … or responsible."

Marley sighed. "I guess not. Speaking of responsible, I should let Jack know we're here." Marley took out her cell and called, filling him in on the details and reassuring him that having Hunter with her was no problem.

"He still hasn't heard from Jasmine," Marley told Abby after she hung up.

"You don't think anything happened to her?" Abby whispered. "I mean … foul play?"

Marley shrugged. "Jack sounded pretty nonchalant, like this happens sometimes."

"Too bad. How about if I make us some tea?"

"Sounds lovely."

Abby was just filling the teapot when Paul came into the kitchen. "Who have we here?" he asked with a puzzled expression.

"This is Hunter," Marley explained.

"Hello, Hunter," Paul said in what seemed a slightly grumpy tone.

"Sorry to crash on you like this," Marley apologized. "But Abby had cookies."

He nodded without a trace of a smile then picked up a couple of cookies and trudged away.

"Maybe Hunter and I should go," Marley said quietly to Abby.

"Oh, Paul's just in one of his growly bear moods." Abby made what looked like a forced smile. "Don't let him scare you off."

Marley looked at the kitchen clock. "It's still three hours until closing time at the gallery. That's a long time to put up with us. Maybe I should take Hunter over to my house, although I don't have a TV."

"I know," Abby said. "I have this little DVD player that I use for Lucy in the car sometimes. Maybe you could take that with you and a couple of movies, too."

"Sure, if you don't mind."

"And some cookies."

Abby scurried about gathering up things, and soon Marley and Hunter were back in the car and driving again.

"They didn't want us there, did they?" Hunter asked as Marley drove.

"Oh, that's not it," Marley said. "I think Abby's husband was just in a grumpy mood. Besides, we'll have fun at my house." Of course, Marley wasn't too sure about this. Really, what did she have that was fun besides the tiny movie player? Still, she decided to give it her best shot.

Which is just what she did. And three hours later, Hunter did not want to leave.

After painting, shell sorting, playing slapjack, doing a puzzle, and watching only half of a movie, Hunter was not happy when it was time to go. "I'll tell you what," Marley said as they loaded Hunter's things into the car. "Maybe we can do this on a regular basis."

"What do you mean?" Hunter sounded suspicious.

"Like, where do you go after school when your mom's working at the gallery?"

Hunter made a scowl. "The babysitter."

"Well, maybe you could visit me—say, once a week—instead of being at the babysitter."

"Really?" Hunter's eyes grew big.

"If your mom's okay with it."

Hunter nodded slowly. "I think she'll be okay with it."

"Great. We'll figure out a day that's good for everyone. Maybe Wednesdays. Does that sound good?"

"Yeah." Hunter smiled now. "That sounds real good."

"It sounds real good to me too." Marley smiled to imagine all the things she and Hunter could do on Wednesday afternoons: arts and crafts and exploring and games and whatever they wanted. This would be almost as good as being a grandma!

Chapter 26

JANIE

Sunday evening, Janie's online research revealed the symbolism of her father's military medals. The one with the eagle was for prisoners of war, the Purple Heart for serious injury. Most impressive was the Medal of Honor, the most elite military award, given only to those who risked life beyond the call of duty in the midst of conflict. Janie's father had been a real war hero.

She'd been tempted to mention her interesting discoveries to Victor several times while they'd been up at parents' weekend with Ben. But something in her made her want to keep this information close to her chest, to figure this mystery out as best she could and to savor it. For whatever reasons, her father had kept this part of his life secret.

She reread the letters and V-mail, this time picking up a few more clues in regard to her father's valiant efforts on the battlefield after being shot down. From what she could tell, he was responsible for the fact that most of his surviving air crew had escaped capture. Why he'd been captured was unclear. Apparently, that was how her father had wanted it to remain.

Janie paced the house, trying to unravel the mystery of why her dad had been so tight-lipped about this whole thing. While other veterans rehashed their war stories and went to the veterans' hall for dances and celebrations, her father remained quietly at home, acting as if the war had never happened.

Except for one thing: The war had changed him. She could tell by his early letters that before going to war, her dad enjoyed life, had friends, and loved her mother dearly. It seemed that being shot down and captured—and who knew what else—had changed him for the worse.

Janie stood in the living room trying to recall the many evenings when her parents sat quietly in here, reading or occasionally watching a TV program. Her father, who rarely engaged in conversation, couldn't tolerate much noise or "silliness." Their home, which always had a place for everything (and everything always stayed in its place), had felt stiff to Janie. Stifling and cold. Most of the time, Janie believed the emotional climate was her fault. Whether she'd left her shoes on the porch or an open book on the coffee table or her bike in the driveway, she was often on the receiving end of her dad's chastisement.

But now Janie realized she hadn't really been responsible for her dad's short fuse. In all likelihood the war, or rather the casualties of war, was to blame. Her mother was probably just as hurt by all this as Janie. She'd married a delightful man, enjoyed a few weeks of marriage, and then her love had left her … only to return as someone else. It was no wonder that Janie's mom ran such a tight ship. It was her way to avoid conflict, to survive.

The fact that Janie had been born about ten years after her dad's return from the war seemed more like a miracle than a coincidence. She'd rarely seen her parents exchange any actual physical affection.

Certainly, they loved each other. But it seemed that romance, for them, died during the war. If only she'd known these things while her parents were still alive. Instead, she had made her own assumptions, and with only her childlike memories to draw from, arrived at her own conclusions—all of which, it seemed, were in error.

Janie boxed up all the correspondence and the war medals and, unsure of what to do with them, placed them in the attic for the time being. She decided to keep her father's desk. Maybe it wasn't exactly her style ... but maybe her style was changing.

The next morning Janie went to the florist and bought two dozen red roses, which she took to the cemetery, laying halves of the bouquet on each of her parents' side-by-side graves. Then she sat down on a nearby bench and wept. Her tears were for her parents, for their lost love and lost lives, as much as they were for all the losses she had suffered as a result. She cried for all three of them. When she was done, she stood and dried her eyes and blew her nose, and then she apologized.

"I'm so sorry I didn't understand," she said quietly. "I'm sorry I judged and misjudged you. I never knew what you'd been through—both of you—I never appreciated the sacrifices you'd made. Please, forgive me. And, please, help me to remember you in a new light from here on out—and to respect you. I'm thankful for the gift you gave to me by bringing me into this world despite how badly this world wounded you both. Thank you." She looked at the dates on their headstones, then remembered something. "Happy anniversary," she said quietly. "I know if you were here, you'd probably wish me happy birthday, too. Thanks."

As Janie was driving away from the cemetery, her cell phone rang and so she pulled over to answer it.

"Oh, Janie," Abby exclaimed. "They accepted our offer."

"Oh ... really ... that's good."

"Are you okay?"

"Yes. I'm fine. I'm just, well, at the cemetery."

"At the cemetery?"

"It's a long story." Janie sighed. "Just remembering my parents. You know it was their anniversary yesterday."

"Oh, that's so sweet you remembered."

"Yes." Janie took in a deep breath. "I remembered it because it was also my birthday." The confession was a step toward healing.

"Well, we're going to have to do something about that!" Suddenly Abby was conjuring up plans for them to celebrate in all sorts of ways, and Janie wasn't even resisting. "I'll see if Marley and Caroline can come," Abby said as their conversation wore down. "Let's meet at my house at eleven thirty so that Caroline can make it during her respite time. Maybe we can coax Darlene into an extra hour."

"Sounds good."

"If you have time, can you swing by the bank and sign off on the final papers?" Abby asked. "I'm about to head over there myself. Leslie said she'll have it all ready for us by ten."

"Not a problem. But I have to get Mario and his wife started on unloading my storage unit first." Janie glanced at her watch. "We're supposed to meet in a few minutes. But once I get them going, I think they'll be good for several hours."

"Hey, I should talk to those two about working for me on the bed-and-breakfast," Abby told her. "I'll need all sorts of help getting that up and running."

"I'll mention that," Janie promised. "I know they're both looking for more steady employment. And I'll vouch for them. They're really good people and hard workers."

"This is so exciting," Abby gushed. "Leslie said that we should have occupancy of the house by the end of the month. Can you believe it?"

"That's great." Janie smiled, remembering her dad's desk. "I already have my first piece of furniture to go into my law office downstairs."

"Great! If I don't see you at the bank, I'll see you at my house at eleven thirty."

"It's a date." As Janie hung up she tried to remember when she'd heard Abby so happy and upbeat. Not since they were kids. Ironically, Abby was the most optimistic of the bunch back then. She'd been the instigator of some of their craziest stunts. "Fearless Leader" is how Janie would've described Abby in those days.

Of course, Janie had probably chalked that up to Abby's parents. Fun and full of life, they had seemed a sharp contrast to Janie's. But now Janie was viewing life from a different angle. Abby's dad hadn't been in the war or the military, but in some ways, looking back through hindsight, he'd been almost shallow. He never took anything terribly seriously. At the time Janie thought he was simply happy-go-lucky. Wasn't it odd that his daughter had turned out to be comparatively unhappy in her own life? Well, at least until now. Things were changing for Abby, and Janie was glad to be a part of it.

The timing of getting the house couldn't be more perfect for Janie. With her other things coming from New York in a week or so, she would now have another place to put them. As she drove toward the mini warehouse company, she imagined how she would set up her law offices in the basement of the B and B.

Ever organized, Janie had brought two sets of Post-it Notes with her. Green stickers meant the item or crate was to be moved to the house. She even wrote which room on some of the larger pieces. The orange sticky notes meant those things would remain in the unit. After less than an hour, she had placed the notes, and Mario and Rosa were already loading her things into the back of Mario's pickup.

"Go ahead and unpack the kitchen things," Janie told Rosa, with Mario acting as interpreter. "Wash them and put them away as best you can." Janie knew that she'd probably have to rearrange some things later, but at least they'd be in the house. "I'll be home around two."

They both nodded, assuring her that they would handle it. Then, as Janie was driving away, she felt a fleeting doubt. Was she a fool to trust them with her things, her house, and her storage unit code numbers? After all, she hardly knew them. But so far, Mario had not disappointed her—not once. Really, what was there to worry about?

Abby had already come and gone at the bank, but Janie took her time going over the last of the paperwork.

"Not all short sales are this smooth," Leslie told her as she signed the last paper. "But because there were no liens and nothing out of the ordinary, it's been pretty slick."

"Well, you've certainly made Abby happy."

Leslie grinned. "I'll say. She was practically walking on air when she sailed in here to sign. Of course, she assured me that you'd be going over the papers more carefully."

Janie handed Leslie back her pen. "Yes, I've always been a bit on the meticulous side." She wanted to add that she hoped that would be changing—that it would feel good to lighten up some. Instead she just smiled and thanked Leslie for her help.

Then, wanting to clean up a bit for Abby's celebration-birthday party, Janie swung by her house and was relieved to see that Mario and Rosa were already there. Mario's brother was there as well, helping him to unload things. Feeling guilty for her unwarranted suspicions, Janie went inside to make some quick notes about what could go where, then quickly cleaned up and changed her clothes.

"You have my number if you need me," she called out to Mario.

Feeling like everything was under control, Janie headed over to Abby's and didn't even feel bad for being a few minutes late.

"Surprise!" her friends yelled when she walked in.

Janie laughed. "Like I didn't know." But she thanked and hugged them, and Abby handed her a margarita.

"You told me you didn't believe in birthdays," Caroline teased.

"People change," Janie told her. "Hey, is this Chuck?" She bent down to pat the head of a pretty golden retriever.

"Yes, meet the newest man in my life." Caroline chuckled.

"She's not kidding," Abby told her. "This weekend, sweet Caroline was inundated with males."

"Really?" Janie peered curiously.

Caroline waved her hand. "Don't ask. Trust me, it was a mess. I'm still working it out. Chuck's my main male at the moment."

They all laughed.

"How was parents' weekend?" Caroline asked Janie.

"It was okay, but I felt a little guilty," Janie admitted.

"Guilty?" Marley's brows shot up. "What did you do?"

"It's not so much what I did, but I got to thinking about my own son off at Princeton. I was wondering if I'd make it to his parents' weekend."

"Did he invite you?"

Janie shook her head. "Matthew kind of played it down this time, saying it was something parents only do during freshman year. Do you think that's true?"

Her friends agreed that it was probably true.

"Think about it," Marley pointed out. "Did you want your parents coming to visit you at college every year?"

Janie considered this. "Not when I was actually *in* college, but maybe I would now."

The phone rang, and Abby excused herself to answer, but Janie could tell by the tone of Abby's voice that something wasn't right. So Janie shushed Caroline and Marley and nodded in Abby's direction. She was holding the phone with a shaking hand.

"Where did it happen?" Abby looked desperately at her friends. "Is he—is he alive?" Then Abby's eyes closed, the phone dropped to the floor, and Abby slumped over with a gasp. In the same instant, all three friends gathered around her, helping her to a chair. Janie grabbed the phone from the floor.

"This is Janie Sorenson, Abby's friend. Please, tell me what's happening," she said. "What's wrong?"

"Abby's husband is being transported to the hospital right now."

"What happened? A car accident?"

"He collapsed on the job," the man told her. "We think it's his heart."

"His heart?"

"Or a stroke. He wasn't breathing. One of the guys gave him CPR, but it didn't seem to work."

Janie took in a sharp breath. "But paramedics came?"

"Yes. They just left with him."

"Thank you," Janie told him. "We're on our way."

"Is he … is he dead?" Abby asked in a tiny voice.

"No," Janie told her firmly. "Paul's being transported to the hospital." She took Abby by the arm. "You come with me."

"We'll follow," Caroline called out as they all rushed to gather their things and head out the door.

"Everyone, drive carefully," Janie warned. "See you there."

Abby was silent as Janie drove away from the house. "He's in good hands," Janie assured Abby. "We'll probably get there, and he'll be sitting up having a soda."

"I don't know." Abby shook her head. "Tom said Paul wasn't breathing, wasn't conscious. I keep thinking about Cathy Gardener at our reunion. She never recovered."

"Cathy is not Paul. And Paul is not Cathy." Janie knew that was a ridiculous thing to say, but it was all she had at the moment. After all, she did know what it felt like to lose a husband. Abby wasn't ready to go there yet.

"He hasn't been feeling well," Abby said weakly. "He hasn't been himself. I should've known something was wrong. It's all my fault."

"There's no point in blaming yourself, Abby. You know as well as I do that hindsight is twenty-twenty."

"If I hadn't been so focused on buying the house, so self-absorbed …" Abby started crying.

"He's going to be okay," Janie told her. "You have to believe that, Abby. You're the one who's been talking about faith lately, about how you've been praying a lot more. You need to hold on to that now."

So, as Janie drove, Abby bowed her head and began mumbling some words that Janie couldn't make out, but she seemed to be praying. That had to be worth something. At least Janie hoped so.

Chapter 27

ABBY

Abby stared down at Paul lying there motionless and pale, his eyes closed, tubes and wires invading his face and body. He looked like someone else, so much older than she normally thought of him … so tired … worn out … fragile, even. This was nothing like the young man she'd fallen for so long ago, back when they were both sixteen and naive enough to believe that their passion and youth and love would last forever.

For all these years—their entire adult lives—their lives had intermingled, meshing together as they shared meals, beds, children, good times, hard times … and everything in between. In all reality, Paul was the one person Abby knew almost as well as she knew herself. Now she couldn't even make a connection with him. It was like he was in another world, already gone, and it was killing her.

"Oh, Paul." She sighed as she pushed a strand of gray hair off his forehead. He was overdue for a haircut … overdue for a lot of things, including that doctor's checkup she'd meant to schedule for him whether he wanted it or not. Why hadn't she done it? Why hadn't she listened to her instincts?

She choked back a sob, willing herself to remain strong for his sake. "I'm here," she said quietly, placing her hand on his, tightening her grasp, trying to infuse warmth, love, life. "Please, come back to me, my darling. I love you so much. I know I say silly, selfish things sometimes. We both say things we don't mean. I'm sorry. Please, come back to me." She felt hot tears streaking down her cheeks. "I need you so much, Paul. I never tell you that, but it's true. I really, really need you. Please, come back to me."

She gently laid her head on his chest, not putting any weight on him for fear of hurting his already damaged heart. But she wanted to feel his closeness, his warmth, and breathe in his scent. She had always loved his scent, even those times when she'd nagged him to take a shower. She silently pleaded with God. She was ready to beg, bargain, or sacrifice whatever it would take to get him to spare Paul.

"I'm sorry, but you must keep your visits to a maximum of fifteen minutes." The nurse placed a hand on Abby's shoulder. "ICU rules."

"Yes." Abby stepped away, slowly removing her hand from his. "I'm sorry."

The nurse nodded, then began checking the monitors and tubes and injected something into the IV. Abby slipped out of the room with trembling knees. Walking down the brightly lit hallway, she felt confused, wondering how this had happened. How had they been blindsided like this? Today had started out like such a normal day. This morning when she'd called Paul to tell him the good news about the house, he actually sounded happy for her. Now they were here, life hanging in the balance. So surreal.

"How's he doing?" Janie asked as Abby rejoined her friends in the waiting area.

Unable to say the words, Abby pressed her lips together, then shook her head. Just like that, the three of them wrapped her in their arms, and she let the tears flow freely. "This feels like it's my fault," she blurted. "Like my selfishness is what killed him."

"But he's not dead, is he?" Caroline looked at Abby with wide eyes.

"No, he's not dead." Abby pulled a tissue out of her pocket and wiped her eyes. "But he's not really alive either. It's only the machines ... keeping him going."

"He will pull through this," Marley said firmly. "I have a very strong feeling he's going to be okay."

Abby stared at her. "How do you know? How can you say that?"

Marley pointed to her chest with a sincere expression. "I sometimes have a sixth sense about things. And I've got a strong one here."

Abby wanted to believe her, but a sixth sense? It just seemed a little far-fetched.

"Did you get hold of the girls?" Abby asked. She'd left her cell phone with Janie, asking her to call family while she was with Paul.

"Just Jessie," Janie told her. "She's on her way here. She and little Lucy promised to call Laurie—"

"And your mom's trying to reach Nicole," Marley added.

"Which won't be easy. What time is it in France?" No one seemed to know. Abby wondered if it might not be better to shelter Nicole from this for the time being. Really, what could she do from the other side of the world? Abby didn't want her to feel pressured to drop everything and come home.

"I asked your mom to swing by your house and make sure the stove's turned off," Marley told her.

"Thank you." Abby shook her head in embarrassment. "I can't believe I didn't think of that. I've never left a stove on in my life. Paul would kill me if I burned the house down."

Caroline put an arm around Abby's shoulders and squeezed her. "No, he would not, Abby. Do you know how much that man loves you?"

Abby let out a jagged sigh. "What just hit me … in there … is *how much* I love him. How much I need him. I can't believe how much I've taken him for granted." She felt the lump in her throat coming back. "I'm still afraid that I'm the reason he's in there right now. It's … it's my fault."

"No, it's not," Caroline insisted. "How can you possibly say that?"

"Because I've been so stubborn about getting that house and starting up the bed-and-breakfast. Paul's been against it, right from the start, but I just kept pushing forward, rolling along like a steamroller, insisting on my way when all the while Paul's been worried about his business and our finances. I'm sure I've completely stressed him out. It's no wonder he's in there … dying." Abby was sobbing again. Once again, her friends gathered her into their arms, this time walking her over to the seating area and easing her onto a sofa.

"I'm sorry," she sobbed. "I wanted to keep it together, but it's just so hard."

"Go ahead and cry as much as you want," Caroline urged. "I usually feel better after a good long cry."

"But you must quit blaming yourself," Marley injected. "You are not responsible for your husband's health. Anyone can have a heart attack, Abby. It's not always stress-related. You do not get to own that."

"That's right," Janie agreed. "Blaming yourself for Paul's heart attack makes as much sense as me blaming myself for Phil's cancer. It's just pointless and wrong. You have to know that."

Abby considered this as she blew her nose. "I'd like to believe that's true."

"It is true." Janie nodded firmly. "Phil had a friend—not an attorney either—who seemed to have this perfect life. He took care of his health and jogged every day and was happily married with kids and loved his job. And one day he just dropped dead from a heart attack. The only reason was a congenital heart defect. You just never know."

"Besides," Marley said quickly. "Paul is *not* going to die. I really have a strong sense that he'll be okay."

Abby hoped Marley was right, but what if she wasn't?

"We've been praying," Caroline told her. "I have to go home to relieve Darlene now, but I'm going to keep praying. I'm going to pray nonstop until Paul pulls through."

"And I'm going over to your house," Marley said, "to clean things up from our little party."

"Sorry you guys didn't get any lunch," Abby said.

"Oh, Abby." Janie shook her head. "Don't be silly."

"I know," Marley said. "I'll pack up the food and bring it back here."

"If the quiche isn't ruined."

"Well, if it's ruined, I'll just pick us something up," Marley promised. Then she and Caroline left.

"I don't want you to feel you need to stay here," Abby told Janie. "I'm sure you have things to—"

"The only thing I have to do is to be with you." Janie patted her back. "So don't try to get rid of me."

Abby looked at her watch. "Is it really only two o'clock? It feels like it's been hours … days … since that phone call."

"It's probably going to be a very long day. How about if I get us some coffee or tea or something?"

Abby just nodded.

"I'll be back soon."

Then Abby was alone. Sitting and waiting felt impossible, so she stood and before long was pacing and praying. She wandered toward the ICU, peering into Paul's window to see that the nurse was still with him, and he still looked exactly the same. Only family was allowed to visit in the ICU, and only for fifteen minutes every two hours. Abby wasn't sure that anyone was really tracking these visitations, but at the same time she didn't want to do anything to impede Paul's recovery. And yet she wanted to be in there, to be by his side, to keep talking to him. Really, how could that hurt?

"There you are." Janie handed Abby a paper cup. "Green tea with a bit of honey. Hope that's okay."

Abby nodded. "Perfect. Thanks."

"Any changes?" Janie nodded toward the ICU.

Abby shook her head. "Not that I've heard. I just wish I could sit with him."

Janie frowned. "I really don't understand their visiting restrictions here. Some hospitals encourage family members to remain with ICU patients because it helps in their recovery."

"What could they do to me if I broke their rules?"

Janie's brow creased. "I doubt they'd resort to any legal action. But, having been in this position before, I wouldn't encourage you to antagonize the people who are caring for your husband."

"No, I suppose not."

They walked back toward the waiting area just as Abby's mom came rushing in. She hugged Abby and inquired about Paul. Abby gave her a quick update, and her mom said that Laurie was trying to get off work and catch a flight up here. "She probably won't arrive until tomorrow."

Abby blinked. "Laurie is coming home?"

Her mom nodded. "Won't it be wonderful to see her?"

Abby just nodded. She wished the circumstances were different, but at least Laurie was coming. That was something. Abby hoped Paul would get to see her and talk to her.

"I left a message for Nicole to call you," her mom told her.

"I was wondering how much I should tell her, Mom. As badly as I want her to come home, I thought maybe I should play this down a bit."

"You need to be honest, Abby. Nicole deserves to know exactly what's going on with her father."

Abby swallowed against the hard lump in her throat. "I don't even know exactly what's going on."

They talked awhile longer, and then the three of them went to the small chapel and just sat there quietly. Abby knew her mom was praying and Janie probably was too. But the only prayer Abby could manage was a silent plea for God to spare Paul. Over and over, she begged God not to take her husband.

Chapter 28

MARLEY

As she drove home from the hospital Monday afternoon, Marley wished there was more she could do for Abby, something more helpful than saying she had a strong feeling that Paul was going to be okay. But the feeling—that confidence that something would turn out a certain way—was real, and it was something she'd experienced only a few times in her life. One time it was in regard to her best friend's daughter, who'd been seriously injured in a horrible car wreck. The doctor was fairly sure that Brianna was going to lose her legs. Even if they could prevent amputation, he said, she would be unable to walk again. Marley, though, had the strongest impression that Brianna was not only going to walk, but dance. A few years later, Brianna and her new husband were dancing at their wedding.

It was when Marley had been driving to the hospital, right after Abby received the bad news, that she got the impression Paul was going to be okay. Marley had actually expected Paul to be perfectly fine by the time they arrived at the hospital. But, even though that wasn't the case, Marley still felt relatively sure that her feeling was right. And that's just what she'd told Abby before she left.

Marley felt a little guilty for leaving, even though she'd taken a meal back to her friends and stayed to help eat it. Abby had Janie, her mom, her granddaughter, and her daughter Jessie. Laurie would be there in the morning. Really, Marley just felt like extra baggage. She still had a painting to finish by the weekend, so she decided to head for home.

She felt a strange sense of loneliness when she parked in front of her beach bungalow. Doris's lights were off next door, because she was with Abby. The fog had rolled in, and the sound of the ocean, which Marley usually loved, seemed strangely haunting tonight.

Marley went into her house, flipped on the lights, turned on some music, and even lit a small fire to take the damp chill out of the air. But when she got set to paint, her creative juices had been sucked dry. So she put her painting things away, puttered around a bit, and eventually crawled into bed with a book. Although she was trying to focus on the story, she was keenly aware of how alone she felt … and lonely. She closed the book and turned off the light and just listened to the sea, wondering where this heavy sense of loneliness had come from.

Certainly, she was concerned about Abby and Paul. Despite her conviction that Paul would be all right, she knew that Abby would be very lonely without him if he did die. Marley supposed that she might be superimposing those emotions onto her own life, but that didn't really seem to be the situation. This was a heavier sort of loneliness, almost spiritual in its depth. As Marley listened to the sea—pondering its never-ending tides and rhythms, she became profoundly aware of her own mortality. Although she'd assured Abby that Paul wasn't going to die, she knew that eventually he would die. They all would die. It was inevitable. For some reason this concept just seemed to devastate her, right in the center of her soul.

She sat up in bed and stared into the darkness. She, Marley Phelps, was going to die someday. And then what? Marley had always believed in God—a higher spiritual power, a creative force in the universe. But her convictions had never been much more substantive than that. Unlike Caroline and even Abby and sometimes Janie, too, Marley had never claimed to have a personal relationship with that higher power. In a way, it seemed presumptuous for anyone to make such a claim. Not that she'd ever said as much to her friends.

Marley thought about Abby's mom. Doris made no bones about how she and God were on very familiar terms. She'd told Marley many times about how she walked on the beach and conversed with God about all sorts of things, big and small. Marley usually just smiled in an indulgent way. But now she wondered. Maybe these women knew something she didn't.

For the first time in her life, Marley decided to knock on the door of the Almighty by asking if he could hear her ... and whether or not he cared. She continued talking, unsure whether she was simply amusing herself or being listened to by God. But when she finally quit, she felt surprisingly better and not nearly so lonely. So, she decided, she might continue this little experiment, just to see where it might take her.

The next morning, she woke before the sun was up. She got out of bed, made coffee, then bundled up and went outside to drink it as the sky began to lighten. Suddenly she realized she was going to follow Doris's advice. She set down her cup and headed out to the beach.

After an hour of walking and talking to God, Marley was back in her house feeling encouraged and refreshed and, to her surprise, very spiritually in tune and inspired. It still seemed too early to call and check on Paul's condition, so she got out her brushes and started to paint.

It was nearly ten when she realized how much time had passed, and she paused to call Janie to find out the latest.

"There's no change in his condition," Janie said in a tired tone.

"How's Abby holding up?"

"It helps having her family around her. But I know she's hurting. She just keeps blaming herself, as if Paul would never have had a heart problem if she hadn't wanted to start a bed-and-breakfast."

"Which is perfectly ridiculous."

"Yes, but she can't see that."

"Poor Abby. You know she really loves Paul."

"I know." Janie let out a long sigh. "It's really hard being in Abby's position, just waiting ... not knowing."

"Do you think I should come to the hospital?" Marley dunked her brush in the jar of water.

"I don't know. With Doris, Jessie, Lucy, and—this afternoon—Laurie, too, well, I'm not even sure that I should stick around. I don't want to be in the way."

"Yes. That's kind of how I felt."

"In fact, after I pick Laurie up from the airport and drop her back here, I might just head for home."

"Well, tell Abby to call me if she needs me to do anything,"

Marley said. "I'll be here all day, and I'm more than willing to drop everything if I can be of any help."

"I will."

Marley poured herself half a cup of coffee, then returned to her canvas and studied it as she sipped. She wasn't sure how to describe her work, but she felt like there was a new kind of energy in this painting. It was more free-spirited and alive. Unless she was imagining things. She stepped back, narrowing her eyes and peering at it. Well, even if it was her imagination, she had to admit that she liked the direction the painting was going, and she couldn't help but wonder if her attempt to connect herself to God might have something to do with it. After all, if God was the Creator of the universe, wasn't it possible that some of his creativity might rub off onto her? Especially if she was spending time with him?

———

After spending all of Tuesday painting, and hearing that Paul's condition had not changed, Marley decided to visit Abby at the hospital. She wasn't sure that her visit would make much difference to Abby, but Marley simply felt she couldn't stay away for another day.

"Oh, I'm so glad to see you," Abby exclaimed as they hugged.

"How's it going?"

Abby just shook her head. "No change."

"I'm sorry."

Abby peered into Marley's eyes. "Do you still have that feeling? That Paul is going to recover?"

Marley considered this, then slowly nodded. "I do. I still do."

Abby let out a sigh.

"Where's your family?" Marley looked around the mostly vacant waiting area as the two of them sat down.

"They went to grab some lunch. They'll bring me something. I just hate to leave, you know, in case something changes."

"I understand."

"Caroline was here for a while. And Janie said she'll stop by later this afternoon. I've missed you guys."

"Really? I just assumed you'd be so busy with your family that—"

"You guys are my family too," Abby declared. "Oh, certainly, I love my daughters and my mom and my darling little Lucy. But you Lindas, well, I really need you a lot."

"You know we're here for you."

Abby was looking over Marley's shoulder. She stood. "I think the nurse is trying to get my attention."

Marley walked with Abby toward the ICU. It did seem the nurse was motioning toward Abby. Hopefully nothing was wrong. Marley remained behind as Abby followed the nurse into the ICU. Feeling that something serious might be happening, Marley began to pray silently. She leaned up against a pillar and, with eyes closed and spirit focused, she asked God to intervene. She stood there a long time, just thinking about Abby and Paul and asking God to do something—something truly miraculous—and finally it was as if she ran out of steam. Feeling tired and slightly empty, Marley went over to the waiting area and sat down. She really had no idea exactly how this whole conversing-with-God thing went. It was still so very new to her. And yet she had a strong feeling that it was real.

After what seemed a long time—but was actually only about fifteen minutes—Abby returned, and she was smiling. "He's awake," Abby told Marley with wide eyes.

"Is he okay?"

"Well, it's hard to say. He's obviously been through a lot. But he could talk, and he knew me, and in some ways he seemed like his old self, only very weak. He got tired after just a few minutes of talking. The doctor came in—they're going to get him ready for an angiogram. The doctor suspects Paul needs bypass surgery."

"Bypass surgery?" Marley questioned. "I wonder why they didn't do that as soon as he came in here."

"The doctor said they had to stabilize him first. Otherwise he could've died on the operating table."

"So is he strong enough for surgery now?"

"I don't know. I'm just so glad he's awake." Abby hugged Marley. "I think you were right. I think he's going to be okay. I really believe it now."

Marley almost reminded Abby that Paul was not out of the woods yet, but then she wondered why she would make such a negative statement. Really, what was she thinking?

Of course, Marley knew exactly where her doubts had come from. It wasn't something she liked to think about, but more than a dozen years ago, Marley's father had undergone bypass surgery right here in this same hospital. Marley had flown down from Seattle to sit with her mom during the procedure. They had both kissed him on the cheek, assuring him that all was well, and then he was wheeled away.

That was the last time Marley saw her father alive. He bled to death several hours after the surgery was proclaimed "successful."

Marley had been furious with the doctor, who actually admitted to Marley's mother that the shunt was too short.

Naturally, Marley had no intention of repeating any of this to Abby. But it did worry her, so much so that Marley began to doubt her earlier sense that Paul was going to be just fine. Before long, Abby was surrounded by family and everyone was so excited over this new turn of events that Marley began to feel like a wet blanket, so she excused herself and went to sit in the chapel, where she prayed some more.

A bit past two, Marley realized that she would need to leave to pick up Hunter, because she'd made a date to pick the little girl up from school. She explained this to Abby.

"Yes, by all means go and get her," Abby said with bright eyes. "The angiogram revealed blockage in three arteries. He's scheduled for surgery at five."

"Five *today?*"

Abby nodded. "Yes, isn't it wonderful that they could do it so soon?"

Marley forced a smile. "Yes." She squeezed Abby's hand. "I'll be praying for him."

"Thank you!"

As Marley was leaving the hospital, she met Janie coming in. She quickly shared the latest news about Paul's scheduled surgery. "I have to go pick up Jack's granddaughter," she explained, "but please keep me in the loop."

"Absolutely." Janie smiled. "That's great news."

"I'll try to make it back here around six," Marley promised. As she hurried on her way, she wondered if that was such a good idea.

Really, it might be best if she kept a low profile throughout this part of the ordeal. Not that she thought her presence would change anything for Paul, but she didn't want to open her mouth and unwittingly play the spoiler while everyone was feeling so hopeful.

As Marley drove to the grade school, she felt grateful that she'd arranged to spend this afternoon with Hunter. It would be a good distraction. Jack had already explained how to go to the office and sign her out. He'd also told Marley how Jasmine came home late on Sunday night, acting like leaving her child home alone was no big deal, like Hunter knew she should call her grandfather and that he would figure things out.

Naturally, Jack had been irritated by that. But he admitted that he had to go easy in regard to his unpredictable daughter. "Otherwise, she might grab Hunter and just take off," he explained to Marley on the phone. "She's said she wants to move to South America before."

"That's got to be frustrating," Marley had told him.

"I'll say."

"But she's okay with me picking up Hunter once a week?"

"Sure. In her mind, it's free babysitting."

"I'll drop Hunter by the gallery before closing," she had promised.

As she walked up to the grade school, she remembered when Ashton had been in school and all the time she'd spent volunteering or chauffeuring him around. It didn't even seem that long ago. Although this was different, she still got a good feeling being here. The familiar musty smell of dust and floor polish and wet tennis shoes, and the sound of kids' voices, actually made her smile. Before long, she and Hunter were on their way.

"What are we going to do?" Hunter asked expectantly.

Marley peered out at the gray sky, which looked like it was about to dump some rain. "What would you like to do?"

"Get ice cream."

Marley chuckled. "Ice cream, huh?"

"Is that okay?"

"I don't see why not. In fact, I'm in the mood for some ice cream myself." So she drove down by the wharfs and parked in front of the old-fashioned ice cream shop, the same place her dad used to take her when she was about Hunter's age. There, they both ordered one scoop of peppermint-candy ice cream on a sugar cone, then sat and slowly ate them.

"Do you like the arcade?" Marley asked as they finished.

Hunter's big brown eyes got bigger as she eagerly nodded. "Yeah!"

"My dad used to take me there for a treat when I was little," Marley told her. "I haven't been there in years."

"I never get to go there," Hunter said. "My mommy hates it."

"Oh?" Now Marley was unsure. "Hates it? Like she doesn't want you to go there?"

"No," Hunter said quickly. "She doesn't like how noisy it is and that it costs money to play."

"Oh." Marley nodded. "Well, I can understand that. But sometimes it's fun to be noisy."

For the next hour they played the silly arcade games and then, when Marley's ears were ringing, she suggested they find something quieter to do. "I've been wanting to get a library card," she told Hunter. "Do you have one?"

"No. I think I'm too little."

"Oh, I don't think so," Marley assured her. "I used to have one when I was about your age. Anyway, we can find out."

At the library, they discovered that Hunter was not too young for her own card, but that she'd need her mom's signature. So Marley got herself a card and checked out some books, both for her and Hunter, and then they took the paperwork with them back to the One-Legged Seagull, where it was just about closing time.

"Do we get to do this every week?" Hunter asked as they went inside the gallery.

"Well, not the same thing," Marley said. "But we'll do something fun. As long as you still want to and if your mom agrees."

Jasmine came out from behind the counter now, stooping to hug Hunter. "Did you have fun with Marley?"

"Yeah." Hunter smiled happily.

"Thanks for doing that," Jasmine told Marley. "And thanks for having her on Sunday, too."

Marley made what she hoped looked like a genuine smile, since she was still a bit irked that a mom could abandon her child like that. "Thank you for sharing her with me. Hunter is a delight."

Jasmine ruffled Hunter's red curls. "Sometimes she's less of a delight."

Marley just nodded. "I hope you don't think I was snooping, but I noticed some of your drawings in your apartment."

Jasmine looked a little uneasy. "You were in my apartment?"

"Grandpa said to let her in," Hunter said.

"Sunday, to pick up Hunter," Marley explained. "I saw your art, and it was really good, Jasmine. I'm surprised you don't have some of it in here."

Jasmine's smile returned now. "Well, it's not really finished …
and not that good."

"I thought it was good."

"Well, thanks."

"So anyway, I guess I'll see you both at the Art Walk on Saturday,"
Marley said brightly. "I better go home and get to work."

"Thanks again," Jasmine called and Hunter echoed. As Marley
drove home, she thought about how spending an afternoon with a
child was really good medicine. She decided then, for the sake of
both Hunter and Jack, she would do everything possible to befriend
Jasmine. It only made sense.

Chapter 29

CAROLINE

Caroline felt so out of it on Tuesday night. Everyone else was rallying around Abby in her time of need. But Caroline, as usual, was stuck at home with her cantankerous mom. At least she had Chuck to brighten things up and keep her company. Caroline was astonished at what a great companion this dog was turning out to be. Although they hadn't been to the beach yet, she looked forward to the days when she would take him there—when her respite time wouldn't be spent at the hospital with her friends.

Caroline had kept her word. Every time she thought about Paul, she prayed for him to recover. She also prayed for Abby and the rest of their family to be comforted throughout their ordeal. Caroline honestly had no idea which way this was going to go, but she knew it wasn't outside the realm of possibility that Paul wouldn't make it. She wondered how Abby would get along without him. The Lindas would be there to help her. Also, Abby had Doris, a mother who was in her right mind—not something to be underestimated.

As Caroline tended to her mom, coaxing her to eat a little vanilla pudding and some Ritz crackers to make up for the barely touched dinner, she kept her phone in her sweatshirt pocket. Janie had promised to let Caroline know as soon as Paul came out of surgery.

But soon it was after seven and time to get her mom to bed. Thankfully she was worn out from being awake most of the day—something Caroline had asked Darlene to help her with—and as a result was fairly cooperative.

It was also helpful that the nurse from social services had secured a prescription for Xanax last week, which was helping her mother sleep better throughout the night. Her suspicious mom wouldn't willingly take any kind of pill, but Caroline had figured out a way to mash it and slip it into the last bite of pudding.

The trick after that was getting her mom into bed before she dozed off and made everything much more difficult. But Caroline's routines were becoming more established, which it seemed her mom appreciated. Sometimes, like tonight, things went almost like clockwork. It wasn't even eight by the time her mom was all tucked in. She'd had her last sip of water, and the plush white toy dog was tucked in next to her when Caroline turned off the light and tiptoed out.

Chuck was waiting eagerly for her in the hallway. She made herself a cup of cocoa, and with the baby monitor in hand and her cell phone still in her pocket, she and Chuck went out to the backyard. She sat beneath awning while Chuck roamed around, sniffing the grass and doing his business, which she would clean up tomorrow.

As usual, she wondered how long she could keep this up. She knew that there were no real rules in regard to Alzheimer's. Even when the hospice nurse had stopped by to do an evaluation, she had seemed unsure as to what stage Caroline's mother was really at. Of course, her mom had been having a fairly good day and actually remembered some things that surprised Caroline. But that wasn't a typical day, which Caroline pointed out. Certainly, she wished her mom always functioned at that level. Wouldn't life be much easier if she did? The hospice nurse promised to come back to check her again in two weeks. And that, to Caroline, seemed sufficient.

She jumped to hear her phone ringing in her pocket. Fumbling to set down her cocoa, she finally extracted it and answered.

"He's out of surgery," Janie told her.

"And is he okay?"

"The doctor just told Abby that the prognosis is good."

"Oh, good." Caroline sighed in relief. "Very, very good."

"Yes. Everyone here is relieved."

"I'll bet." Caroline sighed. "Give my love to Abby. Tell her I wish I were there."

"I'll do that."

"Bye now."

As if sensing Caroline's mood, Chuck came over and laid his head in her lap. She petted his silky ear, twisting it gently in her hand. "You are a good boy, Chuck," she said quietly. "A really good boy."

She remembered her promise to call Mitch if there was any news. Mitch had only met Paul once, on Labor Day, but she'd told him everything when he called Monday night. After a few rings, he answered and she quickly filled him in, but she suspected by his tone that he was busy or distracted. "Did I catch you at a bad time?" she finally asked.

"Just having dinner with clients," he said politely. "But maybe I can call you back later."

"Sure," she told him. "Just not too late. I'm pretty tired."

He chuckled. "But it's only eight thirty, Caroline."

"Yes, I'm aware of that. But it's been a long day." Then she told him good-bye and hung up. It was easy for him to make fun of her for being tired. But how would he manage if he were in her shoes? Caring for someone else twenty-four/seven took its toll.

She leaned back and sighed, telling herself it was senseless to get aggravated at Mitch for being obtuse. Yet it was irritating to think that he was down there in LA right now, probably enjoying a balmy evening at a swanky restaurant. He was probably planning to stay out late, maybe even show his clients the LA nightlife—especially if they were from another country, which was often the case. It was hard not to be just plain jealous. And resentful.

But wasn't this her choice? No one had forced her to take this on. And yet she had imagined moving back to Clifden so differently. Oh, she knew she'd always been the romantic, the optimist, envisioning life through rose-colored glasses. She was the little girl who, if she saw a gigantic pile of horse manure in the backyard, would run to get a shovel—to look for the pony!

Besides, wasn't it this same optimism that had gotten her through some of life's darkest nights? Perhaps that was God's gift to her, his way of seeing her through the tough times. But sometimes Caroline wondered just how much she could really take.

By Friday afternoon, Caroline felt stronger than ever, like she could probably continue taking care of her mom indefinitely. That was probably an overstatement related to a number of factors. First of all, it seemed that the routines she'd established with her mom were finally paying off. Tasks that seemed impossible at first were getting simpler. Second, Darlene had recommended a second caregiver to give Caroline some more time off. Also, Caroline attended an Alzheimer's meeting that had actually been informative and encouraging. Finally, she felt hugely relieved to know that Paul was doing great and would be released from the hospital early next week. Abby had been ecstatic.

"You seem to be in good spirits," Brent said as they walked to the parking lot together after the support meeting. "Is it the dog?"

She laughed. "Well, the dog certainly helps."

"Or is it the boyfriend?" Brent gave her a sideways look.

"You mean Mitch?"

"Wasn't he the one you were more serious about?"

"Look," she said gently. "I'm sorry about last Saturday. Adam acted like a jerk, and that's probably my fault for not making myself more clear with him."

Brent just laughed. "Hey, I actually thought the whole thing was pretty humorous. In fact, it gave me an idea for a screenplay."

"Really?" She turned to see if he was teasing.

"Absolutely. A story about a cougar with three different boyfriends."

Caroline frowned. "Seriously?"

He paused by her car. "Don't you like it?"

"I'm not sure. I'm not really a cougar, you know."

"I know. I'm just saying you were the inspiration for the story." He studied her. "Are you *really* as old as that Adam dude? I mean, he looked like he was about my dad's age."

She laughed. "Well, Adam's a little older. But the truth is, your mom's not that many years older than me."

He patted her on the back. "Well, you look good for your age."

"Thanks."

"I was a little disappointed to find that out."

"So I should have told you sooner?" she asked. "Just blurted out my age the first time we chatted?"

He grinned. "Probably not."

"I enjoy your friendship, Brent. It's nice having someone who knows a little bit about this crazy ride—you know … caring for a parent who sometimes doesn't always remember your name."

He nodded. "Yeah, that's how I feel too."

She stuck out her hand. "So, we're still friends?"

"Absolutely."

They talked awhile longer, and Caroline told him about the Art Walk in town tomorrow night and how she'd already arranged for a caregiver to stay with her mom. "One of my best friends, Marley Phelps, is showing her work at the One-Legged Seagull," she said. "It should be a fun evening."

"Are you inviting me to go with you?"

"Uh … no. I'm sorry. Did I make it sound like that?" She laughed uncomfortably. "Maybe I really am a cougar."

He grinned. "No, I was just jerking your chain."

"Oh, good. Because Mitch said he was going to try to make it up for the weekend again. And I really want to put that cougar image to rest once and for all."

The next day, Caroline did everything possible to make sure that the evening went smoothly. This meant keeping her mom occupied and awake for the best part of the day so that when the part-time caregiver arrived, all was peaceful and quiet because Caroline had already put her mom to bed.

"I could've done that," Andrea told Caroline.

"I know." Caroline reached for her phone to text Mitch that she was ready to go. "But it's less upsetting for her if we stick with our routines."

Despite being tired from a long day, Caroline was excited about the prospect of a night out. It had been a long time. The plan was for her to pick Mitch up at the bed-and-breakfast since he was without a car.

"How was your flight?" she asked as he got into the car.

"A little windy, but at least the fog cleared before I had to land."

"You know, I've never been in a small plane," she admitted.

"Well, that will change as soon as you let me take you up."

She nodded as she turned down Front Street. "Like I told you, I'm working on getting more freedom, but I have to take baby steps with Mom. I can't believe this is the first time I've been out at night in weeks."

"I don't know how you do it," he said as she parked across the street from the One-Legged Seagull.

"One baby step at a time." She felt a thrill of excitement as she got out of the car. Being dressed up and in town in the evening—the lights, the people, music from the band playing at Sailor's Cove— what a rush! "Hey, there's Abby," she said, calling out to her friend as they met in front of the gallery.

"How's Paul doing?" Caroline asked after they exchanged a hug.

Abby shook her head with a dismal expression. "He's fed up."

"Fed up?"

"Meaning he wants out of the hospital *right now.*"

"Sounds like his surgery was a success." Mitch opened the door for them. "Give him my best."

"He must be feeling pretty good," Caroline said as they went inside the crowded gallery.

"Paul says he can't remember the last time he felt this good." Abby looked so happy. "Laurie and Jessie are with him tonight. They told me to get out and see my friends."

"I'm so glad you did." Caroline squeezed Abby's hand. "It's great to see you."

"Abby!" Marley exclaimed when she spotted them. "You made it. And Caroline and Mitch too." Then they all exchanged hugs and began checking out Marley's work, which was even better than Caroline had expected.

Janie and Victor were already there, sipping wine and visiting with Jack, who came over to say hello then seemed to stick to Marley like glue, as if they were really a couple too. For all Caroline knew, they were. In fact, they made a pretty cute pair in their artsy, unique sort of way.

The seven of them gathered in a quiet corner to chat together and Caroline realized that Abby, the only married Linda, was also the only Linda here without a date. Thankfully, it wasn't a permanent situation. Caroline didn't even want to imagine what kind of evening this would've been if Paul hadn't pulled through.

"It's been such a long week," Abby told them as she was getting ready to leave. "It felt like the longest week of my life. I'm just so glad it's over."

"It felt like a long week to me, too." Caroline hugged her again. "I've missed you so much."

"Hey, we need to have a club meeting," Marley said suddenly.

"A club meeting?" Mitch looked confused.

"The Four Lindas," Caroline told him. "Remember?"

He laughed. "Oh, yeah."

"We do need a club meeting," Janie agreed. And before Abby left, they agreed to meet tomorrow at noon, and, weather permitting, they would walk on the beach and follow it up at the Chowder House.

"I hope I can get someone to watch Mom and Chuck," Caroline said as she and Mitch walked back to her car. "Andrea already told me she doesn't work on Sundays, and I'm guessing Darlene doesn't either."

"I'll stay with your mom," he offered.

She blinked. "Seriously?"

"Sure, why not?"

She actually laughed.

"What? You don't think I'm up to it?" He looked slightly indignant.

"I don't know," she admitted. "But, hey, I'm willing to find out."

He nodded. "Okay then. What's the worst that could happen?"

She shrugged as she considered the possibilities, but then decided not to go there. Really, with her mom, *anything* could happen. But if Mitch was as serious about Caroline as he claimed to be, well, then he was more than welcome to her world.

==Chapter 30==

ABBY

Abby got up at seven to make a call to Nicole. By her calculations it should be about four at night in France, and she'd promised to give her youngest daughter an update today.

"I'm so relieved that Dad's better. But it feels like I'm missing out on everything." Nicole sounded blue. "You guys are so far away."

Abby chuckled. "Actually, we're all here. You're the one who's far away."

"Maybe we can all get together for Christmas," Nicole said hopefully. "Do you think Laurie would come?"

"I think it's a possibility."

"So is she actually talking to you, Mom?"

Abby sighed. "Well, we're not exactly chatting, but she's here, staying in the guest room, and she's spent some time with Dad. It's more than I'd hoped for."

"Tell her to call me sometime."

"I will."

"And give everyone my love—and give Dad a great big hug for me."

"I will, honey."

"Hey, you never told me whether you got our old house for the bed-and-breakfast. Or are you still waiting?"

"They accepted our offer," Abby said soberly, "on the same day Dad went into the hospital."

"Wow, that must've been a busy day. But congratulations, Mom. I can't wait to get back and see what you do with it. Maybe you'll let me help."

"I'd love to have you help me, Nicole."

"Cool."

They chatted a bit longer, then Abby heard little footsteps coming into her bedroom, and the next thing she knew Lucy was bouncing on her bed. "Say hi to Auntie Nicole," she said, handing Lucy the phone for a quick hello before they all said good-bye.

"I'm hungry," Lucy said as soon as Abby ended the call.

It wasn't long before Abby had a big breakfast cooking, and Lucy set out to get her mom and Auntie Laurie up.

"Lucy and I are going to head out this morning," Jessie said as she refilled her coffee mug. "We'll pop in to say good-bye to Daddy then hit the road."

"My flight out of Eugene isn't until this evening," Laurie told them. "But I plan to head back over there around four so I can meet some friends for dinner."

"Speaking of friends," Abby began, "I promised to meet my friends at noon for a couple of hours, but you might want to visit with Dad then."

Laurie looked like she was about to protest but then seemed to think better of it. Instead she just nodded. "Sure, I can do that, Mom."

"Thanks." Abby turned her attention back to the Irish oatmeal she was cooking specially for Laurie, since she was a vegetarian, and asked herself why it always seemed that Laurie had a chip on her shoulder. Was it simply middle-daughter syndrome or something more? Abby didn't plan to ask, at least not in front of Jessie and little Lucy. No, that conversation could continue to wait.

After breakfast, Abby cleaned up the kitchen, helped see Jessie and Lucy off, then headed over to have a quick visit with Paul. She wasn't surprised that he was antsy.

"Did you ask the doctor about going home a day early?" she asked.

"He said tomorrow was the soonest he'd release me." Paul frowned. "I told him that the stress of being stuck in the hospital might make me have another heart attack."

"Very funny." Abby leaned over his bed and peered closely at him. "So how are you feeling today?"

"Fine."

"Do you want to get out of bed and walk a little?"

He seemed reluctant, but Abby had heard the doctor telling him that walking and moving around a little would speed up his recovery. So she got Paul's robe and slippers, then helped him out of bed to take a little stroll.

"The doc said I can't play golf for a couple of weeks," Paul said sadly. "But it's okay to do the treadmill."

"What about work?"

"He said no work for a couple of weeks and no actual labor for about a month." As they looped back by his room, Paul's steps seemed to slow. "I think that's enough walking for now."

She helped him back into bed but could tell by his expression that his spirits were sagging. "Are you feeling blue?" She tucked the blanket back up around him.

He just nodded.

"The doctor said that was normal," she told him.

"Yeah, I know."

She took his hand in hers now. "I said a lot of things to you while you were unconscious," she admitted.

"Huh?" He looked curiously at her.

She looked into his eyes. "I was so scared, Paul. I didn't want to lose you." She reached over to push some hair off his forehead. "I told you how much I love you … how I've always loved you … how much you mean to me." She felt her eyes misting. "And I told you how sorry I am for all the times I've blown it, for things I've said and done."

"I'm the one who should say I'm sorry." He squeezed her hand. "I am sorry, Abby. You know, for everything."

She nodded. "I really do want to grow old with you, Paul. I never realized how much I wanted that until I thought I was actually losing you. I'd give up everything and anything—the bed-and-breakfast idea, our beautiful home, fancy vacations, you name it. I'd be willing to live in a camp trailer with you if that was the only way we could be together."

He smiled. "I love you, too, Abby."

She leaned down and hugged him. With her sitting on the edge of his bed, they talked and reminisced, and Paul even offered to help

Abby with the bed-and-breakfast when he was strong enough. "I wonder if anyone sturdied up that old banister yet."

It was a little before noon when Laurie showed up and, like a changing of the guards, Abby left to meet up with her friends. Before long, they were all walking on the beach together.

"Do you guys remember how we used to do weekly highlights at our meetings sometimes?" Abby asked them.

"Yeah," Caroline said eagerly. "We'd go around, and everyone had to tell one thing that made them happy that week."

"Seems like it was your idea," Marley pointed to Caroline. "Our merry little sunshine."

Caroline laughed. "Okay, and since it was my idea, I'll share my highlight first."

"Let's see … does it stand about six feet tall and start with the letter M?" Janie teased.

"No." Caroline shook her head. "Certainly, Mitch is great, and I'm glad he's back in my life. Believe it or not, he's the one staying with my mom today, but I don't want to think about that."

"Then it's Chuck," Marley said quickly.

"No, but that's probably closer."

"Hey, why didn't you bring him today?" Abby asked.

"I promised to bring him later," Caroline explained. "Right now is just for the Lindas. Besides, I think Mitch is glad to have him around."

"Okay, so tell us," Janie pressed. "What was your weekly highlight?"

"It actually started out more as a lowlight. You know how I'd been bummed over that mess with Adam, Brent, and Mitch. But then I realized that I don't have to have a man in my life. It's like I know, way down deep in my soul, that I'll be okay without a guy by my side. The rest of you probably think that's not a big deal, but trust me, for me it was a very big deal. Kind of a liberating moment, you know?"

"That's great." Marley patted her on the back. "So did you tell Mitch you don't need him and can live without him?"

Caroline laughed. "No, of course not."

"Okay, I'll go next," Abby said in a serious tone. "You probably think my highlight was when Paul didn't die. And, naturally, that was a huge highlight. But my real highlight came before that, when I thought I was losing him, because it made me realize just how much I really do love him … and how much I need him … and how empty my life would be without him." She sighed. "I actually told him that this morning."

"That's very cool," Caroline told her.

"Now me," Janie said. "I didn't think I was going to tell anyone, but I know I can trust you guys." Janie explained how her dad had been in the war, but because he never spoke of it, she'd always assumed he was embarrassed about it. "It turns out that he was a real war hero," she said, "and he won some medals, including the Medal of Honor. But the reason it's such a highlight is because, as I was reading old letters and things, I realized how much both my parents had been through. I began to understand why they were the way they were. It was like solving a mystery. I realized that it wasn't really my fault that my parents had some problems—it's just that they'd been broken by the things that happened during the war. And I could forgive them." Janie sighed. "That felt so good."

"That's awesome," Marley told her. "Now I guess it's my turn." She took in a deep breath. "Well, I was in bed one night—when we still didn't know if Paul was going to make it or not—and I started thinking about my own mortality. And for some reason it really got to me, and I felt really alone. So ... I decided to talk to God."

"And?" Caroline asked eagerly.

"And ..." Marley shrugged, then grinned. "The conversation continues."

"Group hug," Abby proclaimed as she stretched out her arms. All four of them huddled into one big embrace. "I need you Lindas so much," Abby told them. "I never could've survived this week without you guys."

"Same back at you," Caroline added as they all stepped away, some of them wiping their eyes.

"I really do believe that God's the one who brought us back together," Marley said.

"And God's the one who will keep us together," Abby added.

"And I am *so* thankful." Janie reached for their hands, and the four of them continued walking down the beach, hand in hand, not so different from how they used to walk down the beach more than forty years before ... and hopefully for decades more.

... a little more ...

When a delightful concert comes to an end,

the orchestra might offer an encore.

When a fine meal comes to an end,

it's always nice to savor a bit of dessert.

When a great story comes to an end,

we think you may want to linger.

And so, we offer ...

AfterWords—just a little something more after you

have finished a David C. Cook novel.

We invite you to stay awhile in the story.

Thanks for reading!

Turn the page for ...

- **Discussion Questions**

DISCUSSION QUESTIONS

1. Examine the conflicting values that affect Caroline's decision to care for her declining mother at home. How do these conflicts play out in real-life situations that you know of?

2. How would Caroline's experience during this season of her life be different if she allowed Mitch, Adam, or Brent to "rescue" her from her feelings of loneliness or helplessness? How is the support that the Four Lindas offer her different from the support she might find in a romantic relationship?

3. What is it about domestic pets that seems to change our perspective for the better?

4. Why was it important for Abby to have her bed-and-breakfast project? What's your opinion of how she went about it? What would you have recommended she do differently, if anything?

5. Why does Marley feel she can only paint when angry? How does this early opinion of her creative process compare to the work she does at the end of the novel, when she is feeling peaceful? How would you explain the difference between these experiences?

6. The prospect of Paul's mortality nudges Marley toward God and Abby toward Paul. Why does it sometimes take an imminent loss to prompt such changes of attitude?

7. Marley feels insecure about her design sense in comparison to Janie's; Abby feels insecure because Paul is typically unsupportive of her interests. What are some of the other insecurities the Four Lindas face? Is insecurity a constant in life, regardless of age, or is it something one can overcome once and for all? Explain.

8. Janie comes to a new understanding of her upbringing and her parents' behavior. Her discoveries make her sympathetic rather than bitter toward them. Why? What is the point of her forgiving them even though they are dead?

9. The Four Lindas are quick to help each other when trouble presents itself. Describe a time when a friend came alongside you and helped you lift a burden. How did their support change the nature of your trouble?

10. What are the sacrifices each of the Four Lindas must make in this story? What are the rewards they experience as a result?